Wedding

of

My Dreams

by

Joyce Good Henderson

Celtic Loom Books

Wedding of My Dreams

Copyright © 2012 by

Joyce Good Henderson

All rights reserved.

Celtic Loom Books

Published in the United States of America

On Beltane, the ancient celebration of May Day
The mortal world comes perilously close to the Otherworld
And portals open allowing a few, a precious few,
To travel between the worlds. While the crossing is rarely
Dangerous, there is always the risk that one might lose
Her heart along with her life.

Moira MacMalley O'Donnell

To the brave Warrior Women in my life
who followed their own paths:
Minnie Hardin Roloson,
Julia Darnell Good
Jeanne, Jennifer, Mary, Anne
Shawn, Heather, Megan, Jennica

Chapter 1

If I had known that my wedding night would be spent on the cold, hard ground, held captive by a crazed terrorist shepherd, I certainly would not have agreed to travel to Ireland, to the tiny village that was my ancestral home for the "wedding of my dreams."

Instead, I would have insisted on a simple service in the chambers of one of my fellow judges, leaving out all the romantic nonsense, tradition and mystery. But, when David planned our dream wedding, how could I suspect my life would change so suddenly and irrevocably?

Six weeks earlier

"I thought all women dreamed about their weddings. You know, the white dress, walking down the aisle, all that traditional stuff."

Standing behind him, I reached my arms around his waist and pressed my cheek against his back. "Not me. Not a wedding bone in my body. I'd just as soon go down to the courthouse and be done with it."

"Seriously?"

He pulled my arms open and turned to face me. "Why would you do that? I can't believe you don't want a big, fancy wedding with all the trimmings. I'm all for saving the money and fuss, but the courthouse is where you work, not where you get married."

"Well, okay. We can have a church wedding, if you want, but I honestly don't have time right now to do anything to get ready for it."

"No problem! Planning a wedding can't be that hard. Let me take care of all the details. I'll give you the wedding of your dreams, baby, even if you don't have any dreams," he said, planting a kiss on my cheek.

"Hey, where are you going?" I asked as he started to walk away.

"I have a lot to do, a wedding to plan."

David was out the door before I could object.

"Keep it simple," I called after him.

True to his promise, David masterminded every detail, clearing the early May calendar with my secretary, buying plane tickets, making arrangements with a village priest, and booking a cottage for a three-week honeymoon. Our best friends, Bill and Linda, begged to come along, and David agreed.

"As long as you get my bride to the church, I'd be happy to book a room at a bed-and-breakfast in Aasleigh," he said.

Aasleigh, a tiny Irish village, perched on a cliff high above a frigid white-foamed sea. I'd always wanted to visit the land of the MacMalleys and O'Donnells, where stone fences lined the road, fragrant purple heather carpeted the hills, and black-faced sheep wandered up to the cottage.

Memories of my grandmother's stories of her childhood home began to come alive in my mind. Would I see the fairies, or hear their music, as she claimed? Or were her stories simply the creations of her imagination and her desire to comfort a lonely and frightened little girl after her parents' sudden deaths?

Only the steady drizzle dampened my first impressions of Aasleigh. We arrived on an overcast Thursday with barely enough daylight left to tour the village. But, we had the next day to get our bearings before Saturday's wedding. I rose early on Friday, anxious to search for the cottage pictured on a black-and-white photograph I had found in my grandmother's Bible.

"If there's time," I told David. "I don't want to spend a whole day looking for it. I'm sure you have plenty you want to do before Saturday morning."

"Not really. Just want to run by the church and confirm with the priest. Bill and I can do that while you and Linda hunt for your cottage. Take your time. You two can meet us for a late lunch at the pub."

The scent of peat fires, wet heather and the nearby sea tickled my nose, as Linda and I set out on my goose chase. Should we walk up and down the streets of the village until we spied a building that could be the right one? I had no clue how to go about the search. Linda suggested we show the photo to some of the shop owners who might be longtime residents and perhaps even remember my grandparents.

We dodged raindrops, popping in and out of a few shops, speaking to everyone we thought might recognize the cottage. I'd decided to make one last stop before going to the pub. Linda pointed to a carved wooden door with a small "Open" sign hanging from a glass doorknob, but no other hint about what we might find inside.

"Odd place, but let's check it out," I said.

We crossed the narrow, cobblestone street and, in spite of the sign, I knocked on the door.

"Don't know why, but it feels like I should knock first," I said, turning the crystal knob slowly.

We entered slowly, expecting to allow our eyes to adjust to dimness, but the interior was bright and cheery, with white walls, lace and silk roses draped along the tops of windows and doorways.

"Welcome to Norah's Bridal Shop."

We heard her voice before we could see her.

"Hello?" I called out.

Fabric rustled in response. I looked at Linda, who shrugged, and grinned. There was something warm and welcoming about the pristine room, and the friendly voice that replied, "Be right out."

Looking around while we waited, I wondered where the bridal dresses were. There should have been racks of gowns, veils, shoes and all the usual trappings. Where were the fitting rooms and floor-to-ceiling mirrors?

Linda migrated over to a round, linen-covered table with three curved-back wrought iron chairs. "Going to sit," she whispered.

"Would ye care for some tea, this fine mornin'? It'll chase away the gloom of a gray day. Just made a pot for me-self. Let me get ye a cup."

We still had no idea who she was, but I answered that we'd love some. The moment the words left my mouth, I regretted it. We were supposed to be meeting the guys in a few minutes. But something about the shop, and the voice reminded me of my grandmother. I felt as if I might finally have found the one person who could tell me about the cottage in the photo I clutched.

After a few minutes of china-clinking and humming in a room beyond the draped doorway, our host finally came in with a silver tray laden with a round rose-patterned teapot, three tea cups, and bowl of sugar cubes.

"Ye've come from the colonies, haven't ye?" The small, white-haired woman asked as she slid the tray onto the table in front of Linda.

"Colonies? Oh, the States, yes. We're from Ohio. In the Midwest. I'm Kat, actually, Kathleen, and this is my friend Linda," I said.

"My name is Norah Kelly. I'm the proprietor of this store. Here, sit down," she pointed to a chair as she began to pour the tea. "It's a wee bit early in the year for tourists. Weather's not yet ready for guests."

Linda stirred a sugar cube into the fragrant black liquid in her cup. I drank mine without sweetener.

"Actually we've come for a wedding. My friend Kat is getting married tomorrow," Linda said.

"Well, ye've come to the right place. That's a bit sudden, but I imagine I can find a dress for ye."

"Oh, no. I'm sorry. We're not here for a dress," I said, feeling very sorry we weren't looking for a dress. "I'm actually looking for information about the location of a cottage that I think might be here in the village."

I handed her the photo, and watched as she studied it. The color in her cheeks drained until her skin matched her hair. Her blue eyes glistened with tears as she turned over the picture to see if anything had been written on the back.

"Aye, the cottage was here, long ago. Burned to the ground back in the 40's. Where did you get this photograph?" Her hand shook slightly as she returned it to me.

My grandmother kept it in her Bible. Perhaps you knew her? Moira MacMalley O'Donnell. She left with my grandfather right after they married. I don't know when but probably in the mid 1940's. Would you have known them?"

The woman put her hand to her mouth. I thought she might faint or become ill.

"I'm sorry? Did I say something wrong?"

She took my hand with both of hers, then cleared her throat, and said, "No, dearie. I should have realized when I saw ye. Ye look just like Moira. Same hair, same eyes. Ye are the image of your grandmother," she said.

"So, you knew my grandparents? Can you tell me anything about their lives here?" I set down my cup a little too quickly and a wave of tea sloshed into the saucer.

"Moira was my cousin. A few years older than I, but I remember her as if she just walked in. I suppose it is seeing ye looking so much like her. Same age as she was when she left. Actually, I remember the stories, too. I was perhaps ten or eleven years old, no, twelve years old, when they left. I remember now, 'twas a few days after my twelfth birthday. I didn't understand everything that had happened, and I certainly couldn't ask." The woman paused and sipped her tea.

"Ask about what?"

"I can't say. It was so long ago and I was so young. No one would talk. There were just whispers and gossip. My mother would never discuss what had happened. Moira was her niece, ye know." Her hands shook slightly, rattling her cup and saucer.

"I don't mean to upset you," I said. "It's just that I have never known much about my family. My parents died in an accident when I was six. Grandmother Moira raised me. There was just the two of us. I think my grandfather died shortly after they moved from Ireland. I grew up with stories of her childhood here, but I was never quite certain what parts of her stories were real and what was fairy tales."

Norah nodded as if she remembered something about my grandmother. "There are others ye must ask about the time before they left. Something happened to Moira. Something that no one in the family would ever speak of. I only know that she was gone for a time. When she returned, they married and then left suddenly. Their home, the cottage of the photograph, burned to the ground that very night."

I startled. "Oh!"

Norah patted my hand. "Let's speak of more pleasant things. How long will ye be visiting Aasleigh?"

"A couple weeks. I'm busy tomorrow, but perhaps I could return next week, and you can tell me more?"

Norah stood abruptly and left from the room. Linda and I exchanged puzzled looks.

"Well, looks like we found someone who knew your grandmother, but what was that all about?"

Before I could answer, the woman returned. She handed me a black velvet box, about the size that would hold a ring. "Moira left something behind. I've kept it all these years hoping she might come back for it. I think ye should have it," she said.

I studied the box. "Do you know what it is?"

She nodded. "I looked at it once, many years ago. It's very old."

I pulled the lid from the box and looked inside to find a blood-red gemstone the size of an unshelled walnut. I lifted the polished oval and held it in my palm, turning it over and over, fascinated by the smoothness of the facets. Nestled in my palm, the rock seemed to pulsate, warming as if it were coming alive as I studied it. The stone was exquisite, yet it had a primitive wildness to its appearance.

"A ruby?"

"Wow," was the only word that Linda could find.

Words failed me. How could I describe something that so fascinated me that I felt as if I was falling into its crimson depths? A crimson fog swirled within the depths of the rock as if its center was liquid. I sensed that the stone held secrets it might reveal. Stroking it, I felt myself being pulled into its mystery as if something deep in the gem longed to reveal itself. I could no longer hear or see anything else around me.

A sense of danger crept across my soul sending shivers down my spine, like hearing the music that warns you something bad is about to happen in the show you've been watching.

I jerked suddenly as if awakening from a bad dream. Shaking my head to clear the remnants of whatever had been happening in my head, I forced myself to set the ruby back into its velvet-lined box. Pushing the lid on, I could almost sense screams of protest coming from the depths of the rock.

How could I explain feeling it throb in my hand or hearing a rock cry out?

Taking a deep breath, I looked up at Norah. "Have you ever held it?"

"I looked at it a few times, but never took it out of the box. It just didn't feel right, since it wasn't mine." Her voice took on a chatty tone, like she was gossiping over the back-fence. "I'm sure it's very valuable, but I could never bring myself to try to sell it. I didn't want to do anything but keep it for her. I kept telling myself that Moira would return for it someday. Now, I'm sure she would want ye to have it. When ye held it, I felt certain of the rightness of that decision. The rock already belongs to ye."

She was right about that. I don't know why. But the rock did belong to me.

I didn't know if I could take it. But, at the same time, I couldn't leave it either. The rock did feel as if it was meant to be mine, or more possibly, I was meant to belong to it.

Chapter 2

David took the credit for perfect weather when clouds finally parted for a bright, May Day sun to rise on the morning of our wedding.

I'd been awake for hours already. Wedding jitters, or missing the customary white noise of traffic outside and my cat's purring-snore. I finally draped a coverlet across my shoulders and slipped out the cottage door just in time to see the stars fade silently as the dawn chased them away. I'd seen plenty of Cleveland sunrises, usually as I drove to work, but for some reason, the very air felt different in Aasleigh.

I could almost believe fairies inhabited the dawn, scurrying about to finish their work before the light of day caught them. I wrapped the blanket tighter against a breeze that whipped my nightshirt around my ankles.

Time to awaken David and send him to the inn where Bill would entertain him while Linda and I got ready. He had not seen my wedding dress, the only detail left to me. I'd picked up a simple white wool sheath with a jacket that I thought would be easy to pack, and practical since I could wear it again throughout the summer.

However, fate apparently had another idea. Even though I hadn't planned to buy anything at Norah's, she insisted I had to have the dress she claimed would be perfect for me. And, I insisted I had to pay for it.

She'd given me a ruby worth a fortune, it would not have been right for me to accept a wedding gown, even if it was the perfect dress. After a few minutes of negotiating tug-of-war, Norah pulled me over to a steamer trunk, opened it and removed a package wrapped in yellowed tissue paper.

"Exquisite" barely described the gown. Antique lace with fragile gossamer roses laid against an underskirt of satin. Old, Irish, and so incredibly beautiful that, when I slipped it over my head, it floated across my hips and swirled around my ankles, barely touching the floor in the front, but puddling into a short train at the back of my ankles.

I looked as if I'd stepped from the pages of a story about castles and princesses. No dress could have been more perfect for the wedding of my dreams. I quickly dismissed the off-the-rack dress I'd brought with me.

After David left, Linda came to help me dress. "What did you bring for *something old, something new, something borrowed, something blue?*"

"You know me. I never even thought of that."

She suggested my dress for old, the lace veil she loaned me for borrowed, and a linen handkerchief embroidered with tiny blue flowers for blue.

"No, even though the dress is old, it's new to me. I think I'll carry the ruby for something old."

"Oh, I don't even know what to say. Just don't lose it."

"I won't." I'd already figured out a way to slip it into a hidden pocket I'd found in the underskirt. I wrapped the stone in the velvet lining from its box and secured the pocket with a small safety pin. The ruby brought my grandmother Moira to mind, and her presence to my wedding. And the gemstone vibrated in agreement as I smooth the pocket against my thigh.

"Perfect," Linda said, as I slowly twirled. With no full-length mirror, I looked to her for an appraisal and encouragement. She gave me a quick hug. "You're so beautiful! Ready?"

I nodded, and she fastened the borrowed, shoulder-length, lace veil over my curls, which had become unmanageably wild in the Irish humidity.

"Let's go then. The guys are probably getting impatient."

David and I had dated for five years that actually seemed much longer. To me, marriage had always been a commitment for others, like Linda and Bill or my grandparents. I never thought I wanted to be married forever. Nothing had been forever in my life. David wanted to be married, and I had finally run out of excuses.

I slipped off my wristwatch, and laid it on the table before we left the cottage. At the last minute, I remembered to move my engagement ring to my right hand. It didn't fit very well, and I worried about losing it, so I decided to leave it with my watch on the table.

A warming breeze flipped the ends of my veil against my cheek as we walked on the uneven cobblestones of the path to the church. We passed Norah's shop and I wished she could have come to the wedding. When I invited her, she declined, saying she couldn't leave her shop unattended when she had fittings already scheduled.

When we reached the church, Linda gave my hand a squeeze and said, "I promise I won't cry, if you try to be as excited about this wedding as everyone else is. I'll go in and make sure the guys are ready. Just wait a couple minutes and join us."

I hugged her and watched as she climbed the broad stone steps. *Try to be excited*, I said to myself, as I fought the feeling that something was missing.

Flowers!

A small bouquet, just enough to fit into my palm. After all, I had to have something to throw to Linda when the ceremony was over.

Just past the churchyard, beyond a weed-choked cemetery, lay a meadow of wild flowers. The soft sea of blossoms swayed, keeping time with the distant surf that brushed against the cliffs.

Wait just one more minute, David.

I hurried past ancient stones and weathered monuments that peered over my shoulder like ghostly residents. As I walked through a part in the thick, knee-high hedge at the far edge of the churchyard, a haunting melody greeted me.

"Fonsheen," grandmother Moira would have called it. The music of the fairies, lyrical, yet moody, like the sound of water, wind and warm sunlight. Delicate bells rang crystal notes as hypnotic as a shepherd's flute. I picked up the hem of my skirt, brushing my hand across the small lump in the hidden pocket, and the ruby began to throb in tune with the strange music.

Remembering that I had come for flowers, I reached for a handful of delicate purple from the fragrant tide lapping at my ankles. I pricked my finger on an unseen thorn, and a droplet of blood appeared on my fingertip.

The music changed to a low rumble. No longer the church bells, nor a shepherd's flute, but the throaty blast of a horn, a deep warning like the thunder of many hooves. A drumbeat with a cadence faster than the surf pulsated the air around me. My heart began to race as the music captured me in a wild rhythm.

I dropped the flowers and followed the hypnotic sound toward the far edge of the meadow. Knee-deep in wild flowers, when the music reached a heart-stopping climax and ended as quickly as it had started, I felt abandoned.

Shaking my head to clear the echo of the drum, I turned back toward the church when a white-hot shaft of pain exploded in my brain.

With both hands, I grabbed my head fearful it might split apart, while a lightning bolt of pain shot from one ear to the other, then spilled out every curl of my hair. I fell to my knees, blinded by waves of nausea, pain and throbbing.

Shouts pierced the curtain of blackness swallowing me.

David, Bill, Linda. They must be coming for me.

Afraid to move in case something had ruptured in my brain, I stayed perfectly still on the bed of wildflowers as the footfalls came closer.

"She is here!" a man shouted in a language I had not heard since childhood.

"Yes," I cried weakly, not even sure whether I spoke Gaelic or English. "Help me, please."

Someone came. He did not ask if I was injured or why I held my head between my hands. He pulled me into his arms, and picked me up as if I were a child. Cradling me against his chest, he began to carry me.

I slowly opened my eyes, amazed that the intense headache had passed, and even more surprised to find that the man was taking me toward a forest on the far side of the meadow.

"No, wait! Go back to the church, please. My fiancé is there. My friends." I pointed toward the church.

When my words had no effect on the man, I switched to Gaelic. It had been years since I'd spoken Gaelic, and I blurted out a few words, hoping they were the correct ones.

"Go back there! Please!" I said, gesturing furiously and repeating my words in English in case he didn't get my rough Gaelic.

The man still did not respond, other than to lengthen his strides away from the churchyard. I squirmed in his arms, and his grip and pace increased. Tapping on his chest to get his attention produced no results. He continued to plow forward, never once looking at me or in the direction I pointed.

"Stop! Put me down!" I said, pounding his chest and pushing against the thick arms that held me fast. He shifted me so that my arms were pinned by his forearms.

Panic bubbled up from my gut. I struggled with all my strength to no effect.

"Sir! Put me down this minute! Who do you think you are?"

"I do not think. I know. I am Connor, son of Malley, chieftain of clan Malley, "he said in thickly-accented Gaelic that I barely understood.

"Okay, fine, Mr. Connor Malley. You can let me go right now and nobody will get into any trouble."

He snorted.

I glanced down at the rock-hard muscles binding me to his chest. *Who was this guy? Mr. Ireland Body Builder?*

"Perhaps you don't understand. I am Kathleen O'Donnell, and I want to go back to the church right now." I tried my sternest, judicial voice.

He set his jaw, and stared straight ahead as he continued in a direct line away from the village.

"You must stop immediately." *Enough Ms. Nice and Polite.* "Kidnapping is a crime, or at least in most parts of the world it is." I alternated between Gaelic and English since my grandmother had never taught me such words as "crime" and "kidnapping."

I did stop short of telling him I was an American. Certainly he'd figure it out eventually, but it didn't seem to be the prudent thing to confess to a kidnapper, especially one whose clenched jaw, and rigid grip should have warned me not to argue with him.

By this time, we had moved from the meadow into a dense forest, heavy with the damp, new growth of spring leftover from the recent rains.

Two other men came alongside, and I repeated my pleas for release in case they were would-be rescuers. Apparently they were his companions because they also ignored me. As my captor bent to walk under a branch, I tried to wriggle free and he nearly dropped my on my backside.

If he were in my court, I'd have fined him for contempt. *Ten minutes ago.* I relished the thought of banging my gavel over his head. But, such thoughts were not going to be productive in securing my release, and I decided to refocus.

Learn as much as you can about a suspect.

I recalled the anti-terrorism classes, the self-defense lessons, the many briefings I had had from the police and FBI. I began to study my captor's buddies.

The men wore their hair long, thick and unkempt, *an Irish version of dreadlocks*, with leather ties at their neck. Clean shaven, I'd give them credit for that much, except for heavy, straggly mustaches that hung over their upper lips and curled down at the corners of their mouths.

Even the worst criminals in my courtroom usually looked more respectable than this guy and his friends. Cleaned up and dressed in suits, they might have been considered good-looking in a rugged, primitive cowboy sort of way. But trying to picture them in suits required a real stretch of any imagination.

I needed a new approach in my attempts to gain release. Persuasion was definitely the better course to take.

Gentle, sweetness, mama bear.

"Do you think you could put me down and let me walk? You're messing up my dress."

From the look and smell of his clothing, he obviously cared little about sweat and dirt, or damage to my antique lace dress. He ignored me, so I returned to making mental notes for the police artist.

He and his companions wore outfits that could be described as voluminous, knee-length shirts of some rough linen-substitute, belted at the waist with leather straps. The fabric appeared to have come off a loom already soiled. The only washing ever given to their clothing was probably from a hard rain.

My nose was suddenly acutely aware of the assault by something unidentifiable, but probably animal in nature.

Over their shirts, each draped a long piece of walnut-brown coarse fabric, fastened with metal pins at the shoulder, tucked in by their leather belts and wrapped around their waists.

The men did not wear pants, but fur-lined leather boots that strapped to their legs with leather cords winding around from ankle to knee.

They looked like shepherds from a Christmas card scene. But not the least bit sanitized by the artist.

Shepherds without sheep.

Even though I had never before been to Aasleigh, I could not believe this was some sort of native costume. It seemed too bizarre even for this remote, time-lost village. And the men carried weapons, large daggers and swords strapped to their waists.

Swords?

Great, I'd been snatched by filthy, sword-bearing shepherds!

So, who were these guys, and why did they kidnap me?

Sudden bright sunlight made me realize we had passed from the woods to the rim of the ocean cliffs. I'd been gone long enough now that David must surely be looking for me. My imagination skipped quickly to *"what if."*

What if I've been kidnapped by terrorists? What if they shoot me and dump my body over the edge of the cliff? What if they go back for David and our friends?

I needed to act. Now. Quickly and decisively. Show these ruffians who they were dealing with.

"That's it!" I said. "If you don't put me down this minute, I'll make you sorry you ever messed with me!" I jerked one hand free and dug my nails into the bare skin of his forearm wrapped around my thighs.

He shook it off as if I were nothing more than an annoying mosquito. "Ye are a most difficult person to steal. I do not want to hurt ye, so be still," he said, tightening his grip on me, his hand pressing so firmly I expected to have a handprint-shaped bruise.

"I will not! How dare you speak to me like that!"

"How dare I? I am chieftain of clan Malley!"

Now I was angry.

"And I am a judge, and an American, so what you are doing is bound to become an international incident." I used my toughest judicial manner and gave him the full benefit of my meanest glare.

"A judge, ye say? Well, I suppose that is possible. There are woman warriors and women priests. I suppose ye may be a judge. That'd be just like Donal to think a woman could learn the tenets of the law," he said with a snort of derision.

"What? Donald, who? Perhaps you misunderstood me. My name is Kathleen O'Donnell. Are you going to let me go or am I going to have to—"

"Talk until the sun is chased away by the moon? Ye are being most difficult, woman. Now, cease or I will drop ye over the edge."

I looked over my shoulder down several hundred feet to the jagged black rocks below.

"Ohhhhh!" I screamed into his ear.

He grimaced. "Ye might as well save your breath, woman. There's no one to hear ye."

"What do you mean? What about the village? It may be small, but I'm sure someone will hear me. Mrs. Kelly or the village priest. My friends, and David." I immediately regretted suggesting someone might be looking for me. After all, they could be walking into a trap.

"Village? David? I know no one called David. Ye talk nonsense. There is no village, only Donal's tower and the tents of the fair, but we're far from there now."

Nothing made sense. The whole kidnapping business had such a disorienting feel I wondered if I might have fallen and hit my head and was now dreaming all of this. But, if this was a dream, it was certainly vivid. I wrinkled my nose at the smell of sweaty, dirty men, and the salty tang of the ocean breeze.

The situation was going from dire to worse quickly. Connor continued walking on the precarious path across the cliffs. My captor apparently had a plan and a destination. Struggling with the Irish equivalent of Arnold Schwarzenegger hadn't accomplished much, and reasoning wasn't part of his vocabulary.

Perhaps pretending to cooperate would persuade him to release me. I sucked in a deep breath, tried to slow my pounding heart, and calmly said, "It can't be easy carrying me. If you put me down, I'll cooperate."

"I've carried heavier loads than ye for greater distances." His snarled words reminded me of a schoolyard bully exercising the first stirrings of testosterone.

The other men now walked ahead and were not paying much attention to us.

Well, Mr. Irish Body-Builder-Kidnapper, no more nice-guy for you. You're about to meet a victim with an attitude!

"Okay, fine. Be stubborn. Throw out your back for all I care."

I jerked one hand free and suddenly jabbed the underside of his chin with the heel of my hand. Then, aimed a fist for his sternum. His head jerked back and he dropped me.

I landed solidly with a thump that knocked the wind out of me, and, I was sure, cracked my tailbone. He quickly planted a foot between my knees, pinning my skirt to the rock beneath me.

So, I smashed my fist into the side of his knee.

He cursed and hopped, releasing me. I rolled quickly away from him, then immediately began to slide down wind-polished slate toward a drop of several hundred feet to the inlet below.

"Help!"

Connor grabbed my outstretched hand, his fingers catching and tightening around my wrist. I kicked my feet, but there was only air beneath them.

Time stood still for several seconds as I stared at the taut muscles of his forearm and the fierce look on his face. A drop of sweat ran down his temple to his clenched jaw as he slowly lifted me until I felt solid rock beneath my feet again.

He encircled my waist with both of his hands, and pulled me toward him until only a few inches separated us. Not wanting to share either my fear or my relief with him, I didn't dare to look up into his eyes.

"Ye are definitely troublesome. I should have let ye fall. But, I have plans for ye and they don't include sending ye to the god of the sea."

"The god of what?"

Facing Connor, I discovered I could see over his shoulder when I stood on tiptoes. I looked toward the village, where I should have seen thatch-roofed cottages or stone fences. Even the thin spire of the stone church where David waited was absent from the horizon.

Straining, I could make out the silhouette of a tower at the point of the inlet's curve. High atop the tower, a flag fluttered and I thought I saw someone standing just below it.

If I were visible to him, he might possibly see me and the man who was stealing me. I raised my hand to wave.

"What do ye think ye are doing now?" Connor leaned into my face, lightning bolts of fury flashing in his black eyes.

I inadvertently glanced toward the tower. He straightened and stared at the figure of a man in the distance.

"He can't save ye now. Go ahead, yell all ye wish. Ye wish to wave?" He reached down and tore the veil from my hair. "Use this! Let him follow. He'll walk right into the trap I have planned for him."

I winced and rubbed the spot where he'd yanked several hairs with the veil. "I have no idea what you're ranting about. Nor do I know that person in the tower."

A trap?

If David came for me … a lump jumped from my stomach to my throat, making it nearly impossible for me to speak if I'd wanted to. I glared at my kidnapper as unbidden tears stung my eyes.

A vein pulsated its way up Connor's right temple and his glare pierced through me as if he were about to pick me up and snap me like a sapling.

He grabbed my upper arm and said, "Ye may walk now. But ye will not slow me down, ye will not try to escape, ye will not give me any more trouble or I will throw ye into the bay and your father may pick up the pieces when he stops cowering in his fort. Do ye understand?"

He dropped the veil which, caught by the wind, fluttered off like a butterfly.

I didn't get all of his angry words, but his tone of voice conveyed that I'd better agree to whatever he said. Trembling within, I lifted my hem and focused on each step, trying to note what direction the men took and how far we had walked.

Traveling on foot, our pace increased slightly and, within a short time, we reached the point where the sea, whipped by the wind into full fury, parted. Some of the water entered an inlet, while most of the waves crashed loudly against the cliffs a hundred feet below them.

Salt spray hung heavily in the air, making the white-crusted rocks as slippery as winter-iced Cleveland sidewalks. I wondered what Connor planned to do now. We'd have to sprout wings to escape from the edge of this cliff.

As if he read my thoughts, Connor pointed. "We will climb down to boats," he shouted above the roar of wind and waves.

Wind as untamed as a Lake Erie winter storm slammed against me. I took one dizzying look at the thunderous waves, the impossible climb and stepped back from the edge.

"Oh, no. First of all, I have this problem with heights. I'm not going near that cliff. Second, there's no way I can climb in a wedding dress."

Without a second of hesitation, Connor said, "Take it off."

Chapter 3

Not a command, not even a request, just a matter-of-fact statement uttered as calmly as if he were accustomed to telling women to remove their clothing.

Giving him my best "Don't-make me-cite-you-for-contempt" look, I said, "What?"

"Take off that shift if it encumbers ye." There was no leer in his voice, only exasperation as if I had tapped into the last of his patience.

I crossed my arms against my chest, crunching salt crystals that clung to the bodice. "I will not!"

He reached out to grab the dress and I slapped away his hand with a stern, "Don't go there, Mister!"

Connor stepped back and said, "By the gods! If I did not need ye—" the wind swallowed the rest of his words.

He shook his fist at the sky, then looked back at me. "Ye are nearly more trouble than ye are worth. I should have tossed ye over the edge long ago."

Planting both hands on my hips, I shouted back, "Well, you have your opportunity now. Go ahead, do it, because if you think I'm going to take off my dress and climb down this cliff, you are crazier than I already think you are."

He turned away suddenly, and stomped over to the other men. Gesturing angrily, he spoke to his companions who nodded, then began climbing down the cliff.

Add anger management to his already numerous faults.

I backed away from my own anger to study Connor.

Tall, several inches over David's six-foot stature. Dark haired with eyes the color of coal, except for the flashes of slate his temper added. He could have been movie-star handsome, and perhaps, a decent guy but for his odorous dress and obnoxious way of ignoring my demands.

Attitude with more than a capital "A."

And, definitely not my type.

While his scruffy, unkempt biker-boy appearance, and "rebel-without-a-cause" aura might attract some women, I would not count myself as one of them. I prefer tidy bankers, well-dressed lawyers, men with education, poise and confidence, rather than brawn, conceit and ego.

Men like David who respected me for my brains as much as they professed to like my looks. I could overlook a lot in a man, but never outright disrespect.

And, Connor was the king of disrespect.

My shepherd-abductor returned as the last of his men disappeared over the edge of the cliff. Giving me no hint of his intentions, he leaned over and said, "Ye will not knock at the gates of the Otherworld yet."

"Huh?"

He grabbed my hands and tied a thin leather cord around my wrists.

"Why are you doing this? Why don't you just kill me and get it over with? David and I don't have money, so there won't be any ransom. And our government doesn't believe in negotiating with kidnappers," I yelled against the wind.

He couldn't be bothered to reply as he began walking away from the cliff, dragging me behind him. I tried sending mental daggers into his broad back where his pony-tailed hair flapped.

Not only was he committing an international crime, but he also had a maddening way of not answering. My Gaelic might be a bit rusty, but he seemed to understand enough of the words.

His direction took us away from the sea and the thunderous surf. In a few minutes, we had moved far enough inland that I could speak without shouting. I'd gone from fear to anger and ping-ponged back again several times. Anger's turn. I stepped alongside him and asked, "Why did you take me?"

He looked at me more boldly than any criminal I had ever faced. "I took ye because I wanted ye."

A chill ran down my spine.

He wanted me? No, it had to be money he was after. Money, notoriety for some cause, a hostage. What else could a kidnapper want? Certainly, not me. He didn't even know me.

"There won't be any ransom," I said calmly, refusing to dwell on his words.

He walked away and yanked the tether that forced me to follow him.

I decided to try a different approach.

It was one against one now. The self-defense course taught by the Cleveland Police Department, and a class in hostage negotiations came to my mind. I never thought I'd need those skills.

I assessed my strengths in the situation. Even if he had the weight, height and muscle advantage, I was quick on my feet, a fast thinker, rational, and at the moment, surprisingly calm. The odds might be in my favor now that the other men had left and the terrain was less treacherous.

On the other side of the ledger, I was wearing a wedding gown and shoes not cut out for running across a meadow, my wrists were tied, and this was his territory.

Tricky, but not bad odds.

Could I somehow grab his sword? There wouldn't be an easy way to pull it from his waistband, and the sword hung down nearly to his knee. I noticed a second weapon, a smaller dagger tucked into the edge of his boot, staring at the ornately carved black handle as if to will it to spring from his leg to my hand. If I could just get close enough, there was a much greater chance I could snatch it. Perhaps at night, when he slept, I'd have an opportunity.

But I would have to be close enough to extract the knife from his boot without awakening him. That would be asking a lot. Getting past the odor emanating from his clothing. Sleeping, or pretending to sleep next to him. Nearly as much courage as stealing his weapon.

And, what would I do with the knife once I had it?

Could I stab him? I didn't think so. I'd spent too much time telling others that violence was never an answer. I'd be hard-pressed to consider stabbing a sleeping man self-defense.

Even if he was a kidnapper. Even if he did ignore me when I demanded he free me. Even if he had told me to remove my clothing.

Connor yanked on the leather tie binding my wrists. I could not begin to match his long-legged stride, especially in a wedding dress that tangled around my ankles with every step as we strode across a huge meadow carpeted with deep grass and heather. I was nearly jogging trying to keep up.

In spite of the spring breeze, sweat dampened my undergarments and plastered my curls to the back of my neck. I could feel my cheeks redden under the bright sun. David, if he ever found me, would chide me for forgetting the sunscreen. But then, I hadn't planned on being kidnapped on my way to our wedding, and then dragged across the Irish countryside. *David!*

I blinked hard as thoughts of him brought tears to my eyes. I couldn't allow my captor to see me cry. I could almost hear Grandmother Moira's words.

You're an O'Donnell, through and through. That usually meant that I was being stubborn and willful like my grandfather.

I refocused on the present moment. How long had we walked? It had to have been hours since I disappeared. David must be frantic with worry. I would be, if he had been the one who was kidnapped.

Well, first I'd be mad at being stood up at the altar.

Then, I'd wonder what happened and start looking for him. David, Bill and Linda would be searching by now. Would they find the veil? Would villagers help in the hunt? It could take a day or longer to notify whatever authorities and get help from the outside world.

Anger and fear changed places again in their little dance around my brain. I slowed my pace slightly. Connor rewarded me with a yank on the binding around my wrists, nearly causing me to trip as I caught the hem with my shoe.

"Hey, I can't walk that fast," I complained.

I pretended to stumble and pulled the leather ties hard, causing Connor to pause. Perhaps if I became more of a nuisance than he wanted to deal with, he'd turn me loose. The anger I'd previously seen in his eyes was gone now. My words were a mosquito buzzing his ear for all the feelings he displayed. He tugged on my wrists and brought me right up against his chest.

Looking down, he asked, "Ye would rather I carried ye again?"

I gasped. "Uh, no thanks. But you could loosen the ropes on my wrists."

He crooked his head and said, "Aye, I could."

With that, he turned and started walking again, leaving the rope exactly as it had been.

I knew then exactly what I'd do with that knife if I got my hands on it!

I lifted my skirt, and crashed through clumps of wildflowers, kicking up a floral scent nearly as heavy as the salt air had been near the ocean. Connor continued to lead me at a brisk pace across the meadow to a grove of tall oak trees.

The coolness of the forest seemed a welcome change from the heat of the sun, but the thick undergrowth and trees made the path just as challenging as the knee-high grasses of the meadow.

"Can we stop for a moment?" I asked, lowering my voice. The stillness of the grove reminded me of a church sanctuary. "My feet hurt, and I need to go to the bathroom."

"Bathroom?" Connor raised one eyebrow at the English word I'd thrown at him.

"You know, restroom? Water closet? Ladies' room? Loo? What do you call it in Gaelic?"

I couldn't think of any other names, in English or Gaelic, and I didn't know why I bothered anyway since there certainly wasn't such a place out in the middle of forest-nowhere.

Finally, he seemed to get the idea, and he pointed to a tree a few yards away.

"Okay, I get it. Primitive, but the best you can offer. You're not going to watch. I need a little privacy." I held out my wrists. "And my hands."

As he removed the rope, he said, "Ye must promise me ye won't try to escape."

"Really? Where would I go? It's not like I know my way around here," I said as I slipped around a tree for a little privacy. I wouldn't try it right then, but later.

That night. Tomorrow. Whenever the opportunity presented.

"Is there a place where we are going? A house?" While I spoke, I quickly tore a small scrap of my hem and tied it to a bush. With any luck, Connor wouldn't hear the sound of ripping fabric and wouldn't find the piece of lace I left as a clue for David and the search party. A needle in a haystack, but I felt better knowing I was doing the best I could to try to escape or be found.

Connor waited until I rejoined him before answering. "Nay, daughter of Donal. Ye will sleep tonight under a canopy of tree branches with stars instead of rush torches to light your dreams." His voice softened slightly, but he still replaced the tie around my wrists.

For the first time, I noticed the telltale bump of a broken nose and a faint scar across his left temple. The lines of his forehead had eased, the vein that pulsated when he grew suddenly angry had disappeared, and the scowl he had worn while we climbed across the rocks was gone.

Keeping him talking seemed to relax him. I hoped enough to drop his guard.

"You remind me of someone I knew in high school," I said lightly.

I neglected to mention that my classmate had cultivated a "bad boy" rep with multiple piercings, chains and full-arm tattoos. I had had a slight crush on him, but never told him or anyone else. My grandmother Moira would never have approved.

But then, if Moira had met Connor, she would have had a few things to say to him also. *Mostly having to do with cleanliness and godliness.*

Connor didn't respond.

"I have to admit I've never slept outdoors before."

Girl Scout camp always had tents or cabins with metal bunk beds.

"Can you tell me more about this place?"

"It is your father's land. What more would ye want to know about it?" Connor said, cocking one eyebrow.

"Why do you keep talking about my father? He died when I was a child. Is it possible you have mistaken me for someone else?"

The vein in his temple started to pulsate. "Nay, ye are Caitrín." He reached out and caught a curl between two of his fingers. "I knew ye would come for flowers today. The blessings of the gods were mine."

I shrank from his touch. His explanation didn't make sense, yet he seemed sincere in his responses. And that was what scared me most. He truly believed in whatever crazy plan he had put into motion. And very little I said seemed to change his direction.

How could he have known I'd come for flowers? And why was he calling me "Caitrín?" Was that the Gaelic version of "Kathleen?"

Perhaps. But then again, maybe I was the wrong person.

"What if I'm not the woman you were looking for?"

Chapter 4

Connor answered with a snort and continued to break his way through the underbrush.

That's it! He's snatched the wrong person. All I have to do is convince him and he'll let me go. Probably even take me back to Aasleigh. I'll promise not to say anything to anyone. He'll apologize and the whole unpleasant episode can be over in a few hours.

I needed to find a crack where I might force him to concede he had taken the wrong woman. *Safer and easier than trying to steal his knife.*

"How much farther until we stop?" I asked as I stumbled over a tree root.

Connor tugged the thong tied to my wrists to keep me from falling.

"Hey, let me fall and break my ankle. That would be better than dislocating my arm. Do you think you could loosen the ties? You're tearing up my wrists, and I won't be going anywhere far since I don't know my way around here."

He agreed this time and removed the binding from my wrists. I rubbed the red welts that marked my wrists. At least my hands were free now.

Score one point.

Shepherd boy didn't know I had been a Girl Scout with a badge in wilderness survival, even if I hadn't slept out under the stars. I hoped that Connor believed I would be unable to find my way in the dark through the forest. As it was, with the trail he had left, I could probably retrace our footsteps blindfolded. I high-fived a tree branch as I bent to walk under it.

"What a place! Nothing like Cleveland! Not a sign of another human being. I didn't know that was possible anymore," I said. "Oak trees? Funny, I never thought of this part of Ireland having such dense forest."

Connor gave me a puzzled look. "This forest is sacred to your father's druid."

"Druid, uh? That's a bit New Age. What does he do?"

"He might accompany your father's men, but he prefers to use the spirit world to do his bidding." Connor held a branch aside for me to pass.

I nodded even though I didn't have the slightest idea what that meant. "So, we're trespassing on land that belongs to a druid who can summon spirits against us?" I bent to free my hem from a tree root that snagged it.

"I am not worried about Ongus. He is an old man who prefers the comfort of his cup these days."

"An old druid with a drinking problem? That could be interesting. Conjure a lion and end up with a rabbit." The thought of a druid's spells gone amok brought a private smile to my face.

Connor paused for a moment to study the trees as if looking for an unmarked path.

"So, how does a shepherd know someone else's forest so well? Did you grow up here?" I asked.

"Shepherd?" Connor's eyes darkened, if it were possible to bring out more ebony in already black-as-night eyes. "I am Connor, son of—"

"'Son of Malley, Chieftain of clan Malley.' Got it. Not that I don't believe you, but you have to admit this is all pretty incredible. Here I am, a bride on my way to being married—"

Connor took my hand in his and said, "Ah, but, ye are still a bride and ye are still on your way to your wedding."

I pulled free. "Aha, so you are going to return me to Aasleigh!" A tone of "I-told-you-so" crept unbidden into my voice.

"Ye speak so strangely, daughter of Donal. It is no wonder your father has betrothed ye to Colum, the warrior. It would take someone like him to control ye."

Connor held my elbow as I climbed over a log. His pace had slowed and he seemed more concerned about my welfare which almost made me more wary.

"Colum, the warrior? And, who might that be?" Visions of professional wrestlers flashed through my mind.

"Ye do not know Colum? Was the betrothal performed before ye were of age? I would not put that past Donal." Connor snorted at some insight he did not share with me as he continued to create a pathway through dense underbrush.

"So, tell me more about this Colum," I said, flicking a leaf from my lace sleeve.

Connor gave me a bewildered look that was beginning to become a permanent part of his visage. "Ye are indeed a most peculiar woman. It is no wonder your father could not find a worthy husband for ye."

"What? I thought you said Donal's daughter was engaged to Colum, the warrior. That sounds pretty worthy to me. If he is a warrior of some sort he must be young and muscular and strong. What's wrong with that?"

Connor looked over his shoulder at me, but instead of glaring as he had been doing every so often, his face softened. And, he actually laughed aloud. "Colum, the Warrior," Connor emphasized the word as if were a last name or title of some sort, "prefers to be a stud, prancing from one village to another seeking mares. There's no telling how many foals he has left behind. And, he is an old man, of perhaps forty winters."

An old man of forty? Then, I must be a middle-aged woman. And Connor had to be only a few years shy of mid-life crisis himself. And, why he doesn't think that being a stud is something to be envied?

"Some women might want to join the stable of Colum, the warrior stud."

This time, Connor's laughter reverberated from the trees as if there were an army of Connors all convulsing at the thought of a woman with Colum, the aging warrior.

I was mystified. But, rather than wonder for long about what he was laughing at, I decided to take advantage of his good humor.

"Do you think we could stop for a moment? There's something in my shoe."

Connor nodded toward a fallen log and I quickly took advantage of the offer. I brushed off a spot, asking myself why I should worry about soiling a dress that was already ruined by now. Sitting, I removed my shoe, taking my time to locate the offending pebble and toss it aside. Before I could replace the shoe, the sound of something crashing through the underbrush caught my attention.

David! He's come to rescue me!

I started to call to him when a huge, wild pig thundered through the trees and stopped a few feet from me. The animal stared, its small black eyes narrowing as though it were trying to decide if I would make a tasty meal.

I froze, tightening the grip on my heel until I felt my hand and the shoe fuse. Not a stiletto heel, unfortunately, but then, a shoe, even with a stiletto heel, was hardly the weapon of choice against a massive porker with vicious-looking teeth and dinner on its mind.

Chapter 5

Aim for the eyes.

Good advice for a shark attack maybe, but would it work on a narrow-eyed boar?

My breath caught in my throat as my heart leapt there and blocked air from coming or going. I started to raise my hand when Connor touched me on the shoulder and whispered in a low voice, "Do not move. Its eyesight is poor. It may not attack if it thinks ye are no threat."

Statue, my brain screamed and my lungs froze in mid-breath. Fused with the log beneath me, I stared at the animal, willing, begging the pig to turn away.

Fat chance. Even I, non-breathing, non-moving woman knew this monster hog ruled these woods, and nothing I did would stop it from making me its lunch.

Making eye contact with a ferocious, near-sighted pile of wild bacon didn't do much to deter it. The boar inched closer, sniffing the ground inches from my shoeless foot. My toes curled under into the dirt on their own.

Meanwhile, Connor's hand slid slowly from my shoulder. I felt the air behind me stir slightly as he stepped away.

He's leaving me! The shepherd-terrorist certainly knows when to jump ship.

It took every ounce of my strength to remain frozen while I waited for the beast to lunge at my throat. I could have been a branch on the log. I didn't move a muscle, not even to breathe or to blink. My attention focused completely on the vicious animal edging so close I could see its nostrils flare as it searched for me.

Its fetid breath nearly gagged me. The boar snorted and showed perfect white and very sharp teeth. Its ears pressed back against its head, and a cork-screw tail pointed straight up. Finished sniffing, the pig dropped its snout, as it prepared to charge.

A drop of sweat trickled down my temple and dripped from my

jaw. I focused on the stain the drop created on my skirt while inside I started to tremble as if my guts had turned to gel that might begin to puddle at any moment.

David, where are you?

Connor, where are you?

The boar took a step closer, sniffed again and its beady eyes darkened to pinpoints. I knew it had finally picked up my scent.

The beast growled low, an unearthly noise that echoed in my ears. Suddenly, it lunged, taking aim for my throat. I gasped and closed my eyes as something whooshed past my ear.

I heard a thud and, opened one eye just in time to see the animal drop a few feet in front of me. A black-handled dagger wobbled between the boar's eyes, and dark red poured out onto the mossy ground where it collapsed.

Letting out my breath, I felt a black hole open in the pit of my belly. The same hand that warned me and that threw the knife now caught me as I slumped backward.

"I ... oh ... " I said, looking into Connor's eyes as I dropped into his arms. "I never ... " I started to say until my mind blanked completely.

Coherent words refused to come., while images, sounds and smells raced through my mind: *The boar's growl, its charge, its teeth, its blood soaking onto the green of the forest floor.*

Connor murmured something, words I could not translate. Gentle sounds of comfort like a mother humming a wordless lullaby. I let myself melt into his arms, finding tenderness at odds with the bravado of the man who called himself chief of the Malley clan. I burrowed against his shoulder unable to look at the dead animal, and unable to stop the shaking and the unbidden tears.

He held me with the patience of a new father. Gently, wiping a finger across my cheek, smearing my tears. When I focused on his eyes, I thought I saw a spark of warmth and caring there. Then, the doorway to his soul closed as quickly as it had opened.

"We must move on," Connor said quietly as he released me.

He stood and walked over to the boar, retrieved his knife and wiped blood from the blade on a mound of moss. Visions of a whole family of wild pigs crashed into my mind, and I found myself unable to move.

"Do not look at it," Connor said, taking the shoe from my hand and gently replacing it on my foot. He pulled me into his arms and steadied me as I stood.

I leaned against him, wrapped myself in the musky fragrance of old trees, and the strength of the man who stroked my shoulder and back tenderly. When my breathing had finally slowed and my heart no longer raced, Connor slowly let go. He caught a single tear before it dripped from my jaw.

And I thought, for a fraction of a second that he might kiss me.

Then, a shudder swept through me as I realized that I wanted him to.

Chapter 6

The day was taking too many unexpected turns, and Connor did not enjoy losing control of his plan. He reviewed the events of the day in his mind.

No one had expected trouble on Beltane, the celebration of the return of light after the season of darkness. A stranger could pass unnoticed through the festival, with all its noise and crowds. Were this any other Beltane festival, Connor would have competed with the warriors and likely won most of the games, but he had not time for contests this day.

Disguised as a traveler from the south so that no one could identify his clan, Connor planned to find the girl, and take her. If he and his men were successful, they would escape before her father even realized she had been abducted. There was no way Donal could mount a swift rescue. The overland route would take days. Since Donal had not been blessed by the gods with ability to navigate the river into Connor's valley, he could only approach Croaghnac by crossing the mountain through a dangerous passage where he would be at the mercy of Connor's warriors.

With the favor of the gods, Connor planned to bundle Donal's daughter across the cliffs to his waiting boats. Returning to Croaghnac, to his own Beltane festival, he'd marry the girl before her father could stop the wedding.

Connor paused at the edge of a great forest. Inhaling the scent of spring, he whispered a prayer of thanksgiving for the day promised to him long before, the day of vengeance the gods set in motion for him. Beltane had never known finer weather. The sun threw off the cloak of gray to greet the meadow flowers and the tender buds of the trees opened wide to welcome new life.

This land, even though it belonged to Donal, smelled of freshness and newness. A gentle breeze stirred the sleeve of Connor's tunic like a spirit walking past. The spirit of his dead father, no doubt here to bless

Connor's efforts.

There was only one flaw in his plan. The path across the cliffs carrying an uncooperative woman would not be easy. Even with the confusion and noise of the games, she might attract attention beyond what Connor and his two men could handle. Donal's daughter was reported to be headstrong, of a temperament that matched her wild, red-gold curls.

How would she be convinced to leave the fair and her guards?

The answer bloomed before him. She needed flowers to weave into a garland for the feast. While he waited and planned, Connor had seen her visit the meadow. Before the games began, she had come to gather spring blossoms.

He might not even need to lure her from the fair. With the excitement of the games, her guards would be distracted. She would leave the crowd and her guards to seek flowers for her hair, and Connor would be there, waiting near the meadow that beckoned her more blatantly than a bridegroom.

Let her come to him. The gods would reward his patience.

Signaling to his companions to hide themselves in the forest and keep watch for any guards who might accompany her, Connor leaned against a tree, the dark brown of his clothing blending into the shadows. One hand rested on the sword hanging from his belt as he studied the tower in the distance, willing the girl to step free of her father's watchful eyes, the merriment of the festival, and most importantly, her father's warriors.

"Come to me," Connor whispered into the wind.

In the distance, a ram's horn sounded, its rich, deep bass blast signaling the official start of the games. Connor smiled. "Come for flowers. Come to the bridegroom who awaits ye."

Now, deep in the druid's wooded lair, Connor knew the gods would turn a deaf ear to his words, so he didn't bother speaking to them. They had blessed him thus far, giving him the woman, and stopping the boar attack. He had never had a truer throw as the boar drop.

He didn't like spending the night in the forest, but even this was preferable to the more exposed foothills. He doubted that Donal's warriors were on their trail yet, but a fire out in the open would be a beacon to anyone.

In the shelter of the trees, he could build a small fire, enough for warmth should the goddess of spring forget to hold some of the sun's heat for the night.

He imagined the scene in Donal's tower. By now, he would have discovered his daughter was missing. He'd send word to Colum inquiring whether the girl had run off with him. But, not waiting for days to get an answer, Donal would dispatch a few warriors to summon the entire army, his fianna, to council. That would take less than one day since most of the warriors were present for the Beltane fair.

The council's discussion would be dramatic and angry. Donal would seize any opportunity to rail against his enemy, Connor whether or not he had any evidence of Connor's involvement in his daughter's absence.

And, when Donal's men searched the surrounding land, they'd find evidence. But not of the fianna. Connor left enough of a trail to make it appear she was with only one person. Donal might believe she had run away on her own.

Connor chuckled.

Donal's warriors would be sent after her. But inexperienced in the ways of the sea, they'd have to take the overland route. The horses could not travel the highlands in the dark. Already a day ahead, Connor would get an early start on the next morning and cross the lowlands before the sun arose. They'd reach Croaghnac before the sun set again.

Connor and his captive came to the edge of the forest where the deep purple, early evening sky, glimmering with huge stars, waited for the moon to outshine them.

Caitrin stretched her hand up, and offered another of her nonsensical proclamations, "I feel as though I'm standing at the top of the world and can reach out and grab a handful of first-wish stars."

Connor didn't look up, but instead began to stamp the ground beneath his feet. "This is where we will spend the night." He motioned for her to sit while he gathered wood for a fire.

Chapter 7

As tired as I was, I didn't need to be persuaded when Connor bade me to sit. And, what was a small grass stain when the dress was, by now, a complete ruin? I folded my legs under myself and sat where I could lean against a tree. Exhaustion was fast catching up with me.

I was perfectly content to allow Connor to clean up the forest or whatever he was doing. Grateful as I was for his rescue from the wild pig, I still wasn't about to help him do anything.

Instead, I picked at twigs and leaves that had hitched a ride on my skirt, and watched his efficient, practiced motions. David would not have known what to do to make a camp.

But then, Connor wouldn't be able find his way around Cleveland's freeways. I mentally ticked off a list of comparisons of the two men. But the more I tried to stack up Connor's shortcomings against David's strengths, the more I had to admit I couldn't really find many beyond Connor's lack of cleanliness, and stubborn insistence I was someone else.

David loves me. Connor wants me.

I could tell from the way he looked at me.

David respects me. Connor protected me.

David is good-looking. Connor is handsome, in his own primitive way.

I stole a glance at the muscles of his upper arms as he passed and I remembered how I felt when he wrapped me in them. He looked at me just then, his dark eyes connecting with mine with such intensity that I hoped he couldn't read my thoughts. I felt my cheeks flush, and I quickly looked down at my skirt.

After stacking wood, he made a small pile of twigs and dried leaves, then pulled two stones from a pouch tied to his belt. A few strikes of one rock against the other produced a spark. He blew gently on the dried leaves until it smoked, and produced a blue flame just large enough to ignite the campfire.

"No matches?" I asked, marveling at how quickly he had lit a fire that would have taken David half a box of matches and a can of lighter fluid. David was the reason a grill had an automatic starter.

Connor ignored my comment. "No wedding feast tonight, but ye shall have something to eat."

From another pouch attached to his belt, he pulled out a handful of dried nuts and berries and a piece of leathery meat and handed them to me. I examined each and tried the nuts first.

I hadn't realized how hungry I was until I sampled the offering. "What sort of nut is this? It tastes pretty good."

He looked surprised by my question. "It was a favorite of my father's."

I pulled up my knees and wrapped my arms around them, resting my chin on my knees. "What did your father do for a living?"

Connor looked puzzled, "For a living?"

"Where did he work? Was he a shepherd also?"

He threw his head back and laughed heartily. I wondered what I had said that was so humorous. I didn't really care so long as he remained in a good mood. If I could summon the energy and courage to try to escape, it would be easiest if he were relaxed and less vigilant.

"A shepherd? He would return from the Otherworld if he heard ye say that." Connor stirred the growing fire and added a few twigs to encourage it.

"Oh, so he's on a trip?"

Connor doubled over as another spasm of laughter coursed through him. Then, he suddenly became serious again, as the light bulb of his laughter clicked off.

"Ye know better. While it did occur before your birth, it surprises me that your father has not bragged of his exploits."

He leaned toward me, his dark eyes boring into mine as he said, "Your father killed my father on the night of my birth, and would have killed me as well had my mother not hidden in a cave."

I gasped at his words. "Oh, I'm so sorry. That is horrible."

So that was the cause of his troubled life.

"But taking Donal's daughter will not return your father. You've wasted your life if you've spent years seeking revenge. You should ... " I stopped in mid-sentence. "I'm sorry, Connor. It's really none of my business, except for the part about your mistaking me for Donal's daughter. But I am sorry."

"I am not one to be pitied by ye or any woman," Connor replied, his heavy brows narrowing as a scowl returned to his face.

"No, I ... " my words were drowned out by the sound of distant rumbling that gathered momentum, building quickly to a deafening roar that shook the ground. Emerging from the shadows of dusk and a cloud of dust, wild horses, and even wilder riders thundered into our small camp.

I looked around quickly for some way to slip into the brush and hide while Connor sprang to his feet, one hand gripping the handle of his still-sheathed sword. His lips curled up slightly disappearing beneath his mustache as the leader of the group slid from a bare-backed horse and strode boldly to face him.

Instead of drawing weapons against each other, the stranger extended a hand that clasped Connor's forearm and pulled him into a boisterous, bear hug.

"It's been too long, brother," the intruder said, walloping Connor on his back. "Too long, and what is this news I have heard?" He craned around Connor's shoulder and stared at me. "Ye have Donal's daughter?"

"Ye know I have planned this for a long time, Basta."

"Everyone knows. And that is why I am here. When your men returned with an empty spot in the boats, I decided to come after ye. To rescue ye."

"Rescue me! From what? The forest is silent. Donal cowers in his tower like a sick, old bear. He does not raise the cry of alarm that his daughter has been taken. He does not care enough about her to put down his mead and chase after her. Or, perhaps he counts the coins of the bride price and laughs because he will not have to deliver her now. Indeed, if anyone were to come for her, it would be Colum. I did not see his colors at the fair, so he is days away from even learning she has been stolen. Nay, I am not worried, and I do not need to be rescued."

"What have ye to eat and drink, brother?" Basta asked.

"Ye see before ye. I did not hunt today."

Basta laughed. "I see a man who has been too busy stealing a woman to feed her or himself. 'Tis a sad state, Connor, but one which I shall rectify since I am here to rescue ye."

Connor backed away from the other man enough that I could see Basta completely. They dressed alike, as did Basta's companions, a half-dozen unkempt shepherds with swords at their waists. Both brothers were taller than the others, broad-shouldered with massive arms the size of most men's thighs, the same midnight-colored eyes, long, dark hair, and straggly, drooping mustaches. An observer could not tell which of them was the younger of the two except for the air of deference Basta seemed to show toward Connor.

With the mention of food, the pendulum had swung in Basta's favor. He puffed with pride at appearing the savior. With one gesture, he directed his men to join them. They brought with them enough food for a football team. Meat—thankfully not the carcass of the boar, but several rabbits and a bird of some sort—was set to roast over a quickly-enlarged fire while they shared chunks of hard, black bread and a pouch containing a drink that they passed from one to another.

I sniffed it and decided not to try it. In less than forty-eight hours, I had arrived in Ireland, discovered a long lost cousin, been kidnapped on my way to my wedding, then dragged in heels and a wedding dress across the countryside.

My head swam from jet lag and lack of food, my legs felt like rubber and whatever energy I had a few minutes before had already soaked into the soft moss beneath me. Tired as I was, I needed to remain alert now that my opportunity to escape would be greatly complicated by the presence of seven more terrorist shepherds.

Basta sat down next to me, annoyingly close, and leaned toward me. One thing these guys could use was some soap and men's cologne.

I scooted a few inches away. Connor sat on my other side, shifting protectively close until I felt as if I were territory being marked. I wanted to squeeze out from between them, but a look from Connor warned me to stay where I was. I ignored his glare and Basta's leer and concentrated on the soiled skirt of my wedding dress, licking my finger to dab at a stain.

The once-beautiful antique dress was ruined. My wedding day was long gone, my fiancé, who knew where? I was surrounded by coarse men who shared a bag of something likely alcoholic, and two brothers who regarded me with almost the same expression as the wild boar.

Tears welled in my eyes. I bit my lower lip and blinked them away. Whatever I did, I didn't want to show any weakness for fear these men would tear me apart like a bone between two dogs. My toughest judicial personality didn't work well when I was exhausted and scared beyond belief, but I clung to it as if I were sitting there, in my black robe before my courtroom at that very moment.

When the meat was well-cooked, Connor skewered a generous hunk on his dagger and broke off a small piece for me. I nodded my thanks and gave him a little smile.

Basta leaned toward me with a piece of dark brown bread, saying, "So tell me, Caitrín, has my brother treated ye well?"

I didn't want to deal with Basta, but playing one brother against the other might work in my favor. Even though I didn't appreciate his invasion of my space, I answered as pleasantly as I could.

"I believe I am not the person he meant to kidnap. My name is Kathleen O'Donnell. I'm a tourist. From all I have gathered so far, he wanted to take Donal's daughter and I am not her. Perhaps you can assist me to convince your brother of his error and to release me and return me to Aasleigh."

Basta nodded his head toward Connor and said, "Why do her words make no sense?"

Connor shrugged his shoulders. "She says she isn't Donal's daughter, but look at her. She has the same red hair as all of Donal's clan, even though someone took a blade to it in such awful fashion. I've watched her come from the tower before. This day, she walked right into the meadow, and dropped at my feet."

"No, I didn't! I was on my way to my wedding. I stopped to pick some flowers. But that's the only part you got right. I heard strange music and must have blacked out for a moment. When I awoke, you were carrying me away. Against my will, I might add."

Basta stroked his mustache and leaned back against one elbow. "No one has ever mentioned that Donal's daughter frightens the aés sídhe. No wonder Donal hasn't married her off yet. Did she hit her head when ye snatched her? But that still would not explain the hair."

"What? Wait just a moment! I do not scare fairies! I am not an old maid yet! I just haven't gotten around to getting married. Call it a commitment phobia, if you want. And, will you get off the hair thing? Women cut their hair. I happen to like my hair shorter. With curls like this, it's easier to manage. You shepherds should talk! When was the last time you so much as washed your hair?"

Connor answered, "Why would we do that? Ye see, Basta, she has been like this all day. She makes no sense."

"A woman," Basta said, wiping his knife across this thigh. "But definitely worse than most. Your patience is commendable. I will gladly take her off your hands."

There was an edge to Basta's voice that I did not like. And in spite of my rusty Gaelic, I understood enough of his words to be more than wary of his intentions. I looked from one brother to the other and decided I would much rather remain with Connor who had made no real attempt to harm me than with Basta whose eyes undressed me as he spoke.

Connor shrugged, and began to toy with his dagger, its blade gleaming in the firelight. I wondered if he was sending his brother a subtle message by the way he turned the knife and ran his finger down the fat-streaked blade.

Just to make sure Connor didn't take Basta up on his offer, I whispered to Connor, "You can't let him do that, you know. Aren't you the one who waited forever to take me? I mean, Donal's daughter. Aren't you the one who wants revenge?"

"Ye know the law, judge," he answered in a low voice. To his brother, Connor gave a grunt and a curt reply. "She is mine."

My mind raced. *Yes, I know the law. But, what law? What law covers terrorist-shepherds and kidnapped brides? What's he talking about?*

I didn't know whether to thank Connor or complain again that I wasn't the woman he thought he was stealing. I stared at his arms, almost wishing he'd put one around me to officially mark his territory so that Basta would back off.

Basta raised one eyebrow as he studied me. His mustached lip turned up in a wry smile as if he got some unspoken, brother-telegraphed message before he turned toward the fire.

Warmth spread across my cheeks at the thought that I actually wanted to stay with this smelly, unkempt, Irish gangster rather than be bargained away to his brother. I tried to tell myself I merely needed to feel the safety and comfort I had found before in his embrace.

Shivering at the thought of being wrapped in his arms, I warned myself to stay in control of my feelings. I had to be able to leave him without a second thought at the first chance to escape. I had to be ready to use his knife if necessary.

Stockholm syndrome, identifying with my captor, would not help me.

Following the meal, the men clustered in twos or threes around the perimeter of the small camp, none so close that they would be a threat to me should I try to flee between them. I intended to remain awake until they went to sleep and then try to slip unnoticed from the camp.

Resting my head on my drawn-up knees, I watched while Connor unwound the length of walnut-colored fabric pinned at his shoulder and wrapped around his waist. He held it out to offer it as a blanket. When I shook my head to refuse it, he ignored me and tucked it around my shoulders.

His hand brushed against my cheek, setting butterflies quivering in my stomach. A spark of caring flashed through his ebony eyes before they returned to being as hard and cold as the night.

I clutched the wrap tightly. It smelled of Connor and reminded me of his arms around me and his body against mine. I pushed away the memories of the boar attack and its aftermath. In spite of his courage and sure throw, he was still a kidnapper.

Stifling a sniffle, I thought of what might have been ... what should have been my wedding night.

What was David feeling and doing? Surely he'd know I hadn't intentionally left him standing at the altar. He knew me better than that.

Linda would have told him I was ready for marriage. He would be looking for me. He'd have rounded up help to search every inch of this country. This camp couldn't be that far from Aasleigh. I was certain he would find me by dawn.

I looked around the campsite, gauging how soon I might be able to escape. One by one, the men's voices silenced and snores soon filled the campsite. Fatigue numbed my mind as well as my body. I rested my head on my arms and, in spite of my intentions, slipped into a dreamless sleep.

I opened my eyes once to find Basta and his men all asleep, but Connor wide awake, watching me. Stretching stiff arms and legs, I said, "Not very comfortable."

Connor reached toward me and pulled me against his chest, wrapping an arm around my shoulder. "Warm enough?"

"Yes." This wasn't exactly what I had in mind. I needed to stay alert. I didn't want to be warmer.

Seductively warmer.

Nor closer, nor more comfortable.

And I certainly didn't want the steady, slow pounding of his heart, a sound like the drum beat I had heard that morning, to lull me to sleep with my head on his chest.

But it did.

Chapter 8

Connor studied the short, coppery curls of the woman asleep against his shoulder. He found it difficult to tell which had brighter color, the glowing embers of the fire or her hair. He knew no woman who took a blade to her hair. Why would anyone want her hair cropped like the wool of sheep?

He had watched her from a distance for so long, he felt her knew her. He'd seen her sun-drenched fiery curls bouncing long and luxurious across her shoulders as she danced at the edge of the meadow.

Every time she came to the meadow, warriors guarded her. This day, she came closer than she had ever been. And, for the first time, without her guards.

His, for the taking. One moment, she paused at the edge of the meadow, the next, she lay amid the flowers at his feet.

Had it not been ordained by the gods?

She reminded him of a child, and her short stature might have led him to believe she was still a young girl. Yet, he knew from the feel of her in his arms and the swell of her breasts that she was no girl-child. She was a woman, the one he sought, even though she was shorter and smaller than he had expected.

He twined a single curl around his finger and marveled at its softness and how her hair smelled incredibly like the spring meadow where he had found her.

She was the most curious of women.

He had never met a woman whose lips wore color as though she had picked a flower and somehow rubbed its rosy pinkness onto her lips. And her lashes were far thicker than most women. He knew that a woman could darken her eyelids by smearing them with a finger dipped in soot. How Caitrín had harnessed the sky's blue and gently laid it on her eyelids, he could not imagine.

He let go of the curl and rested his hand on her shoulder at the edge of her neckline. He had never seen a garment woven to resemble newly fallen snow on roses. Its intricate pattern must have required the work of many weavers. His finger traced a blossom on her sleeve. She must show the weavers of his clan how to create such a fabric.

But it wasn't just her curls and her dress that intrigued him most.

She was beautiful. How could such a simple-minded, evil man as Donal have fathered her? Her courage, her defiance belonged to the daughter of a warrior-king, not a coward like Donal.

She will be a worthy wife and mother for my sons.

His chest puffed slightly at the thought of the children, the sons, she would bear him.

Malley sons and warriors.

While he admired her courage and strength, he had not expected her vulnerability and softness. When she fell into his arms after the boar attack, when she sought his protection from Basta, he felt a strange sensation in his chest.

Tightness.

No, that was not quite right.

An odd feeling of protectiveness. Caring, where there had never been such feelings before. There was no room within his heart of stone for caring. Especially for the daughter of his enemy. He pushed it away to the farthest recesses of his heart.

When his father had been alive, Malley had been the most powerful warrior-king of the land. Had it not been for Connor's birth, Malley would not have been killed by Donal.

Love became Malley's weakness. He had loved his wife, Connor's mother, and sped to her side when he heard her travail had begun. Had he not turned his back on his enemy, he might still be alive this day.

Connor tipped the sleeping woman's face toward his and studied her features.

It was love that cost my father his life. I will never make the same mistake! Ye will bear me sons, but ye will never capture my heart.

The tightness in his chest, now rock-hard, sunk to his gut with a thud. Something troubled him like the gnawing of a small animal he could hear in the darkness of the night forest.

What was it about the woman asleep against his chest that nagged at the edges of his heart?

Could it be her insistence that she was not Donal's daughter?

Could she be telling the truth that I have taken the wrong woman? Nay, not possible!

I watched her leave the tower. I saw her blazing curls as she crossed the meadow.

Once before, he had nearly been close enough to catch the sparkle of her blue eyes as she chased a butterfly. He would have taken her then, but for the guards who always accompanied her.

Through the long nights of the dark season, he wrapped himself in thoughts of her nearly every night. Imagining her body against his warded off the chill of days spent plotting, waiting, preparing. In his mind, he bedded her a thousand times over.

But now the reality of feeling her pressed against him sent doubt niggling at him like a honeybee flitting from blossom to blossom. He ran a finger along the neckline of her garment.

Her clothing, her hair. Perhaps she is, as she claims, not Donal's daughter.

Who could she be then? She is too well-spoken and finely dressed to be the daughter of a freeman, or the wife of a warrior. She must be Donal's daughter.

Yet, she did come to the meadow without her customary guards. Donal's daughter would go to her wedding night with guards. Why had she been alone this time?

Did Donal know I waited there in the meadow? Did he send her out to lure me into a trap?

There was one other possibility.

His hand tightened into a fist, capturing her gown in his grasp, as the fire of anger surged through his veins.

She could be a fairy sent to lead me to my doom! A fairy who could take on the appearance of a woman to steal my heart and spirit.

That would explain much.

The thought hit him like a kick to the gut.

Was it too late? Had her enchantment already taken hold?

Basta saw it. 'Frightens the aes sídhe.' Hadn't he said those very words?

Connor felt a sudden urge to rip off her clothing. Prove to himself and his brother that she was no fairy, but all woman. And all his!

He released the fabric clutched hotly in his hand. Staring into the red embers of the campfire, he considered his original plan to steal his bride and marry her before his clan.

She will be mine soon enough. Before Beltane ends.

Slowly, in the flickering shadows, a new idea came to him.

I will not force her to wed. Caitrín must come willingly to my bed as she came willingly to me this night. She must choose to marry me and choose to bear Malley sons.

How much sweeter the revenge on Donal if his own daughter stuck the blade in his heart!

Chapter 9

In my dreams, I was a little girl again, cuddled against my grandmother in the big wooden rocker on the porch. Her fingers flew as she knit a pair of mittens for me.

Click, click, click, pause, click, click, click.

"Tell me the poem again," I said, catching a loop of yarn with my chubby fingers.

Knitting needles marking the cadence of the poem, Moira whispered in her special language, "In dreams I've seen a Golden Wood that holds the Riddles of the World and I've trod upon a Hidden Path to which shadowed strangers often have led me, to its Gate."

I clapped small hands. "And what did you see?" I answered in the words she had shared with me, the language only we spoke.

My grandmother smiled because I knew the poem by heart.

She continued to recite it. "Strange sights I saw while all alone like candle light encased in stone, and I heard laughter and music low which led me to where I did not know, for I had wandered off the Path."

The path. The magic forest. A place where parents didn't have to die, but stayed with their little girl, even when she was naughty.

I wanted to live in such a place, although my grandmother told me it was far away in Ireland, the place of my dreams. If I were a very good girl, perhaps I could go there one day.

The porch dissolved into emerald mists and golden wood as the pleasant dreams of childhood turned to an unending nightmare. I found myself in a dark forest, fleeing some unknown terror.

At every turn, shepherds and wild boars popped up like figures in a carnival game. I ran from the trees into a church where the priest and David should have been waiting for me.

To the strains of flutes, bagpipes and drum, Irish bridal music, I walked down the aisle. At the altar, my groom turned to face me.

Not David, but Connor.

My mouth opened, but no scream came out. I turned to flee, only to find the pews packed with unwashed, leering shepherds.

"No! This can't be. Where is David?"

"Ye should be asking where ye are," the priest answered.

"Why? I know where I am. I want to know where David is. We're supposed to be married."

Connor, dressed in some sort of full chieftain regalia, took my hand in his. "Ye will be marrying me," he said as if I were property he had already claimed.

I pulled my hand away and cried, "No, I want to marry David. Where is he? What have you done to him? David!"

I awoke with a start, David's name fresh on my lips, but his image dissolving as the dream faded. I sat up and looked around the camp.

Basta had taken his gang and their horses and disappeared. Soft, gray light and fog, like a cat twining around a person's legs, crept through the meadow grasses and trees at the edge of the forest.

I peered through the dimness. I was definitely alone. *Alone!*

Flinging aside Connor's cloak, I stood and listened for any sound that might indicate he was nearby in the woods.

Was the nightmare over? Had Connor also left me? Where had the shepherds gone?

Perhaps the whole kidnap episode had been a bad dream. Perhaps Connor decided he had indeed made a mistake, and he took off with his brother.

Suddenly, I didn't care where he had gone, where his brother and the other shepherds were. Their absence was my ticket to freedom.

I rose, picked up the hem of my skirt and scampered from the camp into the forest as quietly as I could. Even in the pre-dawn shadows, I could easily retrace the path Connor had left. I hurried since I did not know how long it would be until someone returned to discover I was no longer at the camp.

The forest was unnaturally quiet. No squirrels chattered, no birds twittered in response, no burrowing animals rooted among the fallen leaves. I heard only the pounding of my heart, hard breathing and the crunch of leaves underfoot as I ran.

I passed the dead boar, my stomach jumping into my throat at the memory of how close it had come.

A few more feet, and I would be out of the forest. A few more feet, and I would reach the meadow, then the cliffs, then the village. I knew I could find my way back to David and the search party he must be leading.

Suddenly, I froze in my tracks.

Something wasn't right, but I didn't know what. The smell hit me long before I ever saw them. Days-old sweat and campfire smoke, the now-familiar smell of the shepherds.

Basta's men?

I heard voices, but could not understand their words. They must have been unconcerned about being noticed for they talked loudly and laughed. I decided they weren't Basta's men, although I couldn't pinpoint why.

And they also weren't my rescuers. Something akin to a sixth sense told me not to cry out for help.

I melted against a tree wishing I could blend into the foliage. A white lace wedding dress, even one as dirty and grass-stained as mine, in a shadow-filled forest of browns, blacks and a hundred different greens would stand out as much as a shepherd carrying a struggling bride across the cliffs.

Slowly, I backed away from the strangers' camp, and decided to try to circle wide around them. Carefully separating branches and stepping gingerly so as not to make any noise, I moved toward the right, pausing every few feet to listen for their voices. I could find no path to follow through this part of the forest and made several more turns to get around fallen logs and thick underbrush.

Daylight began to filter through the thick canopy of green buds, drawing lace-curtain patterns on the forest floor. Soon, I smelled the meadow, fresh from hibernation. My heart raced as my feet longed to do. But I slowed again, and walked right into the clearing where we'd camped overnight. I had been walking around in circles.

Just as I was about to turn around and flee back into the forest, Connor stepped in front of me, his arms crossed and his feet spread wide as if he were as firmly planted as the great oaks of the forest. I shifted from one side to the other. He followed suit leaning one direction and the other, countering my moves. He was too quick for me to dart past him and too large for me to plow through him.

Finally, I flung my hands up in the air and said, "I give up!"

He chuckled, and I threw myself against his left side, hoping to take him off-guard and knock him to the ground. He stood firm, as if he were accustomed to women throwing themselves into his arms. I buckled and dropped to my knees, angry, frustrated and disappointed I had not gained my freedom.

Connor grabbed me and lifted me, saying, "Ye know I could not allow ye to leave me, Caitrín."

"I suppose it was too good to be true. And, for the record once more, I am not Caitrín and I hope that one day you'll get tired of calling me that and realize you have the wrong person."

"Enough!" he said, taking my hand. He led me to a chestnut-colored, shaggy-haired horse grazing on ankle-deep grasses of the meadow.

"Basta left us a horse," he said "to shorten our trip."

Great! I'd never been on a horse before and he expected me to ride the beast, and with no saddle. How was I supposed to hold on? Never mind riding a wedding dress!

"Me ride a horse?"

Rather than answer a perfectly appropriate question, Connor encircled my waist with his hands and lifted me to the horse's bare back, then climbed up behind me. My skirt would not permit me to sit astride the horse, so he cradled me across his thighs, with his arms securely around me.

I didn't know which was more dangerous, the wildness of the horse beneath me or the fierceness of the man who held me fast against him. Terrified, I grabbed his shirt and squeezed shut my eyes as he prodded the horse into a gallop.

Before long, I realized I was more scared we'd run into something, so I eased one eye open to make sure Connor knew where he was going.

Soon, the warmth of being sheltered in his arms reminded me of the comfort I found as a little girl on my grandmother's lap. As the horse bounced me against Connor and he kept me from sliding or falling, I began to relax and enjoy the exhilaration of the wind whipping my hair into a frenzy. A feeling of untamed freedom like nothing I had ever known began to sprout inside me.

How could I ever explain leaving Cleveland one day, and a few days later, galloping across Ireland with a madman kidnapper who claimed to be a clan chieftain? The hardest to understand was that I was beginning to enjoy this wild, crazy adventure.

And I was starting to trust Connor.

Chapter 10

Had she never ridden?

Connor puzzled at her apparent fear of the horse. She should have been as at home on horseback as he was. Surely, Donal permitted, even encouraged his daughter to ride.

After all, she was a chieftain's daughter and soon to be a warrior's wife. She should have known how to sit astride and control the animal with her thighs, yet she clung to him like a child afraid of the night. She would not even open her eyes.

Her curls tickled his nose as they blew against him. Her body pressing against him kindled a spark of desire he tried to ignore even as it grew more insistent.

He wanted her. Right now on a bed of heather and meadow grass under the warm, pale sun.

Could he wait until nightfall and take her into his chamber where his warriors would hear her moans of pleasure and know she was his by her own accord?

He glanced down and caught a glimpse of her ankles as the wind picked up the edge of her gown. The boots she wore were the strangest leathers he had ever seen.

How had Donal's artisans fashioned such odd shapes? The women of his clan wore boots similar to his own, pieces of leather with straps to secure them to the ankle. She could not even run or climb in hers.

She opened her eyes and glanced up, giving him a strange, small smile that nurtured his kernel of hope for their union.

Tonight. This daughter of a warrior-king, would become the wife of a clan chieftain, a marriage blessed by the gods at the Beltane festival. His body tensed at the thought that Beltane was also the best time to conceive a son.

Yes, the gods would delight in this union.

He merely had to convince Caitrín to come to the marriage bed without a dagger in her hand.

Chapter 11

We sped across a meadow lush with green and purple until the sun climbed high in a pearly sky. Holding one hand to my brow to shade my eyes, I ventured a look toward a silvery streak of a stream tumbling down a slate mountainside.

Without so much as a nudge, the horse slowed to a trot, then stopped when we reached the water's edge, a rock-lined quiet pool at the bottom of the cascade. Connor dropped me gently to the ground before sliding from the horse.

I knelt at the side of the stream and cupped its chilled, clear water to my mouth. "I suppose it's safe to drink this. No pollution."

Connor knelt and splashed a handful over his own face and turned to face me, droplets clinging to his mustache and sparkling like little crystals as he spoke.

"Why do ye say such strange words?"

"I don't know what you're talking about. In this day, that's a perfectly legitimate question. Even in such a pristine wilderness, there can be pollution."

"Pollution? What is this word?"

"Oh, yeah. Sorry. That was English. I forget when I slip from one language to the other. Let's talk about something else." I cautiously sipped the cool water. "I heard men's voices in the forest. I presume they weren't Basta's buddies. Who were they?"

"Warriors. I do not know whose and, until I find out, it is best to avoid them."

"Warriors? Not more shepherds? I realize this isn't Ohio, and I've been kidnapped by a shepherd, clan chieftain, but now you want me to believe there are warriors in the woods. Would that be weekend warriors? Or, some sort of paintball game or extreme sports thing?"

Connor's brow knit in confusion or frustration, I couldn't tell which. And, frankly didn't care much. I was more than ready to be done with the whole kidnap scene.

"My patience is almost at an end. First, you won't believe you have taken the wrong person. I've had very little to eat and drink, nearly been killed by a wild pig, and slept on the ground in my wedding gown, which, by the way, is ruined. Much as I enjoyed the horseback ride through the most incredible scenery in the world, I've had enough. I demand that you return me to Aasleigh now. I do not want to be a part of whatever game you're playing anymore."

Connor cupped my chin with a cold, wet hand and his ebony eyes looked deeply into mine.

"This is no game, Caitrín. Those warriors may be outsiders. If they do not wear the colors of his clan, they are not from Donal. Even Colum wears colors. Ye are at great risk. There are many who hate Donal enough to steal his daughter, ye know."

I pushed him away, and he sat on the grassy bank.

"Swell. I'm not only the wrong person, but now I'm a popular wrong person. This is all so incredible, it's like a bad dream, but I know I'm awake. If I pinch myself one more time, I'll have bruises on my arm to match the ones on my backside. I feel like I've fallen through Alice's hole."

I scooped up another handful of water, and watched as it dripped through my fingers.

"Wait a minute ... that's it! I have fallen through Alice's hole. Actually it's probably Einstein's hole. This makes perfect sense now. Well, not exactly perfect sense, but some kind of sense. Better than I've-completely-lost-my-mind sense. It's probably the only answer that does make sense. Well, if you believe that time is a sort of continuum."

I paused and studied him for a moment. "Sorry, I'm not really a crazy person usually. Connor, what year is this?"

"Year? I do not know this word." He picked a slender blade of grass and began to chew it.

"Year, you know, 2013, 2014, 2015. Who is the president of the United States? Oh, never mind, you might not know that anyway. How's Ireland doing in the World Cup?"

He stared at me and continued to chew the blade of grass.

"None of my questions ring a bell, do they? Time—that's got to be the answer. I'm not in my own time anymore. Somehow, I passed into another time. I don't think I'm unconscious and dreaming all of this. My bottom is too sore from the horseback ride for this to be some sort of nightmare. No, there's a doorway of some kind. My grandmother told me about fairy gates to other worlds, but I thought it was just stories.

54

This is still Ireland, but a different time. One when clans are at war, and warriors roam the forest, and men wear swords and ride horses. That could be almost any time in the past, but chances are, a long time ago. My God, Grandmother was right! She said it was possible to cross time through the fairy portals."

As if to confirm my words, the ruby in my pocket began to vibrate.

"Ye are making even less sense than before, Caitrín." He flipped the blade of grass away.

"Okay, let's try to pinpoint this a little. Ever hear of the English? Soldiers? How about potato blight and famines?"

Connor gave me a bewildered look.

"The coast, where your men climbed down and got into boats. Has there ever been a raid or an attack by tall, blond Norsemen who sailed across the seas in strange-looking ships?"

I could tell by his eyes that I had not yet found the familiar.

"Well, that puts us back to before 500 AD," I said trying to recall the history of Ireland I had studied so many years before. "Ever hear of Patrick the monk? Christians who worship one God? How about the Romans? I know they didn't invade Ireland, but you might have heard stories of their presence in Britain. They had soldiers and chariots and coins with a picture of Caesar stamped on them. Perhaps their ships come to trade. Probably not this far north and west. Well, let's start with what we do know then. You mentioned druids."

Connor nodded slowly. "Your father has the druid Ongus as an advisor."

I tried to think what else might be associated with the ancient Irish. *Celtic warriors.*

I looked at Connor as if seeing him for the first time. Then, I studied him closely from head to toe for some telltale sign of modern times. Tan lines from sunglasses or wristwatch, a tattoo, anything that would prove he could not be what I thought he was.

Basta was one, and Connor mentioned one named Colum.

Not a gang of kidnapping shepherds, but Celtic warriors.

And, Connor, a warrior, too!

I vaguely remembered a college course on the history of ancient cultures. Celts, the fiercest barbarians of the times, a Roman historian's description. Celtic warriors went into battle naked and painted.

I could well imagine how terrifying it would be to see a huge, dark haired, naked Connor, all muscle and determination, wielding that long sword while running at his enemy. The thought of him naked brought a warm rush to my cheeks and I stopped my mind from pursuing those images.

My mind and body began to rebel against the thought that I had somehow been transported back two thousand years. I began to tremble, not knowing whether to feel relieved or terrified that my crazy theory might be true.

It would be easier to accept that I had been drugged by my kidnapper.

I can't be dreaming, or drugged, going crazy, yet the only explanation that makes any sense is time travel.

It had to be true.

From the very first moment I saw Connor, there was no sign of Aasleigh, not of civilization as I knew it. No village buildings, no traffic noise, no jet trails across the sky. I had to have somehow travelled to another time in the distant past.

One thing for certain, I didn't know the rules of the game in a different century.

And, if I did manage to escape and return to the churchyard wherever that was, could I find the portal and cross back again? Could I return to my own time or, heaven forbid, might I land in some other century? This line of thinking greatly complicated my plight.

As if answering my questions, the ruby throbbed against my thigh.

Could it be?

Norah Kelly had said my grandmother Moira had gone missing. Could she have travelled through time as well? Was the ruby somehow a part of this? I had to find out more about what was going on where and when I was.

"What about your brother and his men? Where did they go?" I asked, determined to learn as much as possible, and quickly.

"Basta was offended because I did not want his help."

"Couldn't we use it now?"

"No, I have a plan," Connor said quickly, as if my words had stung his pride.

"Sounds like a Mel Gibson movie. I hope this isn't the part where Danny Glover says, 'We're in big trouble now.'"

"The plan is to keep ye alive and well," Connor said.

"I like that plan. But why? What more do you have in mind for me?"

"I have already told ye. Ye will be my bride." He ran a finger down the slender bone of my jaw. "In the meanwhile, I am waiting for your father to try to rescue ye."

I trembled, as much from his touch as his words.

"And what if he doesn't? Or suppose he sent those warriors in the woods. If Donal is as dastardly as you believe, wouldn't he send his army? Why do you think he'd come for his daughter himself?"

"Honor."

"Would such a man as him be honorable?"

"Ye make a good point." Connor stroked his mustache.

A new plan began to form in my mind. If I could convince Connor that my father, or rather, Caitrín's father, would not come to rescue me, Connor might need some other way to force a confrontation. That might require returning to the place where I had been kidnapped. I might find the time portal again and return to my own time.

If the ruby was the key to the location of the portal, perhaps it could get me back to Aasleigh.

Or, I could always click my heels and repeat, "There's no place like home."

"Suppose Donal doesn't come after me? What if I could help you sneak into Donal's tower? What if there's a secret entrance and you can go right into his home and confront him?"

"That is not the way of a warrior," Connor said, puffing his chest slightly.

"Sorry. I guess the way of a warrior is to wait among the wild flowers and spoil a maiden's spring outing."

"And to steal his enemy's daughter," Connor said, with a leer in his voice.

I made a fist and shook it at him. "Good grief! Why don't you listen to me? I am not Caitrín. I don't have a father named Donal. I've had it with you and with all this craziness. I only want to go home. To go back to my own time and to David." I stood as if I were going to walk back to Aasleigh.

"Your own time? What do ye mean?" Connor asked, this time with a genuineness I could not ignore.

"I'll try to explain, although I don't know why I am wasting my breath. You haven't believed anything I've said so far. Many centuries from now, and I know you don't know what centuries are, but a long time in the future, a man will theorize that time travel is possible. You travel from one place to another. Well, what if you could travel from one time to another? Apparently, I have come to this time and place from the future. I don't know why or how."

I could see Connor had no clue what I was trying to tell him. "Ever hear of gates to the fairy world? The aés sídhe? You know who they are. Do they travel between their world and yours?"

Connor nodded. "Certainly. Although I have never seen them myself."

"Okay, now we're getting somewhere. I must have found the gate, the portal between two worlds and I accidentally wandered through it. I am not from this place or time. That is why my words make no sense to you, my dress seems strange, my hair is cut short, unlike the women of your time."

His eyes lit as if everything was finally became clear to him. He jumped to his feet, put his hand on his sword and said, "Ye are from the fairy world, sent to lead me to my doom. But, I shall outwit even the aés sídhe Donal has summoned to do his evil."

"No, wait, I'm not a fairy. I'm a real woman. No one sent me. Donal isn't my father."

Fists clenched and face suddenly reddened with fury, Connor said, "Donal will soon learn he cannot use warriors, druids, or fairies against the spirit of my father that cries for vengeance."

He put me on the horse, none too gently, and climbed behind me without another word. His arms stiffened around me and did not secure me until the first bounce nearly sent me headfirst off the horse.

As we began to climb the first of the hills leading into the mountains, I glanced over Connor's shoulder and noticed something alarming in the distance. I touched Connor's arm and pointed. "Someone is following us."

Connor shrugged. "We will disappear in the mountains. No one knows them like I do. This is Malley land."

Malley land. His turf.

Gray stubble of rock on a jutting chin of green. Would this be where he meant for the showdown with Donal's warriors to occur? And what if, in the end, they all learned they were fighting over the wrong woman?

I suddenly realized how dangerous this game had become. I felt as if I was being sucked into a whirlpool from which I might never be able to free myself.

The foothills did not stretch for miles as the meadows had. Very quickly, the poorly defined path became rocky and steep. Granite replaced green and each footstep sent an avalanche of pebbles down the mountainside. Finally, when the horse labored and lathered, Connor slid off and pulled me from my perch.

From this vantage point, the most incredible sight I'd ever seen spread across the valley behind us. All of Ireland—slate-colored rocks, grass-covered slopes, flowering meadow—lay below as the land reached out, beckoning me to embrace it, convincing me I belonged to it, to this time, and to the man who stood next to me.

Thoughts of David and the life I had left began to fade as I turned and followed Connor toward a new, completely unknown future in the distant past.

"We must keep moving if we are to reach Croaghnac before nightfall," Connor said.

"Croaghnac?" I recognized part of the word. 'Croag' meant 'hill.'

"My home."

A home on a hill.

"It didn't occur to me that you have a home. You said you prefer to sleep out under the sky."

He threw his head back and laughed. "And so I do. But I also have a home ye shall soon see. It is the home of my father and my clan."

Chapter 12

So was this the ancient equivalent of meeting the parents? Except, he had no parents.

Connor meant to make Caitrín his bride at his ancestral home, exactly as David had meant for us to be married at my ancestral home. I felt a chill snake down my back at the thought that I might soon be married to a first century warrior-chieftain who had mistakenly kidnapped me.

I tried to weigh my options.

If I had to marry him, I supposed I might learn to get along with him over time. He was tall and broad-shouldered, with solid muscles like a Brown's quarterback I'd once known. He knew his way around the wilderness, and had done his best, so it seemed, to keep me safe thus far. Certainly, he wasn't a bad looking man, if I could get past the dirt and smell. Perhaps I could even persuade him to bathe occasionally.

No! Stop!

It's Stockholm Syndrome. The kidnapped victim identifying with her captor. I could understand now how easily that could happen. I really couldn't allow those feelings, or any sort of attraction to grow.

But, try as I might, protecting my heart from Connor was becoming more difficult by the moment. There was something about him, about the way he looked at me with those dark eyes and a possessiveness that made me feel more cherished than stolen.

He made me want to ask why no other man had killed wild boars for me.

Dismounted, we climbed more slowly now over the steep, rocky path, Connor giving me a hand when I needed it, the horse following on its own. My dress and shoes were definitely not made for rock climbing, and I knew I was slowing our escape. Every so often, I glanced over my shoulder to see if we were still being followed, but I could no longer see little puffs of dust in the distance.

Yet, neither did I feel reassured that the pursuers had given up.

"Aye, they're still there." Connor read my mind.

He took my hand and pulled me up over a boulder to a granite ledge where we stood for a moment, my hand resting against his chest over his heart. My gaze met his ebony eyes, no longer dark and fathomless, but sparkling with mystery and desire so tangible he made me blush and stammer like a school girl.

Connor changed as we came closer to his home. He was still a man-on-a-mission, but now he seemed visibly relaxed. The creases on his forehead disappeared, and his eyes softened when he looked at me. Whether because we were on his land or he had forgiven my earlier remarks, I did not know, but I definitely preferred the kinder, gentler version of Celtic warrior.

My feelings surprised me. The gym-jock type never appealed. The Browns quarterback I had dated just before meeting David was the only exception to my unwritten, "date-men-in-suits" rule.

Connor was a far cry from either the locker room or courtroom. His thick arms and expansive shoulders, massive thighs, and the lean angle of his hip came from hiking, climbing, or horseback-riding instead of a treadmill and weight training. The memory of those arms around me set butterflies loose in my stomach and a longing to trace his biceps with my finger, rather than my eyes.

Pushing aside those thoughts to concentrate on the path, I wobbled as I stepped across a large rock, and Connor caught my waist with both hands to steady me.

"The warriors?" I asked, without breaking eye contact.

Connor let his glance caress me before taking my hands to help me. "They know on whose land they trespass, and they move slowly fearing my anger will be visited on their camp."

"I guess you don't like strangers," I said, the words coming in short gasps as I tried to catch my breath. Either his nearness or the unaccustomed exertion took my breath.

Had I known I'd be mountain climbing in May, I'd have taken the stairs instead of the elevator a few more times through the last couple months.

A flash of anger swept across his brow, but I did not regret my words. Obviously, no one ever stood up to a chieftain, and, since he wanted to keep me alive for whatever purpose he had, I decided to speak my mind.

Call it the privilege of a kidnapped bride. Surely if there were a law about chieftains and stolen brides, there'd one about challenging him whenever I wanted.

He ignored my words, and concentrated on the climb.

The terrain had become passable only for mountain goats, and Connor who must have been part goat himself. I bent forward and leaned, palms on my knees. I wasn't trying to delay him this time. I simply felt as if I might collapse and roll back down the mountainside at any moment.

"Ye would like me to carry ye?" he asked, raising one eyebrow. The sparkle in his eyes told me he was teasing this time.

Undoubtedly he could carry me, and still pick his way up the mountainside without breaking a sweat. But did I want to indulge a man who delighted in acting like a caveman? Did I want to be held against his beating heart, my body molded against him as if I had been created to fit him like the pieces of a puzzle?

I didn't think so.

I wouldn't want you to exert yourself like that. I simply need to catch my breath. Are we going all the way to the top of this mountain?"

"Nay. Do ye see the slab of rock cracked by the finger of a god? That is our destination." He pointed to a sheet of granite only a few hundred yards above us.

Lovely, but how does he propose we walk through solid rock?

I straightened and climbed the short distance to the spot where Connor showed me the answer. The cleft was actually an opening in the rock large enough for the two of us and his mount to walk through. Connor entered first, holding my hand.

The horse followed on its own, its snorts bouncing off the rocks as if there were a hundred horses with it. Sunlight never reached the inner depths of the rock, and moss covered the lower reaches and floor making our path slippery at best. The rock smelled aged, like an old cathedral that should have had the windows and doors thrown open every hundred years or so.

I bit my lip. In addition to high places, I didn't like close places, and the thought of being buried alive in this mountain crossed my mind. All it would take would be a rock slide or an earthquake.

What are the odds?

Probably about the same as a twenty-first century woman finding herself in the first or second century, kidnapped by a shepherd—no, excuse me, a body-builder, Celtic warrior-clan-chieftain.

I tightened my grip on Connor's hand and he gave me a reassuring squeeze. "Not much farther," he said, his words echoing like the whispers of a church congregation.

Within a few twists and turns, we passed through the mountain tunnel into a valley drenched in golden sunlight. Connor pulled me in front of him and placed both of his hands on my shoulders.

"This is my home," he said.

The view reminded me of a Monet painting. A landscape of dappled, green velvet, each fold and drape shimmering under the afternoon light and endless azure sky. Like a child surveying an amusement park, I felt as if I could not see it all in one glance.

"It's so beautiful! How could you ever leave such a place?" I said, looking up to catch Connor's smile of pride and ownership.

His fingers strayed along my neck to my ear. I wanted to pull away, but at the same time, the warmth of his hand, the shared intimacy of the moment, and his finger tracing the outline of a curl behind my ear sent delicious shivers down my back. I leaned against him and felt the heat of his body envelope me.

David seemed too far away. I tried to summon his image to distract myself from responding to Connor's touch, but it didn't work. Memories of David only made me long for Connor's arms to comfort me. I pressed back slightly, feeling his hand on my shoulder and his fingers on my neck, at the edge of my gown.

No!

I took a deep breath, and ordered my racing heart to slow. But my breath caught in my throat and my eyes filled with tears. As much as my mind wanted to flee from Connor's caress, my body longed for it, and more. I wanted to hear soothing words of comfort.

What had he said after the boar attack?

I wished I knew. I wished he'd say the words again. I wished he could make this whole nightmare disappear, but I didn't want him to go away with it.

Should I feel guilty? Was I being unfaithful to David? I glanced down at the skirt of my ruined wedding gown, and asked scolded myself.

How can you feel anything for this man? He has stolen you against your will.

Taking a half-step away from him, I tried to distract myself by surveying the valley below.

A ribbon river of wild, white-capped water with heather-covered meadow on either side threaded down the middle of the narrow valley. Across the river, tents with pennants atop them sprouted from the land

and flags fluttering and snapping in the breeze caught my attention.

"What is it?" I asked, pointing to the tent village.

"The games," he said, "the Beltane games. Ye were collecting flowers for your father's games. Ye should not be surprised that we hold them as well."

Beltane? May first. The Celtic celebration of spring. My wedding day.

The words of my grandmother's poem came to my mind.

"On Beltane, the ancient celebration of May Day, the mortal world comes perilously close to the Otherworld and portals open, allowing a few, a precious few, to travel between the worlds."

Grandmother Moira always wove a flower garland for my hair, and recited the poem as she crowned me princess of May Day. She knew about the time portal and believed in it. Probably she'd even crossed through the fairy gate. With the ruby.

Why didn't I pay more attention? Why did I think it was all fairy tales and imagination?

Much as I wanted, and needed a logical reason for all that was happening, I could come up with nothing. I wished I could summon my grandmother's spirit to ask her how to undo all of this, how to find that gate again, and return to my own time.

Or, if that weren't possible, what to do.

Most troubling of all were my growing feelings of attraction to Connor. Should I give in to the feelings and desires that grew more intense by the moment?

My whole body wanted to scream, to fight everything that was happening around me, to flee back to the portal. But I was trapped in the here and now, wherever and whenever that was.

I shifted my attention and my thoughts again to the far side of the valley where a fist of land thrust out boldly, forcing my eyes upward.

Atop a knob of green stood Croagnac, Connor's house on a hill.

Not a ring fort like Tara, the ancient seat of Irish government. Here, there wasn't enough room for concentric rings of trenches and hills. The geography of Croaghnac gave it sufficient natural protection.

To guarantee their security, the clan had built a fortress of rock and timber that looked as if it had already survived centuries of slashing mountain wind and pounding rains. "Weathered" could not begin to describe the wooden-and-stone structure that appeared to be growing from rock, aged to fine gray like the patina of a well-used sword.

This was his home. His home on a hill.

Escape and return to David seemed even farther away now. Yet, part of me, a very small flicker that was quickly diminishing, was still determined not to be trapped in this time.

"Come on!" Connor called, as he started down the slope toward the river.

As I looked at him, my heart did a little flip.

Admit it, girl. It isn't this place that attracts you as much as its chieftain!

I balled my hands into fists. *No, no, no. I've got to concentrate on David and home.*

An internal struggle began as I marched down the hill reciting aloud all the things I loved about Cleveland. "David, downtown, the Lake, the Indians, the opera, David, the art museum, the Browns, my house, spring lilacs, David."

My voice faded in the breeze and restless noise of the river. I neared the river and paused for instructions. Several small boats, the ones his men used after my kidnapping I presumed, rested on the bank. I expected Connor would use one to cross the river which wasn't especially wide, but definitely too deep and swift to walk or swim across.

What more could I do in a wedding gown? I must surely have set a record for hiking, mountain climbing, sleeping on the ground, horse-back riding and boar-baiting in an antique, Irish lace wedding dress.

What now? A swim that would be akin to body surfing through white water rapids?

Followed by a wet wedding dress contest?

As I started walking toward the boats, Connor pointed out boulders lined up as a footbridge requiring nothing but a broad jump between them. He grinned at my look of dismay and swooped me into his arms, then, with glee spilling from his eyes, hopped onto the first rock.

"Ohhhhhh!" I screamed, throwing my arms around his neck and holding tightly as ice-cold spray from the river misted me. I dared not move as he gracefully hopped to the next stepping stone. Twelve jumps later, he set me down on the far shore, and I had the impulse to kneel and kiss the ground.

Instead, I faced him, planted both of my palms against his chest and shoved with all of my strength.

"You are a caveman! You may not go around picking me up whenever it suits you!"

Caught by surprise, Connor fell backward and landed with a thud and a splash in water that was shallow, but cold enough he might have gotten ice splinters in his backside.

"And what's more," I continued, "I don't even like this place! It might be beautiful, but I'll take Cleveland any day! Cleveland, Lake Erie, air pollution, hot summers, and three-foot snow drifts in February! All you have here is untamed wilderness and the barbarian who owns it."

"Ye'll take this!" Connor roared and splashed a handful of water in my direction. I dodged it and scrambled several steps away from the river bank.

Giving me his best "I-am-Connor-chieftain-of-clan-Malley" look, he stood, stepped from the river and caught me.

"Oh, no, you don't!" I squealed as his cold, wet hands encircled my waist and pulled me against his chest.

Drawing up one foot, I kicked his shin with all my strength and pent-up anger. He fell hard and took me with him to the mossy ground. I landed atop him. Then, he rolled to one side, pressing me to the ground beneath him.

Cold, wet and heavy against me.

I opened my mouth to scream, but he silenced me with his lips, kissing me. Accustomed to David's kisses, the feel of his lips and tongue, the urgent, the satisfying, the inviting, the affectionate kisses of long-time lovers, I was surprised by Connor's kiss. He didn't force his tongue into my mouth, nor even tease my lips with it. His kiss could have been hard, eager, forceful, but instead he was shy, gentle, almost sweet.

Like a fourteen-year-old experimental kiss.

His body, with its own agenda, pressed against me, as a force to be reckoned with independently from this kiss of invitation.

He roused something powerful that I had never felt in all the years I'd been with David. A wave of desire crashed over me, sending chills down my backbone. I wanted Connor with a ferocity that frightened me. I started to open my mouth to his.

Then my brain kicked in, and I knew I could not give in to him.

Freeing one hand, I swung a fist at him, connecting with the side of his head. He muttered a Celtic oath, and released me. I quickly jumped to my feet, cheeks aflame and fists clenched, and kicked his thigh for good measure. When I turned to flee, I knew not where, I noticed we had an audience.

Basta and his men, guffawing like sixth-grade boys, blocked my way. "So, ye could na' wait for the marriage bed, brother." Basta chortled.

I slapped Basta hard across the cheek and said, "How dare you!"

Holding a hand to his cheek, he stepped aside and his men followed suit. I stormed past them.

"I see ye have not yet tamed your bride," he said, before I was beyond earshot.

"Nay, brother, and I like her like that," Connor said.

"Can I look forward to a swift wedding?" asked Basta.

"Soon. I assume by your presence, ye are pleased that I will marry Caitrín. No doubt ye plan to witness the ceremony." Connor brushed deliberately past his brother. "We will talk later after I have completed my wedding preparations. I would welcome your companionship, Basta, but I am sure ye have other matters to attend to."

Chapter 13

There was nowhere for me to go but toward the tents assembled for the festivities. The sights and smells felt familiar, almost nostalgic, like a summer county fair in Ohio. Small stands, little more than rough-edged planks anchored to tree stumps displayed goods as people paused to pick something up to examine it and bargain with a vendor.

It amazed me that I attracted so little attention from the crowd. Surely, my once-white dress with rose-embossed lace stood out in sharp contrast to the browns, greens and grays of the homespun clothing of the fair-goers.

These were tall people, dark-haired like Connor, while my fair complexion and short strawberry-red curls made me feel even more foreign. But no one so much as looked me in the eye as I wandered through the throng of people moving from booth to booth.

In spite of the drab clothing they wore, most of the people had gold bracelets and necklaces, and fastened a decorative brooch to one shoulder to secure their wraps. The jewels in these pins reminded me of the ruby Norah had given me.

Stands cluttered with woven baskets of every size and shape, carved gourd mugs, earthenware pottery could have been at the Cuyahoga County Fair. I'd seen jewelry displays at fairs, but none like these booths with hand-crafted delicate gold and silver armbands, rings and collars.

I moved with the crowd toward another stand that displayed knives, arrows and weapons of every kind. Men clustered around it, vying for the merchant's attention. I paused and picked up a dagger for a moment, considered buying it for my own defense. But I had no money and, wasn't about to barter away my ruby, in case it was the key to unlock the portal, and return me to my own time.

Unconsciously, I stroked my left wrist and wished I hadn't removed my watch. It would be a novelty piece here, meaningless but perhaps worth a knife or sword in trade.

Replacing the weapon, I continued walking with the throng. People milled about the merchandise hunting bargains, bartering with salesmen, chasing children away from squares of sticky honeycomb. I tried to pick up conversations, but they spoke too quickly and their words were lost in the noise and music of strolling musicians playing flutes, wide-mouthed horns and goatskin drums.

Jugglers tossed balls high into the air to amaze the young for a fraction of a second. A poet jumped up on a stump in front of me to recite his verse. Adding to the confusion, several tents away, a ballad singer competed with a storyteller for the crowd's attention.

As I paused to listen and absorb everything around me, someone touched my shoulder. I turned to find a young woman fingering the sleeve of my dress. I stood very still, not wishing to offend the stranger, but uncomfortable with the woman's exploration of my clothing. A second woman on my other side picked up the edge of my sleeve, and murmured, attracting the attention of others. A man began to touch my hair.

They pressed against me, talking too rapidly for me to understand their words, but each one blocking my way, touching me, and holding onto my dress. Panic welled up inside and I brought my hands up over my face as I twisted free of the crowd.

Without giving a thought to which direction to flee, I moved toward the open, grassy field where young men had gathered. I refused to make eye contact with them. Tilting my chin, I looked straight ahead and hurried past them.

I needed to be alone, away from Connor and Basta, away from the crowd that pressed me on all sides, away from the young warriors who eyed me as if I was their next conquest.

But I didn't know where to go. Tears filled my eyes to overflowing as I stumbled across the open field, past a row of tents whose walls fluttered slightly in the breeze.

On the other side of the tents, I found a quiet place where no one could see me or bother me. Boxed between the fair and the hill where Croaghnac stood watch over the valley, I collapsed on the grass. Overcome with exhaustion and feeling completely lost in this strange and frightening place, I bent forward, cradling my head in my hands and rocking gently. The tears I'd fought to control now poured freely down my cheeks, landing in angry splotches on my damp and soiled gown.

"Why? Why? Why?" I cried.

I'd always thought of myself as a fighter, a self-reliant, independent woman, but now, I didn't know what to do or where to turn. The thought of trying to find my way back to the coast, to Aasleigh overwhelmed me, but at the same time, I feared staying here even more.

I could not trust Connor, nor myself. He made me want him too much.

I had never felt like that with David. I didn't have to think about what I felt when I was with David. He had been a part of my life for so long he was simply always there. I had been perfectly happy floating along with our relationship, not putting any great effort into analyzing where we were headed or when. My biological clock was on permanent snooze.

Then, along came Connor and everything with him seemed to involve motion. "Got to get there," "going to marry," "before the end of the Beltane fair."

He was driven, intense in his purpose, and his goals. Connor was so different than David, who could be manipulative in his own way, but would never ignore me if I insisted I wasn't the person he thought I was or pick me up and carry me across a river.

"David, where are you?"

I tried to summon his face into my mind, but all I saw was the Cleveland Indians' logo plastered to the bumper of his car. Images of Connor quickly chased the Indian away. Connor brought out the worst in me. I abhorred violence of any sort. That man gave me visions of stealing his dagger and using it on him. He drove me to shove him into the water. He produced in me desire so intense it threatened to consume me.

But, at that moment as even stronger desire raged within me: I wanted to go home. I wanted my life back.

Chapter 14

Connor strode past his brother and began to search the fair for Caitrín. She could not have gone far. His mind was filled with her, how she felt in his arms, how her lips opened to his kiss, how she stirred his blood, and his temper.

With every step, his sodden clothing slapped cold and wet against his thighs. But by the time he worked his way through the fair, he was no longer cold, but steaming.

I will marry her at the end of the fair and seal the marriage whether she wants it or not. She belongs to me. And it is evident from her kiss that she wants me.

How dare she? How dare she capture both mind and body? She is a mere woman.

Or, perhaps fairy?

His brows came together as fear settled over his mind.

She is a fairy. That would explain much. And he'd have to deal with that.

Connor came around the row of tents along the playing field and saw her huddled on the ground. Three of the young warriors started to approach her, but the chieftain held up one hand and gestured to them. He signaled one of the warriors who came to him while the others backed away from the crying woman.

At Connor's bidding, one young man sped up the hill to Croaghnac to summon the only person Connor would allow to go near her. The one person he trusted completely when he could not trust himself with her. He remained silent and still, guarding the woman, until the man came down from the fortress.

A reed-thin, white-haired man walked up to Caitrín, draped fur around her shoulders and helped her to her feet.

"Come with me," the man whispered into her ear. His voice soothed her tears while his arm wrapped around her to calm the shaking. "Ye are safe now."

Connor hung back, satisfied that the man would take care of her and protect her until their wedding.

I wiped my cheeks with the backs of my hands, and allowed the kindly stranger to lead me up the hill toward the fortress of Croaghnac. His grandfatherly demeanor suggested I had nothing to fear. I felt numb as I allowed the man to take me wherever he meant to go.

"No one will harm ye," said the man, with a rich, bass voice that the years had barely weakened.

Did that mean Connor and his brother? Did that mean Donal and his demented druid?

We walked through open, wooden gates into a courtyard. The fortress, built from tree trunks, bark-trimmed and stacked upright one against another, protected crowded beehive-shaped, thatched-roofed huts surrounding a large rectangular building like chicks alongside a hen.

We walked past the huts and entered the building, pausing to allow our eyes to adjust to the dimness. Straw, covering uneven slate stones, crunched as I tried to avoid stepping on remnants of dropped food that wandering beasts hadn't snatched up.

Nothing looked or smelled or felt like home. An odor fouler than the Cleveland sewage treatment plant on a hot, summer afternoon, roiled up from the refuse underfoot.

In the center of the great hall, a circular fire pit glowed with red embers and wisps of smoke smarted my eyes before curling upward to the hole in the roof. I couldn't imagine living in such a place, and wasn't surprised to find the room unoccupied.

Trying to control an urge to bolt from the room, I held one hand over my nose and mouth to block the stench. Something moved near one of the tables. A small dog, mangy and ill-mannered, scrounged for a snack and thought nothing of seizing it from the table, all-the-while growling at me and my companion.

At least it wasn't a rat. That thought didn't really improve the situation.

I had always thought of castles as romantic, ornately decorated with tapestries and coats-of-armor. This fortress didn't deliver on its promise of grandeur as the home of a chieftain. Decorating, or at the least, basic sanitation, were obviously not the clan's strong suits. Even the Cleveland River on the worst day before it was cleaned up wasn't this bad.

On either side of the huge room, cooper and wood screens

partitioned the space into smaller chambers, none of which had doors. I glanced into a few, but they appeared to be empty of both furniture and occupants.

"Let me show ye where ye can rest," the man said. "Do not worry," he said, in response to the look that crossed my face. "Ye are free to come and go, and no one will bother ye here. Ye are under my protection now."

I didn't have a clue why being under his protection was a plus, but I followed him anyway.

Rest in this flea-infested rat hole? The alternatives of being swarmed by the crowd, ridiculed by Basta or kissed by Connor, however, seemed a lot worse at the moment.

The elderly man led me up a narrow, circular stone staircase of uneven steps carved roughly into the side of the mountain, and lit by small slit openings in the foot-thick wall. On the second floor of the building, the stairway opened into another large room, like an alcove built into the rock. Again, copper screens partitioned off smaller chambers that were dark and claustrophobic. Only a few rooms had openings to let in air and light. The man took me to one of them at the far end of the space.

No door to open or close, but after we entered the room, he loosed a curtain over the doorway to allow some privacy. "Rest here. I will send a servant with food and drink for ye," he said.

"No, please, don't leave yet. I don't know where ... I mean, what am I supposed to do here?"

He gave me a gentle, patient smile. "This is Connor's ancestral home. No one will harm ye here. When the ram's horn blows to mark the end of the Beltane games, ye will be his bride. Until then, ye can rest safely here."

"I suppose there could be worse things in life. I'm just not sure what, at the moment. I don't mean to be difficult, but I need some time to adjust to everything. What if I agree to marry Connor, but at some other time. Could the wedding be postponed?"

The man shook his head and started to leave.

"Well, you see, there's a small problem. I'm engaged—betrothed— to someone else. We were supposed to be married yesterday morning. I'm really not the person Connor wants, he took me by mistake."

The old man nodded as a grandfather would if I'd begged to stay up beyond bedtime. I knew what he meant. He listened to me, but there was nothing more he could or would do.

"Honestly, I don't belong here. I'm not Caitrin. Look at this dress. Ever see anything like it? Even if I were from a different clan, do you think I'd have clothing like this? I tell you I need to go back to my own place. I'm not supposed to be here."

He smiled and left the room, shaking down the curtain over the doorway.

My words echoed in my mind. *I'm not supposed to be here. Doesn't anyone believe me?*

I was even beginning to doubt it myself.

Maybe I was supposed to be here. Maybe some quirk of fate sent me here for a strange cosmic reason beyond my comprehension.

Was that even possible?

Should I stop fighting what was, and start to accept what would be? Is this how my grandmother felt when she ventured across the portal of time?

I sighed. This line of reasoning was both frustrating and pointless. Assuming I had truly traveled to a different century, I could be pretty well stuck here.

Even if I thought my grandmother had done the same and returned to her own time, there was no guarantee I could. Perhaps I should be focusing on how to make the best of it. Marrying Connor was one option. One I still wasn't sure I could accept, but worth considering.

After all, if you had to be stuck somewhere for the rest of your life, being the boss' wife, rather than the peasant' wife had to be the better deal.

How much time did I have until the Beltane games ended? Maybe I could change Connor's mind about the wedding. How might I persuade him to wait? What reason could I give? It had to be compelling and believable. And so far, he isn't buying the argument that I'm not Donal's daughter.

How about already married? Secretly married to "what's-his-name," the warrior stud.

Now, there's a possibility. I could tell Connor that I ran off and got married last year. My own father doesn't know. But then Connor would probably marry me anyway thinking he could get even with Donal and that warrior-dude at the same time.

What about Basta? Maybe he could help me convince his brother this marriage isn't so hot an idea

I shuddered at that thought of having to deal with Basta, the scum-bag. Marrying Connor was a far sight better idea than aligning with

Basta.

Suddenly, I felt exhausted, my brain even more tired than my body. I examined the room, which wasn't half-bad. Considerably cleaner than anything I'd seen so far. No nose-tickling straw on the floor, no obvious vermin or rodents in the corners. Fresh air and waning sunlight poured through an open window. I looked out the window to find a dizzying drop straight down.

So much for sneaking out. I'd have to sprout wings and fly or find rappelling equipment and scale down. Neither option was likely.

In the center of the chamber, a square platform covered with furs was probably the bed. I sat on the edge and bounced, hearing a crunch and smelling fresh pine beneath the blanket of brown. Mattresses hadn't been invented yet. Carefully leaning back, certain I would feel every branch under the fur bedding, I was pleasantly surprised when I sank into a cocoon so comfortable that tension drained from me immediately.

I'll deal with this wedding business later, I told myself as I closed tear-swollen eyes and let the warmth of the furs replace the chill of the room and the fresh smell of evergreen soothe me. Within seconds I fell into a peaceful, dream-free sleep.

Chapter 15

A servant scurried from the shadows, following Connor into a small room in the rear of the hall. She set a cup of mead and a platter of food on a table. Connor motioned for her to leave. As he settled into his seat next to the table, he looked up to see a man pausing in the doorway.

"Niall, it is good to see ye. We have much to discuss," Connor greeted the older man whose full head of snowy white hair contrasted with smooth, tanned skin. Niall had served as counselor to every chieftain of the Malley clan for as long as anyone could remember. Connor offered him the cup of mead, but Niall waved it away. Without waiting for permission, Niall sat down on a bench across the table from the younger man.

"She is settled in a chamber. Would ye care to explain to me how ye expect to bed her when ye have done nothing but terrify her? Do ye plan to sleep with one eye open? She is, after all, the daughter of a warrior-king. She'd as leave murder ye in your sleep as allow ye to touch her."

Connor set his cup down a little too hard and splashed mead across the table. The honey-brown liquid pooled on the stained table.

"I need offer no excuses for my behavior. I have done nothing to offend or upset her. It is she who denies her paternity, who babbles about fairy portals and ... "

"And ye expect something different? She is a woman! And ye stole her! Everyone knows ye cannot expect rational behavior. No, I speak of something entirely different. Have ye given no thought at all to her feelings?"

Connor glowered at Niall, then lowered his eyes to the spilled mead. "Why would I do that?"

The counselor ran his hand through his hair with a gesture Connor knew well. He wasn't going to reply, but allow Connor to come up with his own answers.

"Niall, ye know me better than I know myself. What am I to do? I must marry her when the ram's horn blows at the end of the games."

"Aye, I know. But ye would be wise to make peace with your bride since ye cannot guard your own throat when ye sleep with the enemy."

Connor toyed with a piece of bread, then picked up the cup and saluted the counselor. "Ye are right, of course. I have considered that she should marry me of her own will and desire. Let her father go to the Otherworld knowing his only daughter chose to marry a Malley and give him sons. What do ye think of that?" His voice grew louder with every word.

"That is the wisest thing I have heard ye say. But how do ye intend to convince her of the rightness of your plan? How do ye plan to seduce her?"

If any other man were to have said this to him, Connor's sword would already be unsheathed. Both men knew that, yet their conversation continued.

"I am certain I can make her want to marry me," Connor said matter-of-factly.

Niall nodded, then smiled broadly. "Your clothing is damp, and not from her tears."

Connor frowned. "I slipped crossing the river."

Niall raised one eyebrow as if to convey that he knew when Connor shied from the truth. Connor refused eye contact, and Niall pressed his point. "I think ye are right about one thing. If ye kill Donal, or if ye force his daughter into marriage, the war will continue into your sons' generation. If the girl comes willingly to the marriage bed, Donal must surrender. Either way, ye have your work cut out for ye. Donal must believe his daughter desires ye. And ye must first make her want ye."

Connor picked up a piece of bread, but did not eat it immediately. "Ye think I cannot do that? There have been many women who—"

Niall interrupted, "Aye, but none whom ye have stolen from another's bridal bed, and whose father is coming after ye with his fianna."

Connor shrugged.

Niall went on. "There are other concerns as well. What of Basta? He grows stronger by the day. Ye have spent so much time pursuing your enemy's daughter, that ye have neglected the one person who may be your true enemy."

Connor nodded. He knew Basta gobbled up lands the fianna had taken years to recapture from Donal. "Aye, it may be time to put him in his place." Connor dropped the bread and grabbed a hunk of meat, stabbing the air with a leg of lamb as he spoke. "Marrying and producing an heir may take too long for that."

Basta, the first-born of his father's second wife, had as much right as Connor to claim leadership of the clan, but thus far, he was unpopular. Connor and Niall both knew Basta would wait until he was certain of the outcome of any challenge. It would not take a simple brawl or a game of strength to wrest power from Connor.

One of them would have to kill the other.

In the meanwhile, Basta played at being a trouble-maker, leading his warriors in raids of border settlements, stealing crops and livestock from Donal as well as from Connor. And always making it look as if someone else was responsible.

The counselor pursed his lips and nodded. "I can keep an eye on Basta for ye during the fair. And, ye are right. The sooner ye marry and beget an heir, the better. Now, ye must turn your attention to your bride. Convince her to marry ye, but be done with it before the games end. Then after Beltane, ye can deal with Basta once and for all."

Connor lifted the cup of mead to his lips. "Niall, ye may be an old man, yet the light still sparkles in your eye when ye speak of marriage. I need a plan if I am to convince her to come willingly to the marriage bed."

Niall sat upright and laughed. "Do ye have any idea what a woman, that woman wants? No, I suppose ye do not since ye have spent all your life fighting, and have never gone after one before. Especially not one who would might slit your throat in your sleep."

"So, ye see my predicament. Of course, this should not be an impossible task. Other women have wanted me. I did not have to pursue any of them."

Niall stroked his chin. "Hhhmph!" he said. "I've seen Caitrín's tears, the look of confusion and fear in her eyes. I listened to her plea. I have much doubt she could be easily persuaded to wed anyone."

Connor gave him a stern look, but Niall shrugged and rose to leave.

"Before ye go," Connor said, laying his hand on his counselor's forearm. The chieftain leaned forward, lowering his voice to nearly a whisper so that anyone eavesdropping on the other side of the screen would not hear his words. He paused for a moment as if choosing his words carefully.

"There is more ye should know, Niall. Caitrín may be a mad woman, or a fairy."

"What?" Niall asked.

"First, she claimed to be a judge. While that is possible, even if unlikely, she doesn't know the tenets of the law. And her hair. Ye have seen it for yourself. She also speaks a strange language and talks of a fairy gate."

"Hmmm … Donal's daughter a judge with a strange tongue and knowledge of the aés sídhe? Perhaps that also explains why no one has married her yet. Ye are right to be concerned. Ye could lose your spirit to her, or she might taint your seed and the next generation may suffer more than mere war."

Niall turned the cup on the table. "There was another woman many years ago. I did not see her myself but heard of her. She appeared at Donal's tower when his father was chieftain. There was talk of the aés sídhe as well. But she disappeared as suddenly as she'd come."

"Could Donal's druid have gotten power over the aés sídhe to summon one of them to do his bidding? Onghus served Donal's father as well."

"Seems unlikely. Yet what other possibility is there?" Niall dipped one finger into the cup of mead and drew a wet circle on the table. "Perhaps a fairy test would be in order. Take her to the ring of truth and let the druidess examine her."

Connor gave him a horrified look. "But if she is from the spirit world—"

Niall raised a hand to interrupt. "Ye must know. To marry her or even to lie with her without knowing could cost ye more than your life."

"Or the test could cost her hers."

Chapter 16

I awoke suddenly. Shadows crept from the corners of the chamber toward the bed. I didn't know how long I'd slept, but light and the noise of people carrying on their daily chores still filtered in through the window. It took me a few moments to remember where I was.

Then my thoughts immediately jumped to getting away from here. Escaping from this place and returning to Aasleigh, or at least the general vicinity, would not be possible on my own. And, what I'd do when I got there, an even greater mystery. But at least if I went back to the meadow, I'd be closer to finding the time portal, if that were possible.

I needed help. A new game plan.

Dealing with Basta was a definite negative even if I could trust to take me back to the meadow. I strongly doubted I could trust him.

What about the old man who brought me to this room

Who was he? Could he help me escape this nightmare? After all, he had said he would protect me.

Suppose I do find my way back to the meadow. How would I find that portal, if there is such a thing, and get back to my own time?

Would concentrating on David and my own time work? Clicking my heels twice while saying, "There's no place like home?"

I could do the Dorothy-thing, if there was even the remotest possibility that would work.

I sat up on the side of the bed-platform, my heart heavy with the possibility that a two-way fairy gate-time travel was nonsense, crazy talk.

What if I can't go back at all? Could I stay here? What would life be like in this time?

Playing devil's advocate like a certain defense attorney in my court, I wondered about whether I should just accept being stuck here forever. David would move on with his life without me.

Could I?

I guess I could marry Connor since that was the most practical solution. Perhaps it wouldn't be so bad if he could be persuaded to bathe. Perhaps it wouldn't be so bad if I could bathe as well.

I ran my fingers through my hair, and wished for a hot shower.

At times, Connor seemed genuinely concerned about my welfare. He saved me from the boar, and he'd been kind, for the most part. But he had an annoying habit of thinking he was in charge, and acting like a cave man. Well, as it turned out, he did live in a fortress built into a mountainside.

The cons of marrying Connor came next to my mind.

To stay here ... so much could go wrong in such a primitive culture. Yet, there was a certain fascination about living in a time and place not even described in history books.

Perhaps I could improve their lives. Simple things like hand-washing, and cleaning up that dining hall would make huge differences in their lives and health.

What if I am supposed to be here? What if I am supposed to right some wrong or save some life or love someone? If I went back to my own time, would I be tinkering with some law of fate? Like some crazy plot in a movie.

What if I am supposed to be the ancestor of someone famous, and I didn't stay and marry Connor and have his children? Would that change the future in some irrevocable way? Should I stay and try to make the best of this strange twist of fate?

I decided I needed to learn as much about life here as I could. A young girl stood near the doorway, just inside the drape. I motioned for her to come closer, and she crossed the room to place a tray of food on a table near the window.

"Who are you?" I asked.

Eyes wide, cheeks flushed, the girl gave me a deer-in-headlights look.

"It's okay. You can talk to me."

Could it be that there is a person more frightened and out of place here than me?

The girl did not move, nor did she speak. Slight of build, and covered with a lifetime of accumulated dirt, she appeared to be about ten years old. But, what did I know about kids? I avoided them whenever possible. Straggly, black hair hung below her waist and, with a tip of her head, fell over half her face so that I could not see her eyes.

"Are you part of Connor's clan?" I asked slowly, in case the girl might not understand my poorly-spoken Gaelic.

The child neither answered, nor moved. I slowly walked to the table, examined the cup of what looked and smelled like fermented apple cider and the wooden platter with a chunk of soft white cheese and a heel of dark bread. I broke off a piece of cheese and tasted it.

"I didn't realize how hungry I was. Thank you. Did someone ask you to bring it here?"

The girl nodded slightly and edged toward the door.

"I wonder if you might tell me his name." I picked up the bread and bit into it. "The white-haired man?"

The girl hesitated, shifting from one foot to the other.

Connor entered and shooed the girl from the room with a gesture. "Niall. He was my father's counselor and like a father to me."

So, now I've met the father figure. Guess he wouldn't be too keen on saving me from the man who considers himself almost the old man's son.

I choked on a piece of bread. Connor crossed the room and handed me the goblet from the tray. "Here, drink this."

I took the cup and swallowed a mouthful of mead, sweet, and heavy that burned all the way down my throat. I choked and Connor slapped me between my shoulder blades.

"I'm fine now," I gasped, placing a hand against his chest to steady myself as I continued to cough.

His hand rested against my back, gently stroking the place he had just struck. When I'd finished choking, he stepped closer, and with his other hand, cupped my chin and slowly tilted my head back until I gazed into his midnight eyes that made me feel as if I was falling into a bottomless pool.

A blush warmed my cheeks, and my breath caught in my throat as he set everything quivering inside me. He pressed closer until his gaze swallowed me with its intensity. Looking deep into Connor's soul through the window of his eyes, I saw a glimmer that even he might not acknowledge was there.

Deep down, somewhere, he cares for me.

Gone was the bravado of the warrior, the vengeance of the kidnapper, the antagonism of the brother. He was a man who looked at me with eyes of caring and longing.

And he didn't know it.

My mind waved red flags, but my body paid no attention. I suddenly wanted to wrap my arms around his neck and melt into his embrace, but I dared not move and break the spell. He held me suspended between his time and my own, belonging to neither, and yet to both.

I began to tremble inside. Not the quiver of fear when the music in a movie warns you that someone is about to pop out of the dark and grab the heroine. But a soul-quaking quiver that started deep within me and threatened to throw off everything I knew and loved, like a dog scatters the water droplets of his bath.

I had never before felt as if time was suspended, as if I pulled by both my past and future at the same moment, but could not chose which one to let go of.

In the waning light of this room, with Connor, not the chieftain, but just a man, standing so close I could melt into his arms, I wanted to reach up and touch his face, to wait for his mouth to seek mine. An ache so basic to life itself short-circuited my brain's commands to move. My arms were lifeless, weightless. All I could do was breathe. Inhale the scent of forest and fire that clung to him. Taste the honeyed mead. Feel the pounding of my heart as it ached for him, for comfort and security, for answers neither of us had.

At that moment, Connor could take me in his arms, lift me, carry me to the far side of the earth, and I would not fight him. I was his. His for eternity, if we had that much time.

The palm of one hand on her back, her chin cupped by the other hand, Connor felt connected to her as keenly as if he had drawn her naked against his body. He had never before known such fire in the pit of his belly at the mere closeness of a woman. He had never allowed his soul to be probed by a simple gaze. His pulse thundered through him like the drumbeat of a thousand bodrhan gaining both momentum and strength with every stroke against the drum skin.

He felt her chest rise and fall with every breath. And he longed to take her breath away with his kiss. By the gods, he wanted this woman, whether she was mortal or fairy.

He wanted to undress her slowly and possess her quickly. Here. Now. He had never felt this way before. This woman, be she mortal or not, threatened him as no warrior ever had.

Every fiber of his body screamed: *Take her now. Wed her in every way save the exchange of promise before the clan. A warrior, a chieftain takes what he wants.*

But Connor had not spent his lifetime restoring the honor of his clan, regaining its land, and avenging his father's blood by bowing to his own physical desires at crucial times. He would not allow her to possess his body and soul.

He looked into her eyes, as clear and blue as the late-day sky. There was no hint of deception, no beguiling of a fairy. Only desire that might even match his own.

But Niall was right. Connor had to know for certain. He hoped in his heart and in his gut that she was no fairy. He tried to tell himself she could not have stirred his blood so if she were anything else than a woman.

He'd be able to tell if she was a fairy, wouldn't he? Would it really take a visit to the druidess to determine? Couldn't he discover that for himself? Couldn't he just bed her and find the answers he sought?

But could he risk his clan and his own life? If she were a fairy …

Suddenly, he dropped his hands and stepped away from her.

Chapter 17

A rush of cool air separated us.

I blinked and lowered my head. Had I been a fool? Had I misread him, allowed myself to be taken in by the desire I imagined in his eyes? I searched for some reason for his sudden move away that seemed to signal a change of heart.

"What is it you want?" My voice trembled a little.

"The druidess awaits us," Connor said.

"Druidess?"

"She will determine whether we marry."

A druidess premarital counselor?

I sensed an edge to his voice. There was something he wasn't telling me. Something ominous about visiting the druidess.

Was she an elderly drunk like Donal's druid? Did she do magic spells? Or human sacrifice?

I wished I knew more than fairy tales and a smattering of history about the Celts and ancient Ireland. It might be helpful to understand what the druidess was all about, what power, if any, she might have over a chieftain.

"Okay, I'm ready. Let's get this over with." I pulled on my judicial persona, and the best power pose I could assume for a trip to the druidess.

Connor led me from my room back down to the great hall to a tunnel that extended into a cavern. My claustrophobia had been fully awakened by the narrow stairs from the second floor to the hall, but the high ceiling and irregular stone walls of the passageway didn't bother me as much. Our footsteps, muffled by the dirt floor, were the only sounds in a place where I expected to hear the scurrying of rodents or the flapping of bats' wings.

I clenched my fists every few feet to reinforce the power stance that was rapidly slipping away.

Damp and cool, the tunnel looked very much like a cave in central

Ohio I had visited as a child. I tried to reassure myself by imagining I was really at the Olentangy Caverns, and would soon climb slimy steps back to the picnic grounds.

Connor took my hand and squeezed it gently, if not reassuringly. Wherever he was taking me, whatever the druidess wanted, I still believed he would not harm me or allow another to hurt me. His eyes had told me so, no matter what his words might say.

Besides, there was also the old man with white hair. Niall. I had to remember that name. Hadn't he said I was under his protection?

Ahead, a yellow glow illumined the opening into a large chamber lit by a half-dozen hissing torches propped in notches along a soot-stained wall. They gave light, warmth and an acrid smell to the dampness of the chamber.

"What is this place? Why have you brought me here?" I whispered, looking around the high-ceilinged room that resembled a church sanctuary.

In the center of the cavern, six flat-topped, knee-high rocks had been placed in a circle. Connor led me to one of them and put his hands on my shoulders, seating me. Rather than sit next to me, he stood behind the stone stool.

Almost nothing in this strange nightmare could surprise me now.

And a woman with no visible body parts except her face fit that bill perfectly. She glided from the shadows opposite the ring of stones toward the circle. Swathed in a dark cloak with a hood, she reminded me of a spider scurrying to see what it had captured. I sat perfectly still as the woman reached out to touch the sleeve of my dress, my hair, my cheek.

A druidess should be an old crone or a witch, but this woman in a hoodie was the most beautiful woman I'd ever seen. In fact, she could have been a model or an actress. Sparkling azure eyes, naturally long lashes, pouty, red lips, on a perfect face without any make-up.

I alternated between envy, and the thought I must be going crazy to be seeing a beauty queen in a cave in ancient Ireland.

It had to be drugs. Something hallucinogenic in the mead. I knew I hadn't swallowed enough of it to be drunk.

The woman took a seat across the circle of rocks and, with a nod of her head, slid down the hood of her filmy gray cloak. Pale, white-blond hair, straight, and hanging well past her waist, surprised me. Druidess or not, she was an incredibly gorgeous woman. A platinum blond, blue-eyed Kim Kardasian.

Why wouldn't Connor have married her? Wouldn't a chieftain and a druidess have some sort of super, Brangelina-like power base? Never mind the beautiful children these two would have.

The woman held up one long, slender finger to gesture to Connor to leave.

Whoa, someone who can boss around the chieftain of the clan Malley with a simple gesture. I'm going to like this woman after all!

He backed into the shadows of the tunnel, but I knew he had not left. I could feel his presence and, when I concentrated, hear his breathing. And, I was glad he was still there. While I might respect the druidess for ordering Connor around, I didn't trust the woman at all. She reeked of treachery.

The druidess spoke first in a low, husky voice intended for me alone to hear. "I am Niamh. I will ask ye three questions, and ye must answer them or face the blade." The woman's tone was flat, with as much charm as a slap across the cheek.

I sat up a little straighter, trying to bring back my professional bearing.

Face the blade? Wait just a minute, you're supposed to be deciding whether I marry the man who kidnapped me for that purpose. What's this face-the-blade business?

"I'll try, but I'm at a little bit of a handicap here since I have no clue what's going on." I hunted for some hint the woman would help me, but found nothing in the glacial blue stare.

Niamh asked, "Who serves Manannán mac Lir?"

An Irish liqueur?

I looked at the ceiling where soot stains spotted the rocks, and searched my memory for that name in Grandmother's stories and barely-studied Irish history textbooks.

Manannán mac Lir, a Celtic god?

In my mind, I recited parts of a poorly-recalled poem about the woman who served the sea-god until she was lured away to the land of mortals, and drowned in a huge wave. Then I came to the line I needed and said, "From the sward-topped cliffs to the sea-foam waves, from the Land of Promise to the mighty sea, I, Cliona, serve thee, Manannán mac Lir."

I knew immediately I got one. High-five for the woman from Cleveland.

The corner of Niamh's mouth curved up slightly as she nodded, and the curtain of straight, pale hair shifted across one shoulder, snagging on the amber brooch that held her cloak in place.

I didn't know whether to be pleased with myself or not. Perhaps ignorance would be a better response to the next two questions.

Why is the druidess testing me anyway? To determine my worthiness to marry Connor?

Something smelled. Why the test? Being Donal's daughter should have been enough for him. Had I cracked Connor's resolve with my insistence I was not who he thought? If that were the case, this test would verify I wasn't Caitrín, wouldn't it?

Or was he back to the fairy thing? Would a fairy know about Celtic gods or the legends that had become memorialized in poems?

So, which was I supposed to be? Donal's daughter or a literate fairy? Had Connor called on the druidess to determine?

Then what?

There had to be something else, some other reason why I was sitting here on a cold slab of rock being questioned by a woman who appeared to have as much feeling as the stones.

"What are the six gifts of womanhood?" Niamh asked next.

Again, I had no clue.

I stared at my questioner, at the dirt floor, at the scuffed toes of my wedding shoes peeking out from under a filthy hem. If we'd been in my courtroom, I would have banged my gavel and warned the druidess she was a hair shy of contempt of court for the look she gave me.

Six gifts of womanhood?

Would two of them be beauty and brains? No. Beauty and a bust?

How about beauty, a bustline, a dishwasher that unloads itself, a husband who fakes cuddling, a gas tank that never needs to be filled, and someone to cook every day?

Probably not the correct answers.

I ticked off six other things I wished I had and most of them included some way out of here and back to David, but I knew those wouldn't be what Niamh wanted.

Whatever they were, I only knew that I didn't have them. I shrugged my shoulders and looked over my shoulder at Connor. He stood outside the mouth of the chamber, arms crossed, staring back. Our eyes met and, in an instant, I knew he could see my terror.

I also knew he would not help me. He had set in motion some process he couldn't stop, and no matter how much he might want to help me, he would not. I had to face this wild boar alone.

I turned back to Niamh and said, "Can't use a lifeline, can I?"

I shivered at the look from Niamh, as the druidess continued the questioning. "Who lives on the Island of Shadows?"

Not some place on Lake Erie, and that was about it for the islands that came to my mind.

Help me again, Grandmother.

The answer burst from my lips as if it had a life of its own. "Aoife, the warrior queen."

Two out of three. Can I get credit for that much? Maybe with some more time I can get the six gifts thing.

I squirmed like a defendant waiting for the verdict.

Niamh called Connor back into the circle and whispered to him. Connor nodded, handing her a dagger, not the same one he had used on the boar, but a smaller, pearl-handled one, the size of a large kitchen knife. The druidess drew the blade across her own finger, and a streak of blood welled in its path.

Face the blade.

I could only guess what that meant, and it probably did not involve cutting my palm. I had flunked the test. Whatever Connor wanted to find out about me, whatever the druidess had to prove, the verdict was in. It was sentencing time.

Death?

Would it be swift and painless? I swallowed against the lump in my throat and squeezed my palms together.

Then, my thoughts skipped to David.

Would he somehow understand I had disappeared a couple thousand years into the past, and died in a cave because crazy people had tested my worthiness to marry the chieftain? Would he keep on looking for me or return to Cleveland and move on with his life? What would he tell my friends and colleagues? Would he have known the six gifts of womanhood?

I looked at Connor and then at Niamh as they conferred, presumably about my sentence. Then, I felt a storm of anger gathering on the horizon of my mind, rumbling and preparing to blow across me. Leftover bits of the fury I'd felt earlier toward Connor mingled with annoyance with the movie star-witch, but mostly I was angry with myself.

Why had I trusted Connor?

I should have tried harder to get away when I had the chance. And how could I have entertained any thought of marrying him even if it would make the best of a bad situation?

Time travel? Shepherd gangs? A demented druid? And, lastly, a gorgeous, cave-dwelling, black-widow spider woman who wanted to kill me with a pearl-handled dagger because I didn't know the six gifts of womanhood.

Suddenly, I realized how ridiculous this whole mess would seem to David, a twenty-first century man who wouldn't possibly believe my fantastic story if I ever did return to my own time.

Chapter 18

From deep within, laughter boiled up and erupted, convulsing every part of my body. Not an adolescent giggle, not a polite tee-hee but a righteous LMAO. I leaned back, clasped my knees with both hands, tipped my head up and laughed until my sides ached and tears ran from my eyes. Spurred by the scowl on Connor's face, and the shock in Niamh's eyes, wave after wave of laughter spewed from my mouth.

"Go ahead, give me the blade," I gasped between fits. "I can take anything! After all, I've been kidnapped by the chieftain of clan Malley."

Another roll of hysteria.

"Almost eaten by a wild pig!"

I slapped my thigh and laughed again.

"And now you think I'm a fairy goddess. Do I get a broom to ride or a mushroom to live under? Or maybe I'll disappear in a puff of smoke like Glenda, the good witch! Or, drop a house on someone. I dare you."

I rolled to one side laughing so hard my sides ached.

"Kathleen Moira O'Donnell, Court of Common Pleas judge and time-traveling fairy goddess. The tabloids would love it! And David! I wonder if he knew what a bargain he was getting in a bride!"

Suddenly, I stopped laughing, stood straight up and pointed a finger at Connor. "You started this, and you can stop this little exercise in madness. Lay a blade to my skin and we'll see exactly what sort of power I have. Perhaps I am a fairy from some other world. Perhaps I'll turn you into a frog." And whirling to face Niamh, I said, "And your buddy into a lizard."

It was all I could think of in an instant.

I had seen the look of hatred before when sentencing defendants, and I was always glad to have a lot of desk and an armed guard between myself and them. This time, I was face-to-face with a woman who had just smeared her own drop of blood across the blade of a knife she now meant to use on me.

Niamh drew back, raising the dagger above my chest. I faced her squarely and held my breath. In slow motion, the knife came down in a broad arc with all the force the druidess could muster. But before the tip could touch the bodice of my gown, Connor swung out and grabbed Niamh's wrist. He twisted his grip until the dagger dropped to the ground with a thud. Connor held Niamh's arm for a second before she wrenched her arm free. The druidess turned and fled into the shadows from which she had come, like a spider cowering in its web.

My fury rekindled when Connor faced me.

"How dare you? I've told you all along you had the wrong woman. But to kill me because of your mistake? Did you think my blood would bring Donal here faster? Would he avenge the death of a woman he doesn't even know? Or maybe you simply got bored with the whole kidnap thing. Why don't you just let me go? Well, this is it! I'm out of here and you'd better not even think about trying to stop me!"

I turned sharply, walked over to the wall, and grabbed a sputtering torch to light my way back to the hall. My stomach churned, and I swallowed hard. Breathing deeply, I tried to steady my nerves and my pounding heart.

Everything about this place and its people made me want to run until I found the meadow where Aasleigh was supposed to be, where something terrible had happened to catapult me back to whatever time this was. I never thought I'd consider Cleveland heaven on earth, but right now, I was in hell.

And, I didn't know what to do next.

As I reached the end of the tunnel, the smell of the food mingled with rancid straw, sweaty bodies and wood smoke assaulted my nose. While the noise of men gathering for dinner drew me back to the hall, the warriors blocked my way to the stairs, to the exit, and to my chamber. Niall's promise of protection echoed in my ears, but he was nowhere to be seen, and he certainly hadn't protected me from Connor's murderous Niamh.

For years, I had been a woman in a man's world, in law school and in the courts, but this was different. These men didn't respect me or admire me. They didn't know I had flunked the womanhood test. But, they also didn't know Connor and his evil druidess buddy thought I could turn them into lizards and frogs.

And I certainly didn't want them to find out I couldn't transform people into reptiles.

Resisting the impulse to drop the torch on the straw-covered floor and end it all, I propped the torch in a holder on the wall and backed up against a copper screen room divider in the shadowy periphery of the hall while I pondered my situation.

What am I going to do now? Where can I go?

Returning to my own time made the most sense, but how would I do that if I couldn't even get out of Croaghnac?

Standing in semi-darkness, I looked for a way out that didn't involve crossing a room full of half-drunk men. A few of them glanced my way, but made no effort to approach me. I leaned back against the screen and wrapped my arms around myself.

Thirty, or perhaps more, warriors, although I still preferred to think of them as crazy shepherds, clustered around long plank tables. They sat on benches, tree-trunk slab stools or the table itself and picked at communal platters laden with meat and hunks of dark brown bread. None of them used plates or any implements other than their daggers. Dirty hands passed food and tossed an occasional bone to the dog when he crept from the shadows and growled. They shared common goblets and drank as heartily and sloppily as they ate.

I gasped as a cup was upended over one man's head. The altercation that followed gave a whole new meaning to the "food fights" of high school days.

When they were done eating, or passed out from drinking, they rolled up in their clothing and slept on the floor or on a bench. This was a madhouse, and I had to get away from it.

Something brushed across my elbow, and I jumped. The serving girl who earlier had brought me the tray of food stood behind me. She motioned for me to join her, and I slipped unnoticed through an opening in the screen into a small anteroom.

"It is not safe for ye to be here," the girl whispered.

I was inclined to believe her, but at the same time wondered how it could be worse than what I'd already been through?

The girl pulled me out the serving entrance at the rear of the hall. "Come with me," she said. "There's a place away from the warriors where ye won't have to defend yourself or your food while ye eat."

My head buzzed, and my ears rang with the chaos of smells, sights and noise in the hall. The child led me to a nearby hut that appeared to serve as a kitchen. Smoke curled from the central fire pit toward a hole in the thatched roof. A thin, middle-aged woman hunched over a huge, iron cauldron, while two younger women wrested blackened meat from a roasted pig onto an over-sized platter. A square table, held stacks of round bread and several jugs. The girl motioned showed me where to sit on a stool on the other side of the fire, and brought me a hunk of bread and a goblet of sweet-smelling mead.

Fermented, but as sweet as fruit the day it was picked and as warm as the sunlight that ripened the fruit. The same drink Connor had given me earlier. Closing my eyes, I swallowed another mouthful, savoring the warmth that spread through my body. As I bit into the bread, my stomach rumbled in gratitude.

"This is wonderful," I said.

The girl giggled. "Ye do not know mead? Perhaps ye only drink wine."

"Occasionally.

"Ye need more," the girl said.

"This is fine," I said, glancing at the partially stripped carcass hanging over the fire. Fat glistened in the firelight and sizzled when it dropped onto the flames.

"Then, ye must eat this." The girl gave me a generous piece of white cheese. Its smooth, slightly bitter flavor complimented the sweetness of the mead and the coarseness of the bread.

"What is your name?"

"Liadan."

"That's a sweet name." I said. "My name is Kathleen, but my friends call me 'Kat.' How about I call you 'Lia?'"

The child smiled and nodded. I reached up and smoothed a lock of Lia's tangled hair and wished I had a hairbrush. "Can you sit with me for a moment? They won't mind, will they?"

Lia tucked her legs under her and sat on the floor next to my feet. While I ate, I watched the women scurry out of the hut with trays of food and drink and return moments later for more. I couldn't imagine how such a small girl could carry the heavy trays.

"Do you do this every day? I mean, feed that many men?"

Lia shook her head. "Nay, most of the time the warriors are not here. They came for the Beltane games."

"The games. Have you ever gone to them?"

Curiosity spilled from Lia's eyes. "Of course. Before, when I lived with my own clan. Have ye not gone to them?"

"No. Football games and baseball games and an occasional hockey match, but never the Beltane games. What do you like best?"

"Wrestling."

Why couldn't she have answered 'Cotton candy,' or 'the amusement rides?' She's just a kid. She's got no business watching wrestling.

"What else do you like?"

The girl shrugged her shoulders. "We don't get to go to the fair. We must serve the warriors."

Lia's eyes grew dull, and she looked about the room as if she expected a reprimand for wasting time. A chill ran across my heart as I wondered what other things the girl was required to do. She was far too young, far too vulnerable to be alone like this.

Chapter 19

"She is with the slaves," Niall reported to Connor.

"Why would she go there?" Connor asked.

Niall shrugged. "She did not pass the test?"

"Nay, but I could not allow the druidess to kill her either." Connor fingered the blade of his dagger retrieved from the floor of the cave.

"No? Then, the question is, will the woman harm all of us or only you? If she is Donal's daughter, he will come for her, and she must be happily married before he arrives. If she is aés sídhe, marriage to her will seal your doom."

He left unspoken the alternative that Connor should have murdered her while he had the chance.

"Is her father at the gate?"

Niall shook his head.

"He will come. I am certain of that. We are safe for the moment, so long as the Beltane fair continues. Donal would not dare bring his warriors against the valley while mine are here. Post extra guards at the pass. I will marry her soon. But I do not relish the idea of sleeping with one eye open, nor of losing my spirit to a fairy."

All these years he had planned his revenge, he couldn't allow victory to slip through his fingers now. Yet to willingly marry a fairy would doom him and his people.

His body still told him she was a woman. And a woman he wanted fiercely. She had to be Caitrín, no matter what she said or Niamh concluded.

Niall could not advise him this time. Even though the old man had known him since birth, he did not understand the molten fire that surged through Connor's body when Caitrín touched him. Niall would have let the witch's blade make his decisions for him.

Connor could not. Not simply because he desired Caitrín, but because there was still doubt like a shadow lingering across the full moon.

Too much about the woman did not make sense. Could it be possible she was not Donal's daughter in spite of all the evidence? Could she be from another time, as she has claimed?

For the moment, Connor believed she was human.

But if she were, then, who was she?

Chapter 20

I felt safe and calm with the servant-child. Lia showed me to a small beehive hut behind, but not attached to, the cooking room.

"Why are you being so kind to me? I'm a stranger,"

"I was lost once." Her face was solemn, her words empty of emotion.

I studied the child. "You're not part of this clan?"

"Nay, a slave."

"But, slavery is wrong," I said. "You're a child. What happened to your parents?"

"Killed."

"How?"

"The warriors."

"Connor's?" I did not want to hear that Connor would kill a child's parents and take her captive to become a slave. Not so young a child. Not anyone.

Lia shook her head. "Nay. I do not know whose warriors. Only that they came in the night, and killed everyone. I had left the hut in the dark. I wasn't supposed to do that." Her gaze lowered her as eyes grew heavy with tears.

I put my arm around the child's frail shoulders and held her while she cried silently. "It wasn't your fault, Lia. My parents died when I was even younger than you. In an accident. I was lucky. I could live with my grandmother, but I do understand how you feel. It's okay."

Practiced in detachment, I never let any defendant's sob story get to me, but I ached for this little girl. There could be nothing crueler than losing parents, but to become a slave at such a young age, how could such a thing be tolerated? If I did nothing else in this harsh land, I vowed I would change the life of this one, small child. I'd go to Connor to plead for the child's release if I had to.

"Lia, I don't have a child and you don't have a mother. Perhaps while I'm here I could be your mother. Would that be okay with you?"

Lia looked up, eyes brimming with tears that streaked down the dirt on her cheeks, and said, "I do not need a mother, but I would have ye as a friend."

Startled by her rejection, I said, "Yes, you're right. I could be your friend. That would be better."

I wiped the girl's tears with the hem of my dress, and Lia forced a brave smile.

"Got a question for you, friend. This may seem strange, but is there a place where I might bathe? A pool or pond or even a bucket of clean water? Other than the river, of course. It's a wee bit chilly and not very private."

Lia nodded. "I'll show ye, but I do not know why ye wish to bathe. It is evening and the aes sídhe will soon be about. They come for babies."

"You think that being clean would be dangerous, then?"

Lia nodded.

"Okay, then maybe I'll just wash a little. Don't have any shampoo anyway."

Lia took me to the rear of the compound, through a beehive hut that disguised an entrance into the mountain. I hesitated to enter the dark tunnel, but the girl tugged my hand and pulled me in.

"It is safe," she said. "There is no one here."

I estimated we had walked only about fifty feet when the tunnel opened into a cavern lit by two rush torches. Quartz studded the walls and reflected the light, scattering shards of flickering brilliance like a thousand tiny mirrors. In the center of the room was a small and deep pool with rocks lining the edges like a natural ladder.

"Perfect!" I said. "No one will come here for a few minutes?"

Lia nodded. "I'll guard the passageway."

I peeled off my dress, slip, stockings and underwear. When I stuck a foot into the water, I expected it to be icy cold, but didn't care so long as I could splash away some of the dirt. I was surprised to find it warm, so I slid into the inky pool and swam in small circles.

"Lia, you must try this. It feels so good. Do you know how to swim?"

"Swim?"

"See, my head is out of the water and I am moving around the pool. It's perfectly safe. I'll help you. Come try it with me."

Lia tentatively put one foot in the pool, then slowly stepped down the rocks until the water was thigh deep.

"You forgot to take off your shift, but that's okay. It needs to be washed as well," I said, taking the girl's hands and coaxing her into the water. "See how good this feels."

We splashed and played in the pool until some of the dirt and most of the tension soaked away. When we climbed out of the water, I smoothed the water from my arms and legs.

"Next time we bring towels."

Lia giggled.

"Okay, so you don't know what a towel is, but we'll bring something to dry off."

I pulled on my underwear and slip with its precious hidden gem heavy against my thigh, then wrapped my dress around the child's shoulders. "It's cold out there and I don't want you to get a chill."

Back in Lia's hut, the girl shed her wet clothing, and allowed me to tuck her into bed, a pile of sweet-smelling meadow grasses and pine boughs, covered with a sleeping fur. I folded my tattered and now, damp dress, and wrapped a second fur around myself like a sarong.

"I'll sit here a few minutes while you go to sleep," I told her, smoothing a wet lock of hair from the girl's cheek.

I'd never been around children, never baby-sat as a teenager, never had siblings or cousins or nieces or nephews, never discussed having children with David. Being a mother was remote as Cleveland was now.

Would David want them? Would he want to be a father? I couldn't believe that I had no idea how he'd answer such questions.

I looked at Lia and tried to imagine being a friend-mother to her. Being around this small child had evaporated all of the pent-up anger left from the druidess test. Suddenly I wanted to take care of the little girl sleeping next to me.

No matter what Lia says, she needs a mother. She's just a kid. Only a few years older than me when I lost my parents. Thank God, I had a loving grandmother to raise me. This kid has nothing. No one.

I wonder I f... if I stayed, if I could gain her freedom. Could she be the reason I'm here?

The cocoon-like hut oozed with calm and peace, and the slow even breathing of a sleeping child.

I laid down next to her, but stayed awake listening to the night sounds and trying not to think about the events of the past few days. I'd had enough fairies and magic and ancient enchantments in my childhood that I wanted nothing to do with them now. My grandmother had firmly believed in the wee folk and fairy gates. To a lonely child, the stories had brought wonderful dreams.

But, my adult life was built on the practical, logic, and the law with no room for tales of princes and knights in shining armor. I had left all of that nonsense behind years before. Besides, Connor, chieftain of clan Malley was certainly no Prince Charming or Sir Gallahad.

The trip to Ireland had seemed romantic and magical, at first. But, even the wedding of my dreams had turned out to be tarnished by a strange twist of fate.

I should be on my honeymoon. In a small, whitewashed walled cottage on the outskirts of Aasleigh. Is David there looking for me? Waiting for me to return?

Sadness filled my heart to overflowing as images of David brought tears to my eyes. I didn't want to dwell on thoughts of returning to him which seemed so impossible. But could I exchange my life with him for the difficult reality of life in this time and place?

Hot, angry tears started down my cheeks and I smeared them with the backs of my hands. How dare Connor think I was a fairy or a witch or whatever! I didn't even believe in such nonsense. How dare he test me! That alone was sufficient reason for me to return to my own time.

If I could...

One thing I couldn't deny, I was here, somewhere in the past, apparently trapped. I could go on reminiscing, or trying to come up with some scheme to get back to my own time. Or I could make the best of what fate had dropped in my lap.

As exhausted as I was, my mind could not be still.

Croagnac was an awful place. Dirty beyond comprehension. Cruel, and unhealthy. Babies probably died before their first birthdays, and children were enslaved. They feared fairies, and followed witches. They reared their sons to be warriors, and settled their differences with the sword.

I got up and wrapped a sleeping furs around my shoulders. I needed to pace. I looked at the little girl sleeping soundly on a pile of furs.

What can I do here? Can I really change one person's life for the better?

There was the one life I might change. Certainly, I would have more influence as the chieftain's wife than as a slave. I supposed I should be grateful for that much. But staying would mean I'd have to forgive Connor for the test that nearly took my life. My cheeks burned angrily with the memory of the dagger held high above my head.

I wandered out of the hut. The night air felt cool and still. No clouds marred the star-studded sky and a full moon gave the compound a soft silvery glow. Walking past several huts, I found an open space, and a discovery that took away my breath.

A wave of color, first purple, then pink, then green swirled across the black velvet horizon as if a giant had touched a paintbrush to the heavens, but could not decide on one color. The celestial light show seemed to stamp its approval on my conclusion that this was a different world. One where fairies worked their magic after dark.

"Beautiful sight," said a voice behind me.

I jumped and hugged the fur tightly around myself. Turning, I saw Niall, and started to move away from him.

"Do not leave," he said. "Enjoy the night. I will not bother ye."

I froze. I knew Celts didn't stir far from their hearths at night because of the activity of the aés sídhe, the fairies that searched for mischief they might make under cover of darkness.

Would this man think, as Connor did, that I might be one of them? Did he know about the test I had flunked?

"We call it the Northern Lights." I gestured toward the celestial display. "I couldn't sleep."

"Nor I," he said. "Would ye care to sit with me and watch the lights?"

Niall spread his cloak on the ground for me to join him. I felt slightly uneasy sitting next to Connor's pseudo-father and counselor. After all, he had promised me his protection, but that didn't stop Connor from introducing me to Niamh, PMS-with-a-knife.

Niall and I sat for a long time, maybe a quarter-hour mesmerized by the swirling colors. Finally, in a low voice, he said, "I saw the lights of the gods the night Connor was born."

"Really?"

Did that have some special meaning? Was it a blessing of the gods or some portent of greatness?

I recalled Connor's angry words when he told me Donal had murdered his father Malley the night of Connor's birth. Was Niall going to tell the story or did he presume I knew it?

He began slowly as if he was a dispassionate bystander recording history. "When I found Malley, he clutched a wound that bled freely in spite of the cloth wrapped around his waist.

"'Ye canna' survive the trip,' I told him, never one to withhold the truth from the chieftain.

"'I must ... ye will take me,' he said.

"I sent for two warriors to carry Malley, and wiped the war paint from his face. At least Sarina would see her husband as she knew him.

"The warriors lifted him gently to the back of his war pony. I climbed onto the horse, and held him upright until we reached the valley. Croaghnac stood silent guard, both witness and shelter to the generations of this clan who had built it. I felt Malley's life-force slip away, yet his spirit hovered, hesitant to completely sever the connection to his body.

"'We are nearly there, old friend,' I told him as the warriors took him up the slope to the fortress. As he crested the top of the hill, the sky exploded in ever-changing swirls of purple, rose, orange as the stars shed tears every color for the passing of a great warrior-king.

"I hurried ahead to find Sarina and prepare her. The warriors bore their chieftain to a chamber, little more than a hollowed cave at the rear of the fortress. They laid him next to his wife, who struggled against the last stages of childbirth.

"More dead than alive, Malley took Sarina's hand in his and spoke, his words coming out in gasps. 'I ... am ... here.'

"Sarina opened her eyes and focused on his face as a tremendous contraction shuddered through her body. Her spirit left her body, as the midwife grasped the tiny child by his feet, and pulled him from the birth canal.

"A son. The first-born.

"The baby kicked furiously, and drew in his first breath.

"I reached out and took the newborn, and wiped the birth fluids from the infant's face.

"'Ye are your father's son, the first-born. To ye shall be the blessing of the gods and the legacy of Malley.'

"Hand-in-hand, Malley and Sarina now walked the path to the Otherworld. I assumed responsibility for the child they left behind, the son on whom the lights of the gods had shone. The son who would one day avenge their deaths.

"Connor survived only because there are those who remembered he was the first-born."

"What do you mean?"

"Two brothers were born."

"Connor and Basta? Then, they are twins?"

Niall chuckled softly. "No. Connor was born to Sarina, the first wife and Basta several weeks later to Ushna, Malley's second wife."

"Oh," I said, still confused.

Niall's words haunted her.

There were those who remembered he was the first-born. Did Ushna not remember? Did she try to put her own son first? I tried to fill in the blanks in Niall's story.

"Why are you telling me this?"

"Ye need to know."

"Do you think this will make me feel sorry for him and make me want to marry him?"

"No, ye need to know. The day will come when ye must make a choice. Ye need to know what it is ye are choosing."

If it were a choice between Basta and Connor, there'd be no problem. I'd definitely select Connor any day over scum-bag Basta. But why would I ever have to make such a decision? It was Connor who planned to marry me, not Basta. There was no reason I'd ever have to choose between them.

I started to ask Niall about his prediction when he interrupted. "Come, it is time to retire," he said, rising and helping me to my feet. He escorted me back to Lia's hut, and said, "If ye feel more comfortable, stay here the night. No one else knows ye are here."

"Wait. Before you go, I need to ask you a question," I said. "Would you have killed me? If I flunked Niamh's test."

Niall hesitated, which spoke volumes.

"You think I'm a fairy, don't you? But you'd let Connor go ahead with marrying me?"

"What I believe is not important. All that matters is what Connor believes."

He started to turn away, but I laid my hand on his arm. "No, that's not what is important. Connor thinks I am Donal's daughter, which I am not. Then, he decided I'm a fairy, which I am not. He may be the chieftain, but he's wrong about a good many things. Perhaps he's wrong about Donal as well. Maybe Donal won't come here looking for someone who isn't his daughter. What would Connor do then?"

Niall gave me a puzzled look. "So far as Connor is concerned, ye are Donal's daughter, and Connor will marry ye at the end of the games."

I dropped my hand. "I know you don't like the idea. Thanks for being honest with me. I'll remember what you told me about making a choice."

I watched as Niall disappeared into the darkness.

A choice. His words echoed in my mind. *Somehow I don't think that has anything to do with marrying Connor.*

Chapter 21

I awoke the next morning with a start and a hollow feeling in my head. Gray light clung to the mist that swirled through the doorway. My breath added little puffs of condensation the same color. The temperature had dropped during the night, and I didn't want to leave the warmth of the furs.

Looking around the empty hut, I noticed a pile near my feet, a neatly folded tunic, belt, mantle, and boots. I whispered thanks to Lia who must have procured the clothing. Glancing at my wedding gown lying in a heap on the floor, I felt a pang of sadness. It had once been so beautiful and so perfect. But the time had come to put it aside. Not only was the dress ruined beyond repair, but my survival might depend on being able to move about more freely and blend into my surroundings. As it was, I was already at a disadvantage being considerably shorter than the Celtic women of Malley's clan, and possessing short, strawberry-red curls in contrast to their dark looks. At least if I dressed like them, I might be a little safer. And a little warmer.

Setting aside my wedding dress felt like surrendering to being stuck here forever. Was I really ready to abandon life in with David in Cleveland?

No!

But practicality won that argument. I placed my shoes under the dress, and wrapped everything with my stockings, tying the legs into a knot for a neat bundle I could grab and run. If I could escape, I wanted to take the dress with me.

Okay, all set. I can go at a moment's notice. In the meanwhile, I've got to make the best of my life here. And if that means marrying Connor, I'll guess I'll have to do that.

I nodded, pushing aside sentiment with firm resolve, pleased with this decision. Yes, I'd marry Connor, but someday, some way, I'd try to return to my own time. Hiding my bundle behind a wooden box against the wall, I turned to the clothing Lia had left.

Every move felt so permanent. I fought the tears that collected in

111

the corners of my eyes like silent witnesses. The tunic, one piece of woven linen dyed pale yellow reminded me of spring buttercups that had bloomed a week before in Cleveland. I slipped it over my head and smoothed it down over my slip. I refused to leave behind the slip with its secret pocket and hidden jewel.

Wrapping the wide belt around my waist, I tied it at one side as I'd noticed how the other women did. Then, I picked up the pair of incredibly soft deerskin boots and pulled them on. Flat-soled, a little snug, but immensely comfortable and hopefully, practical, they molded to my feet and calves like moccasins. I laced them around my ankles and calves, tying the leather cords in place just under my knees.

When it came to the brat, however, I was lost. I had watched as Connor donned his. He had somehow wrapped around his waist and across one shoulder. The length of fabric, when shaken out, could have been enough to slipcover my sofa at home.

I tossed one end over my left shoulder and began to wrap myself, but I didn't have enough fabric left to tuck in where I could reach and every time I tried, the part that draped over the shoulder fell off. I unwound a few inches, but then the whole thing came loose and puddled around my ankles.

Why didn't I take a college course in ancient costumes or watched the Vikings series?

I started over. This time, I couldn't keep the end over my shoulder from sliding off so I wrapped it around my neck like a mile-long scarf, and held it with my chin. Like a sarong gone awry, the fabric turned around my middle just below my breasts and across one arm. Then, as if it had a mind of its own, the cloth collapsed again in a tangle at my feet.

Undoing my belt, I tried to find some way to tie the over-sized shawl in place. I picked it up and glared at it, feeling like a three-year-old frustrated by buttons and zippers.

How do they do this? Should I wear it like a pashmina, or cut a hole in it and invent the poncho.

I plopped it over my head, trying to gauge how much would drag on the floor if I wore it as a hooded cape.

"I will help ye, if ye wish," the voice in the doorway startled me.

I peeked out from under the edge of the wool to see Connor standing before me. He was the last person I wanted to see since I was still angry with him for trying to have me killed because I didn't know the gifts of womanhood. I'd rather go naked than let him help me with this impossible, over-sized body wrap.

I took a step away from him. "I do not wish!" I said as frostily as the early morning air, my words hanging in little puffs of white.

Without another word, Connor lifted the rectangle of chestnut brown fabric. I glared in response, then ran my fingers through my hair to straighten the mess of curls the heavy cloth had temporarily flattened. I backed down slightly, just enough to allow him to help just this once. But, I vowed to myself that when I figured out how to do it on my own, I'd never let him dress me again.

"I was passing the hut and noticed your struggles."

He eyed my clothing and I began to wish the tunic didn't look as though it had been made specifically for me. Skimming across my waist past my thighs to mid-calf, it moved like second skin, soft and shimmering and inviting more than his gaze.

I gave him a look of annoyance. "If you're done ... I'd like to see some of this place while it's still daylight."

"I'm not done," he answered, holding out the brat and gesturing for me to turn.

I folded my arms across my chest.

"I can show ye how to don this brat, if ye stand still, but ye must hold out your arms. Like this." He stretched his arms out to either side. "Like ye are going to wrap them around my neck."

He got a second glare for that.

"Almost right," I said. "It's my hands I'd like to wrap around your neck."

One corner of his mouth turned up slightly in the beginnings of a smile. "I imagine ye do. And not without reason. But, if ye really want a piece of me, it would be easier to use this." He pulled a small dagger from his waistband sheath and extended the handle toward me.

I stared at it both fascinated and repulsed. I had seen plenty of knives of all kinds, used in all ways to hurt and maim people. Even in self-defense, I could not imagine myself plunging a knife into someone, no matter how much he tempted me.

"No, thank you," I said.

He placed the knife on the ground between us. And while he was bent, I raised my arms as he'd demonstrated.

He held the fabric, and I twirled this way and that until he had me tied in knots with the piece of wool.

"Once more," he said, "and this time, do not move. I will walk it around ye."

My anger began to melt at the mirth I saw light his eyes. Connor piled the brat over his arm. Laying one edge over my right shoulder and placing my right hand to hold it, he draped the rest around my waist, under my left arm, across the small of my back, to the front and tucked it in on the side.

Then, he pulled a hammered cooper brooch from the small doeskin bag hanging from his belt and fastened it at my shoulder to gather the width of cloth so that it did not hang down my arm and encumber me. The entire process took less than thirty seconds.

His hand lingered at my neck, and he wrapped a curl around one finger. Slipping a finger under my chin, he tipped my face up until our eyes met. Gazing, barely touching, yet keenly aware of his proximity, of the intimate ease I felt being so close to him, I stood perfectly still for a long, breath-held moment.

I finally broke the spell. "I'm not a fairy."

"I know," Connor said.

"No more tests?"

"None. Will ye forgive me?"

I waited a few seconds to answer, then said, "Maybe."

He picked up the dagger and slid it carefully into the top of my boot into a pocket I had not noticed before.

"Am I ready now? How do I look?"

"Ye look as though ye are ready for the games," he said.

"The games?"

"The Beltane fair. The warriors' games are about to begin." He gestured toward the valley below. "I have come to take ye to the fair, if ye will go with me."

His voice conveyed an invitation that signaled he was giving me a choice. I hesitated slightly, remembering the people closing in on me yesterday, the warriors leering, Basta's humiliating comments, Niall's belief that I was a fairy, and most of all, Connor's plan to marry me before the ram's horn sounded.

But instead of allowing doubts and fears to control me, I decided to step forward, to embrace this new and strange life. I deliberately chose to make the best of the circumstances, even if I couldn't dress myself completely. Yet.

I placed my hand in Connor's outstretched hand.

When he escorted me from the hut to the gate of the fortress, I gasped at the splendor of the meadow. Under a pearly white sky awaiting the sun that silhouetted the rim of mountains to the east, the scene was a muted painting in a poorly-lit room, waiting for the lights to be turned on. The colors of the valley, heather and grasses, the ribbon of river, the pennants waiting for a breeze had not yet brightened. Yet, even in the shadows, everything glowed.

Tents hovered on the morning mist like dandelion fluff bobbing on a stream. Far-off sounds drifted up the slope, people beginning to stir, animals braying and snorting to be fed, merchants setting out the wares for the day, warriors gathering at the edge of the field. Shouts and calls mixed with the low rumble of a drumbeat. The smell of fires being stirred and stoked added another texture as the day was quickly coming to life.

"Come!" said Connor, excitement evident in his voice as we started down the slope.

"Wait. The games. What will happen there?"

Connor drew his shoulders back and answered, "I will compete in all."

"Why?"

"It is what the chieftain does."

"Okay. And what sort of games are these? Games of chance?"

He laughed heartily. "Nay, games of strength, courage and teamwork."

"Good, I mean, there's a whole bunch of men—warriors—playing at one time. I presume they look out for each other. No one gets hurt?" I didn't know what possessed me to ask such a question. "It's not like a battle to the death, is it?"

Connor stared at me as if uncertain how to answer such a peculiar query. "Are ye worried for my welfare?"

"No, of course not," I stammered, feeling color rise in my cheeks. "Do you do this sort of thing every Beltane?"

"The clan needs to know I am worthy to be their chieftain."

"You have to continually prove yourself? I thought you are chieftain because your father was."

"No, any man may be chieftain if he defeats me and has the support of the council."

An image of Basta suddenly sprang into my mind. I shuddered at the thought he might someday be the chieftain.

"Uh, could you get hurt in these games?" A storm cloud of premonition gathered the horizon of my mind.

His eyes darkened and his brows knit in a glower nearly as fierce as when I had refused to remove my gown at the cliff. "Nay! No danger! I am chieftain—"

"Yeah, I know, 'chieftain of clan Malley.' But, there's also that slimy brother of yours. Maybe, just maybe, he'd like to keep you from getting married. And one way might be to make sure you never make it to your wedding. I'm not one to borrow trouble, of course, but seems to me—"

"Enough! Basta does not even participate in the games. There is no danger. I am a warrior!" Connor dropped my hand and walked away.

I stared at him as he disappeared into a group of warriors.

This man infuriated me like no other, not even Jim Lewis, an attorney I usually tried to reassign to someone else whenever his name appeared on my case list.

Why should I care? Let Connor get himself killed. One less groom for me!

I would have turned and marched right back to the hut had not Niall walked up just then to take Connor's place as my escort. The cadence of a drum directed our steps down the hillside following Connor. The crowds drawn to the field parted to allow us to walk through until we reached a spot Niall pronounced as perfect to watch the games. A slight rise gave us a view of the entire field and each sport.

"This is all safe, isn't it? I mean nothing bad can happen to ... "

I didn't want to let Niall know I was either worried about Connor's safety or more than pleased to send him off to another bride.

Niall smiled and gave my arm a gentle squeeze. "He's perfectly safe. He usually wins all contests."

"Because he's good at them, or because he's the chieftain?"

Niall grinned at my words. "Both."

Standing slightly behind me, the counselor played the part of an announcer to perfection, describing each of the four contests about to begin.

Two warriors engaged in sword play in one corner, others tossed a huge log in the farthest corner and, in the middle of the field, men played a sort of ball game with an object Niall identified as a sheep's bladder. Closest to us was a wrestling match between two unclothed and painted warriors.

I didn't know which contest to watch first, but the naked, blue-painted men wrestling did catch my attention. Better than a Vegas show. The enthusiasm of the cheering onlookers was contagious, although I had no clear idea which side or opponent I should prefer. Completely engrossed in the competitions, I didn't notice the sun break free of the mountains and quickly burn off the lingering wisps of smoky mist. But I didn't miss the arrival of the chieftain. No one could.

The blast of a horn suddenly silenced the noise of the crowd like a thunderclap stills the air before a storm. I jumped, and must have given Niall a look of panic because he touched my shoulder to direct my attention.

"Connor arrives." Niall gestured toward the edge of the field where six men walked across the playing field. In the center of the group, Connor walked with the confidence of, well, a chieftain.

And there was certainly no doubt about that!

He wore a shirt of woven gold that caught the first rays of the sun with glints of amber, and copper, shimmering as he moved. In one hand, he carried a heavy sword, larger and longer than the one normally strapped to his waist. On his left arm, he had had a round shield, hammered and polished like a multi-faceted mirror. He commanded the attention of contestants and the audience, with equal authority.

My heart jumped into my throat and pounded as if it would explode at any moment. I had never seen anyone so—I could not even think of a word except—majestic.

Connor raised his sword to signal the contests to continue and shouts erupted from the crowd. Beyond their obvious excitement, I noticed admiration and awe on their faces. They loved their chieftain. A shiver of apprehension coursed down my spine. In spite of the reassuring cheers of the crowd, and Niall's calming presence, a shadow crept over me like a cloud wandering across the morning sun.

I watched as Connor moved from game to game. He tossed his log the farthest distance, took on three opponents in sword fights, raced up and down the field in the ball game. Each match seemed safe enough. And true to his word Connor was the victor in every contest. His opponents didn't appear to give him deference. He seemed genuinely to be the champion.

Then, it came time to wrestle.

The wrestling matches resembled a no-holds-barred brawl unlike the Greco-Roman wrestling of the Olympics or choreographed fights on television. No referee, no judges, no time out bell. A fight to the death or, at the least, the incapacitation of one of the wrestlers.

One very large bear of a man had, thus far, defeated every opponent. I could see his face as he turned toward Connor. His expression was dead. Completely devoid of emotion.

Connor handed one of his companions his sword and shield. Then he glanced in my direction. I started to raise a hand to wave when an unexpected wave of premonition swept over me.

I should signal to him not to fight. But my arm froze.

He turned away, and stripped off his shirt before I could warn him.

I grabbed Niall's arm to express some sort of warning, and he put his hand over mine in paternal reassurance. His expression told me he was not worried. But I could not be placated. Something terrible was about to happen. I knew it, yet felt powerless to stop it. I needed to warn Connor, but how?

I wanted to look away, but my eyes would not obey.

Connor, blue geometric designs like hand-painted tattoos decorating his broad shoulders and muscular upper back, bowed low as if to offer homage to the man about to pummel him. His opponent grunted in acknowledgment of the challenge.

Facing each other, both men walked slowly in a circle, assessing each other. They nodded and backed away for the last time before engaging.

The ritual dance finished, both of them, and everyone now watching, knew that only one would walk away from this contest.

Chapter 22

"See how he struts before the crowd," Basta said to a man standing with him on the edge of the playing field.

"I see a chieftain who is adored by his clan," the man said.

"A chieftain who must fight to maintain leadership," said Basta.

"Aye, he fights, all do. But does he need to prove his courage and strength to remain the chieftain? I think not. He competes in the games because he enjoys them. He keeps himself ready for battle. If ye think he is worried about any challenges to his leadership, ye are mistaken," the man said, before moving away.

Basta cursed under his breath. The man was right. Connor never needed to worry about a challenge, even from his own half-brother. From the day of Connor's birth, he had been the heir to his father's position in the clan. There had never been a question in anyone's mind that Connor would grow up to lead the clan.

Why Connor? Basta wanted to know. *Why not me?*

Basta was not crippled by bitterness and revenge like his elder brother. Greed was his primary and only motivator. He knew it. He readily admitted it.

After all, wouldn't the clan benefit from being led by someone who sought better for it? More land. More wealth.

He'd go after Donal, but for land and riches, not for a sad-eyed, little witch with such ridiculous hair. Abducting Donal's daughter was a fool's errand. He had tried to warn his brother. Nothing good could come from Connor's crazy ideas of revenge.

And that woman certainly wasn't worth Connor's efforts. She wouldn't bear him strong sons, warriors worthy of the clan. Not that one. Basta could tell from the looks of her. Too small-boned. If she were a mare, he'd sell her.

She didn't stand tall and proud like the women of their clan. What kind of warrior would she make? She couldn't carry a spear, he surmised. He studied his brother's intended bride as she stood next to the old counselor.

Her tunic clung to her hips as she moved. Breasts strained against the fabric when she turned to speak to the counselor. She was a temptress, not the proper bride of a chieftain.

But perhaps I have misjudged her.

Basta licked his lips as he let his imagination roam freely. He might pull her into one of the tents across the field. He considered how he could entertain her while his brother played the crowd.

She was rumored to have a temper. Hadn't he tasted a sample when his brother carried her across the river? Something could be said for taming a woman with spirit, and he decided that he was just the man to do it. He needed only to find an opportunity to lure her from the games, and from the old man who had taken on protecting her.

Reluctantly, Basta shifted his attention to the wrestling match as Connor faced the farmer. Slowly, a plan developed while he watched the opponents. He might not have to do anything if Fodor took care of Connor.

If the brute were successful, Basta could have it all. The land, the wealth, the clan, and Connor's bride. All that should have been his all along.

Fodor, as a wrestler, was neither stupid, nor slow, in spite of his immense size. A farmer, he was accustomed to wrestling recalcitrant livestock. He swung an ax with the strength of three men. He could lift and hold a chariot while another replaced its wheel. He was a giant of a man, heavily-muscled.

And he hated warriors.

He had once longed to become a warrior, but he could not memorize the epics, a task required of every young lad who aspired to be a warrior.

Instead of reciting chants, Fodor called sheep. Instead of wielding a sword, he plowed. The high point of his life was the Beltane fair where year after year, he would trounce any warrior foolish enough to challenge him. He enjoyed crunching their bones, and grinding their faces into the dirt. He never intended to kill anyone, but when it happened, he didn't regret it. He always made sure they would never forget the mistake of taking him on.

Made no difference to him that this time it was the chieftain who challenged him. He had persisted through three Beltane fairs waiting for the right moment to challenge the chieftain.

Fodor snorted and sized up his opponent.

He knew Connor well, but had never fought him. He had watched the chieftain compete in all of the other games. Connor was quick-footed, probably almost as strong as the farmer, but Fodor had one advantage other than brute strength.

He could outlast most of his opponents, wear them down slowly, like a determined bear, pursuing, pawing, pummeling until the other gave up. Then, he'd pounce, snap a limb, crush a head or break a neck.

Connor would not see this as a contest to the death, as Fodor always did. In the farmer's estimation, Connor was a crowd-pleaser, not a serious contestant.

The giant, eager for first contact, took a step toward the chieftain. Connor circled slowly and steadily, allowing the bigger man to start the match. Fodor lunged with one meaty hand outstretched, and grabbed hold of Connor's upper arm. The chieftain twisted slightly, and Fodor's grasp was lost.

At the same time, Connor kicked one of his opponent's legs. The farmer stumbled, but stayed upright.

So it began.

Like a parry without their swords. They assessed each other, exchanged first blows, retreated, and then got down to serious fighting.

The crowd cheered them on, taunting the farmer, rooting for their chieftain. Taking my cue from Niall, I watched silently.

Connor held up both arms, palms open and perpendicular to the ground, ready to grab his opponent or to defend his upper body.

He tightened already-firm abdominal muscles, tucked his chin before stepping forward with his first blow, a straight punch aimed at Fodor's head.

The farmer saw him coming, and shifted toward the hit so that the impact glanced off his temple, doing little damage.

Groans from the closest observers spurned on the fighters.

Fodor's turn. He charged Connor suddenly, catching him in the mid-section and knocking him to the ground with a thud.

Connor rolled as Fodor dove atop him. Moving quickly, the chieftain eluded the farmer, and scrambled back to his feet. Instead of setting upon his opponent, Connor backed away and allowed Fodor to rise.

They exchanged several quick fists to the face. A bruise welled up just below Connor's eye, and a small cut at one side of Fodor's mouth bled freely.

My own fists clenched, and my breaths quickened. Much as I was unsure about my feelings for Connor, I didn't like seeing the giant hit him. I felt like punching the best myself. But then again, I also felt like slugging Connor.

And I didn't like that I felt that way.

The men circled again before fists flew once more. Punch, smack, thump. Uppercut to the farmer's chin, side blow to Connor's left ear.

The mood of the men gathered to watch shifted suddenly as if they sensed the wrestling was intensifying.

Connor and Fodor responded to the buzz around them by dancing closer. They caught each other in a sweaty embrace, leaning together, arms locked, heads jammed side-by-side.

Pummeling each other, Connor landed the first major blow. Fodor's head whipped back with a snap, but not before one of the farmer's strikes caught Connor's left cheek.

I said a word I was pretty confident Niall did not know but would probably guess its meaning.

They broke apart long enough for Fodor to catch his opponent in a headlock. But Connor wrapped his powerful arms around Fodor's waist, lifted him off the ground before slamming him down on his back.

Fodor snatched Connor's ankles, and pulled him to the ground as well. The warriors backed slightly to give them room to roll around on the ground.

Although the morning air had barely begun to warm, the wrestlers' muscles rippled and glistened with sweat now, and Connor's blue body paint smeared, some of it rubbed off onto Fodor.

The crowd roared approval as the combatants rolled as one unit, exchanging hits to belly, chest and head. I caught a glimpse of the determination frozen on Fodor's face. His ebony eyes narrowed to slits from the blows to his face. The corner of his mouth still bled.

I felt my heart skip a beat, and my breath catch in my throat as I realized this was no longer a game, nor an exhibition of strength. Fodor meant to kill Connor. I could feel it in my gut.

Connor took a blow to the belly. Fodor on top, straddling Connor's back, punched his flanks, then grabbed his hair, and wrapped it around his fist. Yanking, the farmer slammed Connor's head into the ground.

Then, repeated the vicious assault, making known to all that this was a contest to the death.

Chapter23

"Enough!" I said to Niall. "You must stop this!"

The fight had become fierce, disgusting and brutal. I'd seen plenty of photos from crime scenes, victims of beatings in staged poses for police files, but I had never witnessed a fight like this in progress.

I didn't want to watch any longer, but neither could I tear myself away. My stomach contracted, and I was glad I had not yet eaten anything that might threaten to come up.

No amount of glory, no political office, no chieftainship was worth a fight to the death, in my book. And, if someone didn't intervene soon, that was what the outcome would be.

Niall stood motionless, except for tightening his grip on my arm to prevent me from intervening in this madness.

The warriors grew strangely quiet. You could have heard a pin drop, except pins had not yet been invented.

I shifted as the two combatants circled each other again, and the observers crowded closer. I didn't want to lose sight of Connor.

"Please stop them before someone is killed."

"I cannot," Niall said, releasing his hold on me, and crossing his arms over his chest. The old man could not or would not be swayed.

I tried to tell myself I didn't care. Really. After all, I had no real stake in who became the new leader of the clan. And I didn't even want to root for Connor since I was supposed to be trying to plot an escape from him anyway.

But, on the other hand, if I had to be stuck in this time and place, I'd rather be married to a live Connor than a brain-dead one. And, Fodor was definitely not my type, so I'd prefer to see him defeated.

However, it didn't appear that the fight was going Connor's way and I wasn't couldn't stand by and watch a massacre. If Niall wouldn't interrupt it, I'd stop it myself if I had to.

I pushed my way through the throng to the edge of the field, Niall following. My ill-considered plan was to throw myself between the men to stop them.

Apparently Niall figured that out and grabbed my arm, spinning me around. "Ye cannot interfere! This must be!"

I twisted free as cheers erupted from the warriors. Screams filled the air indicating that the fight was over.

I turned back toward the field, but the crowd of men blocked my view of the two bodies on the ground. Their voices echoed as they surged forward. I caught bits and pieces of their shouts rose above the din.

"No!"

"A broken neck."

"It canna' be!"

"He's dead!"

"Connor, son of Malley?"

"Connor!"

Shock, not victory resounded in their cries.

I strained and pushed to get to the wrestling field.

"Has Connor been hurt?" I asked, grabbing Niall to steady myself as the mob surged toward the wrestling area.

Fear and shock etched across his face answered me.

Could it be true? Connor was not the victor?

As the throng moved forward, a solid crush of men suddenly pulled me away from Niall. Warriors jostled and shoved me in their stampede across the playing fields.

"Connor!" I shouted. "Niall!"

But the noise of the crowd swallowed my words, and the mob threatened to knock me off my feet. Just then, Basta stepped up, shoving aside everyone in his path. He pulled me toward him, and tucked me against his body so that I would not be trampled.

"Come with me," he said, wrapping me into the shelter of his arms. "Connor's dead. Niall must see to his body. He can no longer protect ye."

A warning bell went off in my head telling me not to go with Basta, but I feared the warriors were heading toward mass hysteria and violence. Basta offered the only way out of the mayhem erupting around us. He shouldered through the human torrent toward a row of tents.

Several times, I stood on tiptoes, straining to back, but could not see the contestants, or Niall.

Basta said, "Don't look. Ye will only upset yourself."

I could not believe that Connor might be dead, but I had seen with my own eyes the demonic look on Fodor's face, and the ferocious blows he delivered.

I had heard the cries of the crowd. Niall had left my side, and now Basta had confirmed it.

Connor was dead.

I shook with the thought that somehow I knew this would happen, that I could have prevented it had I been more insistent with Niall.

Connor, the shepherd who had carried me away from Aasleigh, the warrior who had saved me from the wild boar, the man who refused to believe my story of time travel, the chieftain to whom I was inexplicably tied, was dead.

The nightmare that had become my life was taking a turn I had not expected.

I didn't want to care, but suddenly, I did.

There had not been time yet to mourn for the loss of David and my perfect life-to-be with him. Now, in quick succession, I had also lost Connor, and whatever life I was just beginning to accept with him.

My eyes began to burn and my vision blurred as tears gathered for a procession across my cheeks. I smeared them with the backs of my hands.

Paying little attention to Basta, I was only dimly aware that he led me to the row of tents. He pulled me into one of them, and unloosed the flap hanging over the doorway.

"Ye are safe here and ye have privacy. I will stay with ye until the crowds calm. Cry, if ye wish," Basta said, offering to comfort me.

No!

I didn't want to cry for Connor, especially not in front of Basta, yet the tears poured down my cheeks unbidden and uncontrollably.

Outside the tent, people hurried past, anxious to see what the uproar was all about. The muffled shouts of the warriors lingered in the distance, but I scarcely noticed as sorrow wrapped around me like the brat Connor had placed over my shoulders the night we slept in the forest.

Small, gulped sobs began to escape as I detached from my surroundings and held tightly to the memory of Connor's arms around me. Anger, fear, and now, loss mingled into the nightmare that would not stop unfolding.

Basta appeared kind and solicitous. He let me lean against him while pain flowed from my heart. He stroked my shoulders and arms tenderly, and murmured soothing words that reminded me of Connor.

Had I misjudged Basta, misunderstood his intentions?

Even though he held me in his arms, I refused to allow Connor's brother to intrude on my grief. Overwhelmed by emotions I could neither explain nor dismiss, I pulled away from everything and everyone.

I sank to the floor and rested my head in my hands, unaware someone lifted the door flap. Basta knelt next to me, and stroked my back with his hand.

"Aye, love, I can give ye what ye want. Forget Connor," he said.

I lifted my head as the tent flap fluttered down, and asked, "Uh, is someone there? Who was that?"

"Someone who realized he had come to the wrong tent." Basta stood up and gave me an odd half-smile.

"Let me take ye away from here. There is nothing here for ye. I can return ye to your father."

"My father?" I wiped the tears from my cheeks and sniffled.

Suddenly Basta's offer sunk in.

Not my father, Caitrín's, but the place where I might find the portal. Before I could answer, Niall came into the tent.

"I've been searching for ye," he said.

"She has been safe with me," said Basta.

Niall raised an eyebrow, and I nodded to confirm what Basta had claimed. "He saved me from the mob." My voice sounded hoarse with grief.

"Ye'll not mind if escort her back to Croaghnac," Niall said, with an insistence that left no room for Basta to object.

He held out one hand to me, and I rose slowly.

"My offer still stands," Basta whispered as I brushed past him.

"He means ye no good," said Niall, taking me from the tent.

I cleared my throat and steadied myself. "He was polite and kind. I know I originally thought he was not so, but today, he saved me from the crush of the warriors' stampede, and comforted me when I heard the news."

"Then, he wants something."

"Well, you'll probably have to be more charitable to him now. He'll be the next chieftain now that Connor is gone."

"Connor is gone?"

I sniffled. "You don't have to hide anything from me. I know he was killed. And, it's my fault! I'm so sorry. I tried to stop him. I told him I had this feeling something would happen. He wouldn't believe me. And, now see what's happened. It's so awful!"

Niall remained silent as we completed the climb to the fortress. We parted at the gate. I went to Lia's hut, and Niall toward the great hall.

Alone in Lia's hut, I said aloud, "I don't know whether I should be happy or sad."

I picked up the bundle of my clothing and hugged it close.

Connor dead. Could it really be possible?

I had heard the crowds, and Basta had confirmed my fears. Part of me felt immense sadness. Sadness for what might have been. Even sadness at having to leave Croaghnac and Lia.

"Why did you have to die, Connor, and leave me in such a mess?"

I didn't yet know why I was here. I was so certain it had been for some reason. Now, I could return to Donal's land, possibly to my own time, and yet that felt so wrong.

Like something was missing, or incomplete.

Ever since my grandmother's death, I had been on my own. Alone. There had been a hole in my heart that even David could not fill. It felt like it had opened again.

I thought about my parents and my grandmother. Those who had loved me and left. I hadn't known Connor long enough to relegate him to their status, but that didn't seem to matter right now. The hole in my heart was big enough for him as well.

Would there be some sort of funeral for Connor?

Should I attend?

Probably not. I wasn't a part of his life, his culture, his clan.

No, I should leave before any sort of ceremony.

I wondered what Basta intended to do. Would he take me back to Donal before the funeral? Would there be some sort of coronation event to name him the new chieftain, or would that honor be passing on to Fodor?

I sat on the bed and propped my elbows on my knees, chin on my hands, an occasional tear sliding unceremoniously down my cheek. After a few moments, I decided I should go and find Basta to see how soon he planned to leave for Donal's land.

Bleeeh, Basta in charge!

I shivered at the sudden thought of the slimy brother being the boss of the clan. Even the giant Fodor might have been a better choice.

But, if Basta made good on the offer to take me back to Donal's land, I could tolerate his presence long enough to get to the portal.

I grabbed my satchel of clothing, dried the last tears with the edge of the brat, and left to search for Connor's brother before he forgot his offer.

Chapter 24

"She thought me dead?" Connor said to Niall. "How can that be?"

Niall touched the swelling around Connor's eye. "Perhaps because Basta convinced her. Does your eye hurt much?"

The old counselor damped a piece of cloth with water and touched the bruise on Connor's temple. Connor shied from Niall's hand and his question.

"Did she not see me when I opened the tent flap? Or, was she too eager to seek comfort in my brother's arms! Perhaps comfort is not what she wanted. It certainly isn't what he had in mind. I saw them together."

"Aye, I had the girl with me, but then the crowd separated us. Basta moved in very quickly and spirited her away from the match. I am sorry I did not anticipate his treachery."

Niall handed Connor a cup of wine. "Drink. This will dull the pain."

"I feel no pain, nor do I wish to dull anything."

"I referred only to the pain these bruises must be causing, not the girl."

Connor took a sip and continued to glare at his counselor.

Niall said, "There's more you should know. She still does not know ye are alive. I brought her back to the fortress. She was quite desolate in her grief." Niall sat on a stool while Connor paced the small chamber.

"How could she think I am dead?"

Niall shrugged. "The crowds. The noise. I am certain that, in the confusion Basta encouraged deception."

"He must be up to more than merely chasing a filly. That bastard." Connor turned in his tracks. "Ye did not clear up her misconception?"

"Nay, I thought it might be useful to ye to be dead a little longer."

"If she doesn't run off with my brother first." Connor pounded a fist into the palm of his other hand. "Well, then, if I am dead, my spirit must first pay my kin a visit, and invite him to join me in the Otherworld. He needs to be dispossessed of the notion he can have my bride, whether I am dead or not. He will know that I am alive and strong when he feels my wrath."

On the way to find Basta, I met Lia outside the cooking hut, and the girl pointed toward the fortress gate. "Time to go down," she said breathlessly as she tried to hoist three heavily-ladened baskets.

"Here, let me help you with that." I dropped my bundle of clothing onto a flat stump, and took two of the baskets. "Where are you heading with these?"

"The feast," said Liadan.

"Feast?" *Were they honoring their dead chieftain with a feast?*

"The warriors' feast."

I felt a wave of sorrow, tinged with a sense of responsibility. I should have been more persistent in trying to get Niall to stop the fight.

Tears welled up again, but I focused on the task at hand to will them away. I followed Lia down the slope toward long plank tables that had been erected near the tents. Warriors gathered around one, drinking freely and bragging about their exploits during the games. The slave girl placed her basket on one of the tables, and motioned for me to do likewise.

As I straightened, one of the warriors laid a hand on my hip. At first, I thought I was imagining it, or it had been an accident. But when he slid it down and squeezed my buttocks like a melon in the grocery, I took offense.

I turned and gave him the most scathing look I could muster, accompanied by a loudly spoken, "Excuse me!" as I removed his hand from my posterior.

"What did ye bring us, woman?" he asked, helping himself to the basket. He tossed a heel of bread to another warrior and caught Lia, pulling her onto his lap. She screamed in terror.

I grabbed a large cup of mead from the table and dumped it over the warrior's head. "Your manners leave a great deal to be desired," I said, extracting Lia from the man's lap.

"Come along, Lia, I'm sure we have other baskets to bring down. This fool obviously doesn't know what he's doing."

Lia suppressed a smile. When we were out of earshot of the warriors, she thanked me.

"Are they like that all the time?"

The child shook her head. "Most of the time. Too much mead. That is all. Ye learn to move quickly, dodge their hands."

"Or you learn to fight back. I wonder how many of them want to wear their mead instead of drinking it?"

"Slaves do not fight back," said Lia, her mouth agape at my words.

"No, but women do. Don't let them enslave you. Fight, Lia. Don't let them have your body and soul. What about the other women? There's enough of you that if you stand together, someone will listen. I think Connor might have. But it's too late now. Perhaps the new chieftain will make some changes."

"New chieftain?"

"The one who replaces Connor. Basta or Fodor? Well, whoever it is, if I can help in any way, I will. Now, let's get the rest of the baskets down there."

We climbed the hill quickly, and brought another load of baskets from the cooking hut. This time, word had spread throughout the warriors, and they gave the two of us plenty of space.

"See, Lia," I whispered. "Don't take anything from them."

Lia looked at me wide-eyed, her small mouth forming an "O" as though this was an entirely new concept for her. We quickly finished our serving duties and returned to the fortress where we had a meal of our own waiting.

"Where do you suppose Basta is? I didn't see him at the feast."

The girl answered, "I don't know, but he is one to stay away from."

"You're probably right about that. But he promised to take me back to Donal's land. I suppose we'll have to wait until after the funeral, but I was hoping to get some idea of when we might be able to leave."

Chapter 25

A shadow passed the doorway of Lia's hut, and paused outside the thin wall to eavesdrop. Bits of their conversation drifted toward the unseen listener. Connor rankled at the thought of Caitrín and Basta together.

How dare she choose Basta over him?

I am barely started on my journey to the Otherworld and she already makes plans with my brother.

Her words turned the knife his brother had put in his back and he clenched his hands into fists.

So, I did not imagine what I saw! She wants Basta. Plans to take him with her to Donal's land. The three of them are likely conspiring against me.

It was past time for Basta to leave Croaghnac, and Connor would be happy to issue the invitation. Then, he would deal with Caitrín. In his own time and his own way.

I did not find Basta that evening as I'd hoped. I trudged down to the playing field and back up to the fortress feeling more depressed by the moment. Basta had apparently disappeared, and with him, my hopes of returning to the meadow and the time portal.

Until he showed up again, I needed something to occupy my time. Helping Lia and the other women would work. Perhaps I could even improve their lot in life.

Early the next morning, I joined Lia and the other slaves in the cooking hut. With the day's chores underway, Lia took me on a quick tour of the weaving hut, where four women huddled over their work.

"Do they sell their work at the fair?" I asked, marveling at the speed of the fingers as they shifted strands in an intricate pattern.

Lia smiled, "Nay, the cloth ye saw in the market comes from another clan. Likely taken in a raid. This cloth is for the needs of the clan."

I immediately felt guilty for having admired the swaths and bolts of linen at the fair. I imagined the poor women working so diligently only to have it all stolen by foreign warriors. I didn't even want to think what became of the weavers.

Lia led me to the next stop, the grain hut. Or, cavern, as I soon discovered. A beehive hut covered the entrance to a cavern extending a few feet into the mountainside. Roughly parallel to the cave with the pool where I had bathed, the grain storage cave was cool, dark and not nearly so threatening as the tunnel where the druidess lived. This cave could also be used as a shelter in times of invasion, Lia explained as she filled a small basket with wheat.

"Supplies are low, but now that the warm season is coming, we will be able to replenish them soon."

"Okay, you've got space here for the women and children to hide, and food supplies for an emergency. What about water?"

Lia pointed to large pottery jugs. "Ye know about the pool in the other cavern. There are many springs and pools within the mountain. The people used to live here in the caverns before the fortress was built."

"How long ago was that?"

Lia shrugged. She did not know. Stories shared by firelight and shrouded in the mists of time could not be assigned to one lifetime. She handed me a bag of grain, and we started the trek back to the cooking hut.

Throughout the morning, I worked alongside the women, planting a small garden, feeding farm animals, and tending children. There was no school, no day care, no health care. There were also no old women. It appeared that few lived beyond their child-bearing years.

In spite of Lia's insistence she was better off here than under her father's rule, she had no future and no rights. Nor did any of the women.

The men, their husbands? A rough lot of warrior-shepherd-terrorists who needed to learn some manners, and poor farmers.

And I was just the person to teach them. Not just manners, but lessons in civility and basic health. I would have started with their chieftain had he not been dispatched by the brutish farmer.

So, now it was up to me to lay down a new law for behavior in the dining hall.

Beginning with cleaning up the place. I mentally divided what I planned to teach the men into several classes. Interpersonal relationships, similar to the anger management classes I ordered for the majority of people who graced my courtroom, sounded like a good place to start. From there, basic cleanliness would be next.

"Can ye imagine a different life for yourself?" I asked Lia.

School? Dating? Career? Marriage? Children? In any other world.

Lia shook her head and a tear trickled down her cheek.

I could not imagine such a young life with no future, and no dreams.

Finally, I knew my purpose for being here, a better life for the women of Croaghnac. I'd call it breaking the straw ceiling, since glass wasn't part of their culture.

"Well, I can. And perhaps I can help make it a better one. Do you think you can get the women together to talk with me? I think I've got a plan. But we need to work on it together."

Chapter 26

"She has done what?" Connor exploded.

"Gathered the women. They refuse to serve the feast. Some of the men tried to force them, and others grew angry with the ones who confronted the women. They brawled. Ye now have four warriors nursing lumps on their heads, a few with black eyes, and a dozen or more with bruised pride."

"All from fighting with each other?"

"Nay. With the women. Some of them bore weapons."

"Swords? Spears?" Connor stood and started toward the doorway.

"Iron pots," said Niall, barely able to conceal a grin.

"The serving women struck warriors with cooking pots?" The image did not amuse him so much as it apparently did Niall.

As if he were reporting a battle, Niall said, "The fiercest and largest of the warriors felled by a blow from a reed-thin woman. Ye should see Fergus' black eye, too. His own wife gave it to him."

"And the cause of all of this discontent? One woman? How can one woman cause so much trouble? The sun has barely broken the horizon. First, she allies with Basta, now she foments insurrection." As he stomped down the hallway Connor said, "I should expect nothing less from Donal's daughter. But this? Apparently, it is not the men she will lead to doom, but the women."

"If ye go to the hall, she will discover ye are still alive."

"Not just alive, Niall, but a force to be reckoned with. She cannot charm my brother, incite my slaves to rebellion, attack my warriors, and get away with it!"

The vein in Connor's temple throbbed, but it wasn't the only one. Every vessel in his body pulsated, alive with the heat of his temper. He balled his fists ready for a fight.

"By the gods, she has brought me nothing but grief. After the trouble I had with Basta, he has surely gone to join forces with Donal. And now, my enemy's daughter rallies my slaves against me. What will she do next? Enchant the warriors to lay down their swords?"

Niall said, "Perhaps ye should take a lesson from her strategy. The women have joined arms, and almost without a word of command, they break to assault anyone who gets too near them. Without training. Without so much as a gesture of command."

"And all of this amuses ye? Have ye a full belly already? Or perhaps ye wish to join their ranks," Connor said, his own stomach rumbling with hunger.

"My belly is as empty as yours, and likely to remain so for most of the day if the women continue as they are."

Connor pointed a finger at Niall. "Well, they won't!"

"Ye have much to learn about women, I think," Niall muttered.

Unprepared for the sight of a battlefield in his dining hall, Connor paused at the doorway to survey the damages. Tables and benches were toppled, at least two appeared to have been broken over the heads of the warriors who lay under their wreckage.

Three other men lay unmoving, but presumably not dead. Connor wondered briefly if the warriors would be permitted to enter the Otherworld if they died from being struck by a cooking pot instead of a spear.

These were not warrior women. They had not been trained with bow and arrow, nor learned the epics of the forefathers. Yet, they wielded their utensils, cooking pots, better than some of his men.

How could this be? How could one small woman train the others to act in chorus? Was this part of some plan of Donal's? Allowing his daughter to be taken so that she might defeat his enemy within the enemy's own camp?

Or, by the gods, has she proven that she is a fairy sent to cause our doom?

At the same time, Connor could also understand why Niall had nearly been overcome with the humor of the situation. The sight of Fergus' swollen eye nearly undid the chieftain.

But mostly, he felt irritation. Irritation and frustration.

Why couldn't Caitrín be what she was supposed to be?

I should have sent her away with Basta. Let her father deal with her. Let him try to find a husband for her now.

As Connor surveyed the wreckage of his dining hall, he noticed the women gathered in one corner. Their leader, the red-haired curse of his life, stood with them, no doubt inciting further rebellion. Fortunately, she had not seen him enter the hall.

He motioned to the uninjured men to carry their companions from the room. While he waited for the hall to clear, he studied the line of women.

He recognized most of them. Slaves, wives of freemen, daughters of the clan. For many winters, they had lived in the mountains while he and their husbands drove Donal and his fianna from their land.

What could they want now? Have I not restored the land of their clan to them? They have a home, land for planting, work to do. Food in their bellies, sheep in their meadows. Why would they want anything else?

And the slaves? Did I not treat them justly? Give them shelter and food for their labors?

Why would this woman think anything should be different? Her own father's household was surely the same. He has slaves. The wives of his freemen serve his warriors.

Has she stirred discontent there as well?

Perhaps Donal welcomed his daughter's absence. Perhaps he now has peace in his household.

Connor turned to Niall and said, in a low voice, "This is why she came out of the tower without her guards. She meant to be taken. This is Donal's plan to defeat me. He knows he canna' attack the stronghold, so he slipped a more powerful weapon right into my household. I had not thought him capable of such shrewdness."

"So, what will ye do about it?" Niall asked.

"Post warriors at the gate, and send the rest into the valley, and to the cleft. Prepare for an attack. I will handle the women alone."

"Alone?" Niall raised one eyebrow.

Connor rewarded him with a glare that reminded the counselor of his father Malley.

"Don't get within striking distance," Niall warned as he left on his mission.

As the room cleared of men, Connor picked his way through the debris to the line of women. He walked slowly, studying each face until he reached the center of the group where he stopped just out of range of a swung pot. He righted a bench, and sat down on it, facing Caitrín.

At the thump of a bench being set down behind her, she turned and saw him.

Chapter 27

"You! You're alive!"

I felt as if I'd been kicked in the stomach. If there had been a chair behind me, I'd have collapsed into it. Instead, I swayed for a moment, then caught myself.

He's alive!

I wanted to break ranks and run to him and throw my arms around his neck to be certain he was really here.

How could this have happened? I heard the warriors shout that he had fallen. I heard the cries of the crowd.

Basta ... Basta had said Connor was dead.

Anger quickly replaced any relief.

How dare Basta lie like that?

How dare Connor show up alive when he's supposed to be dead?

Here I was trying to better the lives of the women of this clan, trying to teach the new chieftain a lesson, trying to improve the manners of these ruffian warriors.

How dare Connor show up alive! How dare he let me think he'd been killed.

Well, let either one of the Malley brothers come within spitting distance, and it will be all over for them!

I picked up a pot lid and clutched it tightly to my chest as I gave him a look that warned him to keep his distance or taste iron. I'd spent all morning organizing the women and explaining the concept of a protest. Hoping the new chieftain would listen to their grievances, I had stationed the women in the hall, and immediately gotten the warriors' attention.

"No Respect, No Feast" was the women's motto. I taught them to chant it until Connor showed up and silenced the room. So now that he was once again among the living, it was time for him to learn a lesson as well.

As I took a half-step closer, I noticed the yellowing bruise near his eye. But the pang of sympathy it engendered reminded me he was supposed to be dead, and had let me think that for nearly a day.

Placing both palms on his knees, he waited silently for my next move. I spread my feet slightly to signal I meant business here.

It wasn't really about me and my feelings any longer. The women had legitimate complaints. I had heard each one, from putting up with ill-mannered men to outright sexual harassment. If I did nothing else in my time with these people, at least I might improve the lot of these women.

Heaven knew their own druidess hadn't done much for them.

Gesturing to the line behind me, I began to sing in full voice, "We will not be moved, we will not be moved."

Of course, none of the others knew the song, but they linked arms and hummed along. The Gaelic translation sounded strange, so I sang it in English, disregarding Connor's previous concern about my speaking in a strange tongue. If he wanted to believe I was a fairy, fine, I'd give him plenty of reason this day.

"We will not be moved this day-ay-ay-ay-ay."

I raised my voice to encourage the women to join in a repetition of the same verse.

"One more time," I called to them.

Connor sat unmoved. He tipped his head slightly and listened. He could out-wait her any day. Even when the rumbling of his gut played the bass notes of her song, he did not move. He ignored the bounce of her curls as she swayed back and forth with her song. He would not notice the color in her cheeks as she waved her arms trying to encourage the women to sing with her. He declined to think of her lips and what he longed to do with them. He refused to be drawn into her web of charm. He stared at the curve of her hip, and remembered the sight of Basta running his hand down it.

A dull ache spread across Connor's chest and tightened around his heart. He would feel nothing for her until there could be no question about her identity, her intentions and her feelings for his half-brother.

His eyes drifted up and down the line of women. Caitrín stood out, unlike any other woman he had ever met. No one dared speak to him as she did. No one pushed him as she did. No one ever presumed to organize his slaves and women folk into a female fianna.

A drop of sweat beaded on his temple and ran down his cheek. He ignored it, sucked in a slow breath, reminding himself that Donal's daughter, whether aés sídhe or woman, must remain simply another prize in his quest for vengeance and restoration of his clan. He could not allow himself any feelings for her. She had proven herself to be nothing but trouble, and the true offspring of his enemy, in her own right.

Connor waited while the woman continued to sing until her throat was surely parched. At the end of the row, one woman, large with child, broke ranks when her baby decided to be born. Two others went along to assist. Children began to fuss, and several mothers left to tend them.

As late afternoon approached, and the women's resolve began to fade, Connor finally spoke, quietly, but in a firm voice. "What do ye want?"

They all looked to Donal's daughter to speak for them.

"It isn't about what I want, but what these women need," she said, her voice cracking.

"I see. What do ye think my clanswomen and slaves need?" He kept his voice steady and calm. He leaned slightly forward, and looked at her as if he were engaging her in a staring contest.

She had his full attention, but she refused to be drawn into his challenge. With a grand sweep of both arms, she gestured to the lines of women on either side of her.

Then, she tipped her chin up, cleared her throat and answered, "Respect. It all boils down to that. I know you can't do much to change some conditions. No women's clinic, no child care center, no schools, but you could improve their lot by insisting that the men show them respect. Women are not property to be passed from father to husband."

She paused for a few seconds so that he could consider her words, then she continued. "The women of your clan grow and gather food, prepare and serve it, make and mend your clothing, bear and rear children, and what are their rewards? A warrior may accost one any time he wishes. A father may sell his daughter to the highest bidder. A husband may beat his wife if she displeases him. And, then, there's the slaves. You cannot own another person. This is where you can begin. Make rules that protect women. Your clan will grow stronger, and your people, all of them, will prosper."

Her words made no sense. Why would Caitrín suggest a different way of treating women? They were women. Not cattle, but not much above that.

Why should I listen to the daughter of my enemy? Things are no different in her father's camp.

And if she was not a woman?

Why should I consider the words of a fairy? Why would a fairy champion the cause of women? Hadn't she just sung in the language of the Otherworld and tried to teach the women strange words? Would she steal their spirits and leave the menfolk without their women?

He clenched his fists. One glance at her intense blue eyes, still moist with the earnest plea she had made, and at the body he longed to possess, made his blood boil.

If she wanted to be treated differently, by the gods, he'd give her a taste of her own blood. There was no time for all this foolishness. He had to put into action his plan to wed and bed her quickly.

And, all must be done before the Beltane horn blew this day.

Already the clan should have gathered for the feast, that from the looks of his dining hall was not going to be served. Niall had gone to prepare for the ceremony. On top of all this nonsense, there was the attack he expected from Donal. His warriors waited even now for his direction.

Why could this have not been a simple bridal abduction? Why should I not already be enjoying my wedding night instead of facing my bride and an iron pot lid?

His temper pushed to near-explosion, Connor decided to leave the room before he acted on the murderous thoughts that raced through his mind. He pressed his hands against his thighs and rose.

"I will think on what ye have said," he said, then turned and marched from the hall.

"Is it over?" Lia whispered.

"I think so," I said, feeling a mixture of relief and puzzlement.

I wasn't sure what I expected, but not this. I circled the remaining women, and thanked each one for her courage and persistence.

"There will be changes. You have brought attention to your plight. And, I believe Connor will act honorably now."

They slipped away into the growing shadows of late afternoon. There were children to be bedded down soon, animals to be tended, chores to be completed before darkness sent them into their huts. They each thanked me. None felt the day had been a waste.

The lid slipped from my hands and thudded to the floor.

"Is that it?" My voice echoed as I surveyed the empty hall. I set up a tipped bench and noticed the mongrel sleeping in a corner. "I've made a mess, haven't I?"

As I continued to set the furniture back into place, I felt like an alien who had landed among a less advanced people, tried to make their lives better, but still had nothing of my own life.

I was no closer to going home. Basta had disappeared, and now Connor was back from the grave.

I felt terribly alone. Trapped in a strange place, in a strange time and most likely, unable to return to my own time. I had just antagonized the man whom I was supposed to marry, and for that matter, the man who held power over everything and everyone. It was a likely bet that I'd never fit in here.

Even if I wanted to.

"What do you think, dog? Any more surprises for today?"

I slumped onto the bench, and remembered a conversation with my grandmother when I was about eight years old. I had asked why my parents had left me. My grandmother's answer, meant to reassure, had left me feeling hollow. If they had truly loved me, they wouldn't gone away, and nothing anyone said would ever make sense of their deaths.

So, why did I feel the same way now? Like my life had died, and nothing would ever make sense again.

I held my head in my hands as tears fell unbidden and unwanted. I hated crying. I never let myself be moved to tears by a defendant's sad tale or by a sappy movie. I prided myself in steely control, yet it seemed as though all I could do this day was weep.

I'd had tears for Connor when I thought him dead and now, when I knew he was alive, I was bawling again. I was sad and angry.

Both at the same time.

Angry with Connor for letting me think he was dead, then for coming back from the dead. Angry with myself for ever believing I might be able to make a real difference here.

Angry because I felt ... what?

"Don't make me love you, damn you, Connor! I won't! I can't!"

At the sound of my voice, the scraggly dog stirred from its nap and walked over to me. I reached out and scratched his ears, starting his tail wagging. He sat expectantly while I gave his neck and back the same attention. Then, he plopped down and rolled over presenting his belly to my hand. I smeared my cheeks with the backs of my hands, then rubbed his belly until he squirmed.

"I sure hope you don't have rabies, you flea-ridden little beast," I said.

"No one touches that dog without being rewarded with a growl and a bite," Connor said, as he stepped from the shadows.

The hound rolled over quickly and gave a teeth-baring snarl at the chieftain's approach. I gestured to the little mutt, which stopped growling and sat at my feet.

"It seems I have a friend."

"Ye would be the only one to have befriended him."

I shrugged my shoulders. Animal-charming, never my forte at home, was probably just another piece of evidence that I was some sort of fairy.

Connor held out his hand, palm up. "Would ye come with me?"

I shook my head.

He stood impassively, arm extended, eyes locking mine.

"You'd have to give me a pretty darn good reason. Let's begin with, why did you and Niall and everyone else let me go on believing you were dead? Why are you playing games with me? I'm hungry and tired, but mostly I'm sick of your Cro-Magnon approach. You lied. You pick me up and carry me off whenever you have the notion to do so. I am an adult, not a child. And even though you kidnapped me, you have no right to take me anywhere!"

The dog, my new defender, growled low at Connor.

Connor's face reddened and he spoke in slow, even words. "By the gods, I do not have to answer to ye, woman!"

"Yes, you do. It's high time you realized that. I won't go with you now or any time."

"Ye will come with me now." His voice was soft and steady like the warning growl of the mongrel sitting at my feet.

"And if I don't? What will you do?"

"By the gods, why do ye do this, woman? Why did ye throw yourself at my brother, stir up trouble with my slaves and now refuse me?"

He gave me a look that said he could swat me like a mosquito and think nothing of it.

But I knew better. I'd seen caring in his eyes at least once.

"If you want me to go somewhere with you, you'll have to give me some very good reason. Where were you when I was talking about respect? Well, this is what it's all about! You can't just waltz in here after being dead for twenty-four hours, and expect me to drop everything, and swoon all over you."

"Am I supposed to understand what ye just said?"

I thought about my words for a few seconds and replied, "Well, no.

But that's beside the point. You do not own me. You stole me. Stole me from the man I was supposed to marry, from my home, my career, my whole life."

I stood and stepped behind a stool, then continued. "Then, there was that test with the crazy druidess. I could have died because of your stupid prejudices. I'm no fairy, never have been. And let's not forget Basta. He's a scumbag. We both know it, but so far, he's the only one who has offered to help me return to my own time."

"Scumbag?"

The effort of arguing took every bit of strength I had left, and the roller coaster of emotion I had ridden for the last several days was on the downhill rush.

My shoulders sagged, and every part of me wanted to collapse in a heap on the floor.

"Scumbag. Slimy, nasty, gross, self-serving, not the kind of guy you want to bring home to meet the folks."

Connor's visage softened slightly. "And I?"

I smiled a little. "You are definitely not a scumbag. Difficult and stubborn, but not vile."

His impatience began to surface again, but he checked it. "I am asking ye to come with me."

He lowered his voice so that it sounded more like a request than a demand.

I still did not move.

"I could tell ye it is for your own safety. Or I could tell ye I wish to have some time alone with ye."

"Or, novel idea, you could tell me the real reason you want me to go with you."

"Ye must come with me before enemy warriors reach this valley."

Warriors? The ones who had followed them, or Donal's? That darned Caitrín—why'd she have to be so popular?

I had no desire to inflict war on the women who suffered enough already. I thought about his words for a few seconds, then said, "See, that wasn't so hard. All you had to do was give me a reason and that sounds like a darn good one. Okay, I'll go with you."

I wagged a finger at him. "But don't think you've won anything here."

Chapter 28

Basta had had enough of his half-brother's leadership of clan Malley. Aye, Connor had restored most of the Malley lands, but his insane quest to steal Donal's daughter would bring ruin to the clan.

Basta knew he could not defeat his brother in a conquest of strength and bravery and that was the only way, short of murder that would convince the council to choose him as their chieftain.

To make matters worse, Fodor, the farmer had not delivered on the promise to kill Connor.

Even Basta's attempt to incite a jealous rage in his brother had not worked. But, when Basta had held Caitrín in his arms, he understood what fueled his brother's passion. She was both girl and woman. Her petite size and fully developed figure excited him like no other woman had before.

Basta rubbed his hands together. He must have Caitrín. If he could seal his brother's fate, and secure his brother's land at the same time, so much the better. Basta could hire a private assassin, perhaps one of his warriors could be entrusted with such a mission.

But, he did not want to jeopardize Caitrín's safety. Such a man, one who could be bought, might not be trustworthy to bring the grieving woman back to him. Once he had her, he knew what he'd do next.

Besides, he wanted to see pleasure and pain in her eyes, inflicted by him alone, not by the memory of Connor's death. Dispatching his brother to the Otherworld would have to be done very carefully. And after the girl left him. That would be the tricky part, freeing the girl from his brother.

Slowly, a more devious plan came to Basta.

Connor's foolishness could be turned to Basta's advantage. Basta decided to go to Donal and offer to assist him to retrieve his daughter. He knew Donal would not forgive the insult of his daughter's kidnapping, nor accept a forced marriage to Connor. The chieftain cared only for himself, his daughter, and his feud with Connor. Basta could turn that hatred to meet his own goals.

Basta's mouth watered at the thought of the reward he would negotiate with Donal.

Croaghnac. The valley, the hill, the fortress weren't Donal's to begin with. He'd be happy to let go of any claim to them. Then Basta would ask for the girl. After Connor had had her, no other man would want her. Basta would be doing Donal a favor keeping her, covering up Donal's shame by taking her off his hands.

Let the old chieftain do what he liked with Connor. It did not even matter if Connor had taken Caitrín as his bride. In fact, it would be all the better, for once used, she would be of no further value to Donal. Basta would not have to soil his hands killing his half-brother.

He licked his lips.

I will no longer be the other son, born to the second wife. I will have it all.

Donal paced.

He had thrown out his advisors, and told the guards to let no one enter his chambers. He fumed and plotted how many ways he would punish his daughter when he caught her.

How dare she run away on the eve of her marriage. She had ruined the Beltane celebration with her foolish flight before her wedding night.

He thought about replacing his wayward daughter with one of the slaves since Colum had never seen Caitrín and might be fooled into marrying another woman. But Caitrín's fiery red hair was well-known, and none of Donal's slaves matched her appearance.

To make matters even worse, now Basta had shown up. Donal did not want to be bothered with his constant complaints about Connor.

"Ye would be wrong to turn me away this time," Basta announced as he pushed past the guards and strode into the room. "I presume ye are looking for your missing daughter."

What? Donal spun around, and gestured for his guards to leave the room.

What could Basta know about Caitrín's disappearance? He is scarcely more than an outlaw, unwelcome even among his own clan. Surely she had not gone with him.

Donal rested a hand on the handle of his sword. "Ye have some knowledge of her whereabouts?"

"I know enough to be of help to ye if ye wish to get her back."

Donal did not remove his hand from his sword. "And of course, ye would provide that information for the proper incentive. What sort of price do ye have in mind?"

Basta folded his arms across his chest and said, "To begin with, Croaghnac."

Donal threw his head back and laughed. He didn't want the useless valley anyway. That was easily granted and confirmed his opinion that Basta was a fool.

"Yours," said Donal, with a wave of his hand.

"And your daughter as my wife," added Basta.

"She is betrothed, and the bride price paid."

"Then, ye'll think of some excuse to keep the money, and marry her to me. Tell Colum another man has already tasted her sweetness. Tell him whatever ye wish. She will be mine. And ye should be glad ye do not have to pay a bride price to be rid of her."

Donal's hand tightened on his sword. He took a half step toward the man, then stopped to reconsider.

I should kill Basta, and do everyone a favor. But, perhaps he has a good idea after all. Marriage to Basta might be fitting punishment for Caitrín's defiance of me.

Donal relaxed his hand. "I will think on your proposal."

Would it do to have a son-in-law as avaricious as him? I'd have to watch that one all the time. But if I left him at Croaghnac, at least I'd know where he was all the time.

Basta was not willing to wait for Donal's decision.

"Your warriors are assembled, and ye could enter the valley this evening," he said.

Donal stared at Basta. Entering the valley through the cleft was an invitation to a slaughter. A few of Connor's well-placed warriors would pick off the warriors faster than he could send them trough the pass.

Could this be a trick?

"Ye would lead the way?" Donal asked.

He shook his head. "I just came through the cleft. I can certainly return to Croaghnac. My own warriors can take care of the guards to allow you and your fianna to follow. Connor is greatly distracted by the feast and his wedding plans."

He said the last few words slowly, emphasizing "wedding."

Then he added, "If I lead ye in, Caitrín will be mine before the ram's horn sounds the end of Beltane?"

"As ye say," Donal said through gritted teeth, waved a hand to dismiss Basta, then added an after-thought, "Of course, ye may have to deal with Colum since he has paid the bride price for her."

"Colum is an old man. He wouldn't know what to do with a young bride anyway."

Chapter 29

Connor could not shake the sight of Caitrín touching that mongrel dog. Surely that was a sign of her fairy powers. Yet if she were a fairy, why had she not charmed the boar in the forest?

He stroked his mustache.

There were too many contradictions. He had studied her clear blue eyes for some sign of deception, and found none.

Aye, she still insisted she wasn't Donal's daughter, yet Connor knew she had to be. Her fiery red hair, although shorn in some unruly fashion, her legendary temper, everything about her declared she was the woman he watched for so long.

On the other hand, she had not known even the simplest answers of Niamh's test. Any woman of his or Donal's clans should have been able to answer those questions.

Her dress and speech were so vastly different from any clanswoman or slave he knew. She argued with him about participating in the games, when she should have known the rules of succession. She should have understood how a chieftain was vulnerable to challenges. Her own father had won the games to claim and continue in leadership of his clan and fianna.

Then, there was the insurrection of the women and slaves. She demanded respect for the women, and defied him. Any other woman would have accepted the way things naturally were.

But, if she were truly not Donal's daughter, who could she possibly be?

His bruised eye throbbed, and his head pounded as if it might explode. Worst of all, the more difficult she was, the more he desired her. The more she stood up to him, the more he wanted to capture her lips with his own, and smother her complaints with kisses.

It made no sense to him!

He was the chieftain. He led his fianna and his clan.

How could one small woman be such a threat to him, the greatest warrior of clan Malley, the man who had outsmarted Donal?

Not only did she herself bother him, but the feelings she engendered in him troubled him greatly as well.

Desire? Lust was one thing, but love? Could this be love?

The thought nearly floored him. He ran one hand through his hair and looked at her as if he had never truly seen her before.

I cannot love her. Love killed my father and mother. There is no room in my life for such a weakness!

Steal her, yes. Force her into marriage, aye. Make her want me. But never give her my heart. Never, never love her.

The chill in the breeze brought Connor back to the present. Nightfall would soon be upon them. The ram's horn would sound as soon as the sun set.

Their wedding ceremony had to begin immediately.

She must come with him now.

Whether she wanted to marry him or not.

He touched the handle of his sword and hoped he would not need it to enforce his plan.

The clan had gathered. Niall waited. All Connor had to do was bring a bride to the ceremony. He held out his hand again to Kat.

Decision time.

I had made up my mind not to trust Connor, but his lowlife half-brother was by far even less trust-worthy, and apparently no longer around.

With no other realistic choice at hand, it was time to decide. I knew, from the look in Connor's eyes, that if I took his hand, I would become his wife within the hour.

I stepped forward, but didn't put my hand into his. If I was going to do this, it had to be at least partly on my terms. We walked side-by-side thought the courtyard.

The fortress was strangely quiet, the warriors having been posted to the cleft while the clan assembled at the foot of the hill for the feast to mark the end of the Beltane fair.

Connor, a gentle smile lighting his face, brought me first to Lia's hut where two women waited me. He whispered instructions to them, then disappeared.

The women began to help me don an ivory tunic so soft I thought of brushed leather as I swept my palm across the nap. They wrapped a dark red leather criss around my waist and looped a new brat of a deep shade of burgundy across my shoulder.

They fussed with my hair, but could do little with my short curls, other than remark about its strangeness. Finally, they decided to weave a braid of gold like a headband across my crown. I wished for a mirror that I might see how it looked.

Satisfied with their work, the women clucked their approval and whispered their wishes of good fortune for the bride before surrendering me to Connor who appeared outside the hut.

I gasped when I saw him.

He wore a robin's egg blue tunic embroidered with an intricate design along the neckline and hem. His brat was a darker blue, almost black, changing shades with his movement as the light caught it from a different angle. At his shoulder, a brooch of polished gold with a large purple stone, easily the size of my ruby, glimmered in the afternoon sunlight.

But his clothing, lovely as it was, could not match the glow on his face.

Deep in the pocket of my slip, the ruby began to hum. I positioned my hand near my hip to conceal its vibrations. It responded by stilling once again, but not before I felt a sensation that I was meant to be here in this place and at this time for a purpose.

This time, Connor held out his arm to escort me formally.

I did not hesitate. I placed my hand on his forearm, conscious of the strength of his intention, and of my own resolve. I'd marry this man, because I had to, but he would never know how I really felt. He'd never know the struggle within me.

He might be the chieftain of clan Malley, but he would never own my heart.

Without speaking, we left the hut fortress, proceeded through the courtyard to the fortress gates, and walked out and down the slope toward the field below.

How strangely surreal! A few days ago I was on my way to meet David in a tiny church. Now, I'm about to marry another man.

One who infuriated me one moment, but made me crave his touch the next. One whom I didn't want to love, but who had turned my entire life upside down. One whose kiss made me want to be swallowed in his arms, in a way David could never imagine. One who could never understand me or the life I left, but whose world would now be my world and my life.

I pushed aside thoughts of what it would be like to be married to this man and instead, thought of Lia and the clanwomen, of Niall and even of the strange, little mutt I had befriended. I could make changes here. I could help them.

Love would indeed play no part in this wedding.

Necessity, perhaps. Maybe even desire. But mostly it was about fate.

Chapter 30

Under a perfect, cloudless sky with a golden, late-afternoon sun sitting directly atop the western mountain, we calmly walked down the slope toward the meadow. I felt strangely at peace, but detached, as if I were watching a movie unfold around me. The people gathered for the ceremony murmured their approval as we approached, and parted to let us pass.

A small riser had been erected on almost the same spot where I had watched the competition. Niall stood there, smiling broadly as he extended a hand to help me step up. I looked into his mellow, brown eyes and soft wrinkled face, and found the same expression my grandmother had when she told me, "It's going to be all right."

I returned a look that said, "I trust you to make it so," and continued to face him as Connor took his place next to me. The ruby hidden deep in its hidden pocket began to hum, but only I was aware of its vibration. I shifted my leg so that it had less contact with the stone.

With a nod of approval from Niall, Connor began to speak. "I give ye that which is mine to give and freely share all with ye." His voice, firm and resolute, rose above the murmur of approval of the crowd.

The people hushed expectantly, anticipating my response. The blood drained from my head. I didn't know what to say, and I wanted to shout.

Stop! I don't have something old and something new, something borrowed, something blue.

I stepped back from the edge of panic, and put on my judge persona that allowed me to be dispassionate in the most difficult courtroom situations. But the only words I could think of were, "I do," and that clearly wasn't what Connor wanted to hear.

Niall offered me a reassuring smile and touched my elbow. With his prompting, I said, "I belong to myself and I give you that which is mine to give as a free person."

I swallowed, my mouth so dry I thought I might choke on the next words.

Connor's turn. He turned me to face him and looked deep into my eyes, saying, "Yours shall be the name I call in the night, and your face the one I look for in the morn."

Ooooh. I liked that. It was much prettier than the vows David and I would have said, even though we wrote them ourselves. Right now, I couldn't remember a word of the ceremony David and I had planned.

I wondered if Niall would ask the assemblage if anyone objected to our vows. *Please let someone stick up the hand and object.*

Would we exchange rings? I glanced at my left hand, where my ring finger suddenly felt naked without my engagement ring.

Would Connor be instructed to kiss the bride? My mind raced ahead in the pause that followed Connor's vow.

Then, realizing I was supposed to be saying something, I looked to Niall to supply the next words.

"I shall serve ye, and the honeycomb shall taste sweeter because it comes from my hands."

Honeycomb? Yeah, like I'd ever handled honeycomb before. Sticky mess attracting bees ... popped into my mind.

Looking into Connor's eyes pulled me back to the moment. His in-charge, commander-in-chief demeanor was gone. Instead, I saw the little boy raised without a mother's love, the young man who had to go through life proving himself over and over, never really finding the affection he needed.

I longed to reach out to him and tell him I understood, and that ... I loved him.

Everything froze. The ruby stopped vibrating. The crowd stopped murmuring. Connor held his breath. My heart skipped a beat.

At that moment, that crazy, how-could-this-possibly-be-happening moment, I realized that I loved him.

Wild and insane though it may be.

Like no other man. Not even David.

Completely without reason. Or thought. Or sense.

A body slam to the heart.

I love Connor.

My hands shook, but Connor held them steady as he promised that he would give me the first bite of his meat, the first drink from his cup. I had no vows to respond, but, that didn't matter.

In my heart, I vowed to love him until death parted us.

In spite of the crowd, silence descended on the valley like the gathering dusk. Niall handed us a gold cup, and Connor took the first sip before passing it to me. Fearful that I might choke, I barely wet my lips with the sweet wine.

Niall took the cup and handed Connor a small, round oat cake that, the counselor explained, symbolized the promise of fertility.

Fertility? Like the thing that produces children?

Wait just a minute.

I hadn't signed on for kids. David and I had never even talked about that. I knew Connor wanted heirs, but it didn't really sink in that I had to provide them.

So, if I ate the oak cake, I'd get pregnant?

I might be sensitive to gluten. Definitely allergic to babies.

I slowly broke off a small piece and forced it down, swallowing carefully to keep from losing it right then and there.

Connor ate his without hesitation, and then said, "As long as I live and breathe I shall honor ye and keep ye in my heart."

To which Niall helped me to respond, "My life and death are equally in your care, and I shall honor you above all others until the day I die."

My voice sounded as if it belonged to someone else. The words could not have come from me. They were in my heart but I didn't know how they found their way to my throat.

I looked into Connor's ebony eyes, and saw something that almost made me believe this could work. I could be his wife. And, no matter what he said, he loved me.

He may not have even known it yet himself, but I could see in his eyes that he loved me.

Connor could feel her trembling as they exchanged their vows. She was incredibly beautiful, her hair aflame in the late day sun, her eyes as blue as the sky. Fragile like a child, yet full-bodied as a woman.

He longed to sweep her into his arms, to carry her off to his chamber amid the cheers of his clan.

Yet, at the same time, he felt a new respect for her because of her concern for the women, because of the way she stood up to him, and because of the tenderness she displayed to the mongrel.

Silently, he promised himself and her, *once we're married, and I have claimed your body and spirit, I will give ye time before I claim your heart.*

They drank from the cup and ate the oat cake before Niall spoke again. "By the gods your people honor, these vows ye swear, that ye will be full partners to each other. Ye make these promises before your kin and clan, the gods of the sun and moon, fire and water, earth and sky, day and night. Where two stood before, ye are now one."

The assembled throng burst into cheers as the first arrows began to fly.

Chapter 31

Connor heard a rush of air, a high pitched whine and a thud as an arrow whooshed past his ear, and struck the ground beyond them.

Caitrín could not react quickly enough. As he reached for her, she lost her balance and stumbled. The next arrow would have connected with its intended target had she not fallen into its path. The arrow aimed at his heart embedded in her left shoulder.

She didn't fully realize she had been hit until she looked over her shoulder to see the shaft protruding from her back and a crimson stain spreading down from it. She screamed as Connor threw himself backward, carrying her to the ground, and taking the blow himself to cushion her fall.

All around them, people ran and dropped to the ground as they were hit. Covering their heads with their arms and crouching as they ran, women and children fled in chaos. Screams and moans filled the air where moments before, the crowd had cheered.

Warriors, armed only with their swords, were defenseless against the rain of arrows. They scrambled to grab their shields and hold them overhead. Most of the arrows missed victims, landing in the soft ground of the field, but the panic they caused gave Donal's men an advantage that enabled them to move quickly into the valley.

Connor didn't need to tell Caitrín not to move. She could not. She bit her lip to keep from screaming as Connor held her tightly in his arms to keep her from aggravating the injury.

"Take it out," she pleaded.

He did not answer her. Niall reached them first. He helped Connor carefully shift her from atop himself to the ground, placing her on her right side.

Connor quickly looked around to assess their situation. The enemy had not yet reached them as his fianna engaged in sword or hand-to-hand fighting. Climbing the slope to the fortress would expose them to the worst of the arrow barrage. They might be able to make it to the tents, but not the fortress.

He scooped Caitrín into his arms and, with Niall's help, they ran toward the shelters. The rain of arrows had not yet reached the tents and Connor and Niall stopped there momentarily.

Every movement sent spasms of pain through her, Connor knew. He could see it in her eyes, large with fear and wet with unshed tears.

"I can't pull it out yet," he told her, knowing she would bleed more if he pulled the arrowhead out now. "Do ye understand me?"

She nodded slowly.

"But I must break it off so that I can carry ye. This will hurt."

Her eyes gave him her reply. *Do it, quickly.*

He turned her onto her right side and, clasping the arrow with both hands, he snapped the shaft in half so that the head remained embedded in her shoulder. When they reached safe haven, he could cut out the remaining part to minimize the damage and blood loss.

"I've got to go and lead my men," Connor said to Niall, "Stay with her."

Niall shook his head, "Nay, ye must get her to safety first. She is your first priority. All is lost if she dies. Donal will not curb his revenge."

Connor looked back at the field.

What had first seemed to be a slaughter was not as serious as he had thought. Most of the arrows missed their targets, and in the panic that cleared the field, only a few more had been hit. He counted six bodies down.

His men had found shelter from which they could regroup and continue the battle. There wasn't time to figure out how the enemy had gotten past his sentries at the cleft. He could not see any advancing enemy warriors, but he knew they were there, not yet across the river.

The river.

"We've got to get her to the river. It's our way out."

In the few minutes since the attack began, the sun had disappeared below the western mountain and darkness descended rapidly on the valley. Their escape might go unnoticed as Donal's warriors focused on the meadow and the slope to the fortress.

"Yes, the river," Niall agreed. "Take her quickly."

All around them they could hear the sounds of the battle beginning, as the enemy reached the field. Connor and Niall moved swiftly through the booths where many of the women and children had taken refuge.

"Get to the fort!" Niall instructed them as he and Connor carried Caitrín toward the boats.

By the time they reached the boats, the moon was beginning to crest over the far mountains giving the twilight a gray pallor.

Connor wondered if she was still breathing, but there was no time to check. He placed her gently in the bottom of a curragh and pushed it into the water. Turning to Niall, he said, "Take her to safety. I must stay here. My place is with my people."

Niall grabbed his arm and said, "No! Ye must go with her. I cannot travel the white water. Ye know the islands. Get your bride to safety. Then, come back, when ye can. I will stay with the clan."

In his heart, Connor knew Niall was right, but he had spent a lifetime defending his clan. He could not leave them now.

He hesitated. If he did not take her away, Caitrín might die. Darkness would soon be upon them, and the warriors would stop fighting and regroup in the morning. He could see her to safety and come back to lead the clan.

Niall shoved him toward the boat.

Connor abandoned the argument, and plunged into the curragh with a push that sent it streaking into the river toward the rocks and cascading, white water. The river, nearly concealed in shadow, took every bit of skill and concentration Connor could muster.

The tide was in, pushing against his small vessel. He felt his way through the rocks as if he were reaching out for walls of a darkened room and stepping with uncertainty into it.

The boat bobbed past the first obstacle, gently scraped the second and third, and thudded against the next. Connor pushed off and sent them back into the current for a clean pass of several more large boulders. He paddled with all his strength, knowing that Caitrín fought an even greater battle than he.

The noise of the raid faded as the river carried them away from the valley. Connor had little time to wonder how the warriors fared. His entire attention focused on keeping the curragh away from the rocks.

Drifting in and out of consciousness, Caitrín was only vaguely aware of jarring against the boulders, and the cold river spray that soaked her clothing. The boat lurched to one side and jarred her shoulder, causing her to moan, and Connor laid a hand on her thigh to reassure her.

The gods of the river are with us.

Connor said a prayer of thanksgiving as they reached the calm waters beyond the rocks. He had no time to consider the outcome of the battle in his valley.Ahead lay a half-dozen small islands, any one of which could harbor them for a day or two before Donal realized they were not at Croaghnac, and came looking for them.

Connor reached down to check Caitrín. She felt cool and clammy to his touch, misted by river spray, but, most importantly, she still breathed.

"I will not let ye die, muirnin," he told her, aware she might die no matter what he promised.

He jumped from the boat as it began to scrape bottom in the shallows off the third island. Dragging the curragh ashore until it was far enough from the waves that it would not wash back out into the river, he left her where she was while he scouted for a place of natural shelter. Tall trees came nearly to the waterline on this island and Connor chose a grove near his landing.

The curragh, pushed between two trees, nearly disappeared and, when tipped to its side, would provide shelter against the night chill and morning dew. There would be no fire this night, even though he desperately needed the light to remove the arrow and the heat to cauterize the wound.

Connor gently turned the boat and crawled under. Caitrín lay on her right side, with the broken shaft of the arrow still protruding from her left shoulder. His fingers touched the stickiness that soaked through her garment. The bleeding seemed to have slowed.

Carefully, he fit his body against hers to cradle her and keep her warm. With first morning light, he would find a better shelter, build a fire, and treat her wound. He dozed lightly, aware of every sound, most especially of her shallow breathing.

Morning brought a thick fog on the river, a blessing because it allowed him to move Caitrín to safety before any warriors began searching for them.

He found a small clearing where two boulders came together, providing two sides of a natural shelter. There was space enough for a fire pit, and the smoke would disperse before it rose above the trees and rocks.

With a flint he carried in his waist pouch, he started a fire. He cut tree branches and covered them with his own brat to make a bed for her. Not as soft as the bridal bed of furs he had intended to use, but off the ground and warmer.

As he gently carried her from the beach to the camp, he sensed her spirit barely clung to her body. Her breathing was shallow and she no longer murmured or tried to open her eyes.

"Do not leave me, muirnin," he whispered in her ear.

Once the fire had produced dancing flames, he laid his sword on a rock with the blade resting among the glowing coals. Then, he tore the blood-crusted edges of Caitrín's shift to expose her shoulder.

The wound began to ooze again, adding a sense of urgency to his work. He slid the tip of the knife gently alongside the embedded arrow head.

Connor had removed many an arrow and knew how deep to cut yet avoid doing more damage. With the skill of a surgeon, he excised the arrowhead, then used the tip of sword, heated to cauterize the wound and stop the bleeding.

He pressed a handful of river weed into the wound and tore a strip from the hem of her shift for a dressing. The original wound was not as deep as he feared it might be, and the edges looked clean. She would have a scar there, but it would heal and she would recover.

If he could stop any bleeding, and keep away fever.

She had lost much blood, and she had been unconscious since they left the valley. A blessing for she would be in great pain if she were awake. But both neither were good signs, Connor knew.

His heart was troubled with more than just her wound. She had stepped in front of an arrow intended for him. Of course, neither of them knew, at the time what was happening. And he could not have prevented it.

One other woman, his mother, had given her life for him.

He looked at Caitrín still lying across his lap, peacefully sleeping. Suddenly, a wave of anger swept across him. He didn't want to lose her. Every instinct, every fiber of his being demanded she must live. Not merely because she was now his wife. Not because he had fulfilled his quest for revenge.

But because, she had taken an arrow meant for him.

He nestled her onto the brat-covered tree branches, and watched her slow breathing for a few moments. When she appeared to be stable with no more bleeding, he decided he would have to leave her to find food and water before nightfall.

He stroked her pale cheek, and whispered the words of a chant for a fallen warrior. The rest of the plea to the guardian of the gates of the Otherworld would have to wait until he finished a few necessary chores.

As he studied her face, the line of her jaw, the soft swell of her cheekbone, the brush of fine lashes against ivory skin, he marveled at her delicate beauty. He had watched her sleep the first night after he'd taken her, but this time, something seemed different.

That first night, he basked in the glow of accomplishment of his plan. The gods were on his side and his future had begun to unfold. Now, as he smoothed a curl from her cheek, he wondered how his plan had gone awry.

What happened to the warriors I posted to guard the entrance to the valley? Had Basta led Donal through the cleft?

How could my brother betray his clan by helping Donal? For this woman? Would Basta have risked all and surrendered his heritage for a woman?

Connor shook with rage. *Aye, he would.*

Especially with this woman to encourage him. Had she enticed his brother to break the trust of his people?

He felt heaviness in his chest as his own heart turned to stone. He had pledged himself to her. He had saved her life.

Saved the life of the woman who was responsible for his brother's defection, the probable defeat of his clan, and the loss of Croaghnac.

Let her die. Let her die for what she has done to me and my people.

He rose and left her to return to his curragh. How simple it would be to leave her there! She'd die before anyone could reach her. He glanced at the river, where a heavy fog swirled in defiance of the sunlight that had not burned it off.

Soon, warriors would begin searching the islands for them. Whether Donal won the battle for the valley or not, he would not give up looking for his daughter.

As Connor studied the river, debating about leaving her there, he heard the muffled cry of an eagle seeking its home in the gray mist.

Ye are lost? Connor wondered as he listened for a reply from the bird's mate.

None came. Connor picked up a small, smooth pebble and rolled it around in his hand, wishing he had his slingshot. If the bird came close enough ...

A second, stronger caw met Connor's ear. Then, in the distance, he heard a faint answer. The male bird fell silent as he winged toward his mate's continuing call, the beacon to guide him to home and safety. Connor let the pebble slip from his fingers.

In that moment, Connor understood something that had troubled him his entire life.

His father Malley had faced a decision. He had left the fianna to go to his wife during Connor's birth. One small decision, one moment of conscience, cost the clan its leader, but gave the clan a second chance in

Connor.

He dragged the small boat to the water and shoved it into the water until the current picked it up. It would be carried a distance, he hoped, then smashed on the rocks. If any debris were found, the warriors would assume he and the woman had drowned.

He watched the curragh bob along until it swallowed by the fog and the black waters of the river.

Chapter 32

As the god of the heavens sent late afternoon shadows into the valley, Niall summed the clan's losses. Ten of the warriors died in the initial attack. The remaining men had managed to kill most of the enemy over a long, hard day of fighting.

He missed Connor.

The fianna had fought without him before, but not since the boy was old enough to pick up his father's sword and shield. From that first day, the young warrior's mission was clear, to restore the clan, to honor his father. Nothing had deterred him.

Nothing, save the woman.

Niall did not understand Connor's obsession with Donal's daughter, until he met Caitrín. There was something about her that could possess a man's soul. Whether she were fairy or witch, or simply mortal, she had certainly captured Connor.

The counselor prayed they had made it to safe harbor and had not been found by any of the warriors fleeing the valley. Then, he added a prayer that Donal's daughter, now Connor's wife, still lived.

As darkness came to the fortress, Niall left the hall to speak with the warriors stationed as guards along the berm-and-wood wall of the fortress.

Beltane was the first time the warriors had gathered since the dark season. They spend the cold months in small settlements, scattered across Malley land. Connor instructed them at Samhain, the autumn festival, to maintain their fighting edge through the dark season by practicing with the bow, and keeping their sword arm ready.

Niall was glad now that Connor had continued the training for the warriors who wintered at Croaghnac. Without that edge, the clan would have been doomed by the element of surprise Donal had used.

Connor had grown into a seasoned leader, mature beyond his years. But, would he also be a wise husband? Niall feared that only time would answer that, and the young chieftain might not have that on his side.

Meanwhile, on the island, Connor did not greet nightfall with ease. He needed all of his strength and faith to fight the battle for Caitrín's spirit. He sensed the presence of the guardian of the gates to the Otherworld in the gray aura that surrounded her.

Her spirit hovered as though it was uncertain whether to leave her body.

I must call her back. He knew that he was her only link to life now.

He sat on the ground next to her and gently lifted her onto his lap. Bending low to speak into her ear, he repeated the words of an ancient chant, not to the guardians to ease the passage of one about to die, but to the goddess for healing to return Caitrín to the living.

Squeezing closed his eyes and lifting his head, he pleaded, in an urgent and low voice, "Do not take this woman. She has much to do here yet."

He stroked her hand, pale and lifeless in his own. "Caitrín, muirnin, come back to me."

If he could, he'd infuse his own strength into her. Merely willing her to return to the living had not yet convinced the guardians of the gates to release her spirit.

Her chest barely rose and fell with every breath. Connor frowned. She had lost much blood and the wound continued to ooze every time he removed and replaced the riverweed dressing.

Color slowly returned to her cheeks, but Connor was concerned. He recalled the old saying, "From pallor to red, by the morrow, dead."

He laid the back of his hand against her cheek, then her forehead.

Aye, she had a fever.

Unless he worked quickly, a fever would kill her even when the wound did not. He surveyed their small camp. He needed only to build a lean-to wall and roof to enclose the third side of their natural shelter.

He went to work immediately and continued through the night. By morning, he had cut and bound branches into a lean-to wall and propped it against the boulders. With vines, he tied the branches in place for a roof, and brought a stack of firewood into the make-shift hut.

Then, he hurried to the river to fill his water bag. This time, he approached the shore with caution. There could be warriors searching for them now.

But no curraghs sliced through the calm of the river, no cries of discovery pierced the sun-drenched calm. Could the battle for Croaghnac be over? Sounds from the valley were too distant, yet Connor imagined them in his mind. His heart pounded as he clutched the water bag and dipped it into the river.

Does my brother sit in my place now? Or Donal?

What of Niall? Was he successful in rallying the warriors?

Is anyone looking for us?

Ever since Connor was old enough to pick up the sword, he had led his people. He would rather be there fighting alongside his warriors, leading his clan now.

But, he also realized Niall had been right. Connor was the only one who could save Caitrín. The old counselor might have tried but he wouldn't have had the skills and intentions to help her.

A dull ache spread across Connor's chest. For the first time since he first held his father's sword, Connor felt powerless to control the future of his clan. He who regained their homeland, plotted against his enemy to avenge his father's death now raged against his exile.

Connor shook his fist at the river.

"I should be there!" he shouted.

I should be there to fight with my clan and die with my clan.

Rage and sadness competed for control as he turned to go back to the shelter.

Ye must live, Caitrín! No matter what is happening in the valley, it is not over yet.

On the trek back, Connor imagined her as she had appeared the day before, sitting in the hall, talking to and petting the dog.

Who is this woman who has regard for slaves and a hearth stray?

He thought he knew her.

She is the daughter of my enemy. She is the woman I planned to force into marriage. She is the woman I would have seduced into my bed. She is the woman I want to bear my sons. She is the woman who betrayed me and my clan.

"Headstrong, difficult." The words Niall had used to warn him of her reputation sprang into his mind.

Yet, she came willingly to the ceremony, head held high, voice clear as she repeated the words of the promises.

What had he seen in her eyes during the binding ceremony?

No defiance certainly. She had not even complained that she was the wrong woman.

Connor didn't like the confusion that currently inhabited his thoughts. He kicked a tree root that snaked across the path in front of him. Life had been simple before. He knew who his enemies were, and he plotted against them.

How could this one woman have turned his life so upside down?

In his mind, he saw her as she stood next to him, radiant in the wedding garment he had selected for her. She looked at him with trusting eyes. Then, she stepped in front of the arrow aimed at him.

Why had she taken his punishment? Why did she now walk the perilous path to the gates of the Otherworld when it should have been him?

Connor took her brat and draped it over the entrance of the shelter he had built. Slivers of early-evening crimson and violet light slipped between the branches and danced on the floor as a soft breeze rustled the leaves, but most of the chamber was shrouded in shadow. He paused to allow his eyes to adjust to the dimness. The faint sound of Caitrín breathing brought a sigh of relief from him.

He recalled the last words she had said to him. "My life and death are equally in your care, and I shall honor you above all others until the day I die."

Had his father remembered the same words as his wife lay dying in childbirth? How could either of them have known that day might come so soon?

Connor cursed, railed at the very gods he had thanked for blessing his plan. His prayers would not matter now. The guardians of the gates to the Otherworld had thus far turned a deaf ear toward him, and now held Caitrín's hand. He did not know if he could summon her spirit back. If the goddess would answer his pleas ...

First, though, he must break the fever that burned her. He lined the fire pit with river rocks and added wood to the fire until the flames leapt high and heated the stones.

Then, he poured water on the rocks surrounding the fire pit until steam mixed with the smoke and filled the small chamber.

A steam hut would break a fever, but only if he could induce sweating. He ran his hand down Caitrín's arm. Her skin felt hot, but dry. He splashed more water onto the stones and watched the steam billow around her.

Perhaps removing her clothing would help.

He unlaced her boots and slid them from her feet. His fingers brushed across the pale skin of her ankles sending a wave of heat through his body unrelated to the rising temperature in the makeshift hut.

Trying not to jostle her too much, he slid her wedding shift over her head and tossed it aside. She wore a second shift of slippery fabric with strange strips of fabric holding it across her shoulders. He pulled it over her head as well and dumped it in a heap with the shift.

In the nearly dark hut, she was incredibly beautiful. Her skin took on a golden glow in the yellow-orange of the fire's light. He drank the sight of her as slowly as he would savor the finest wine.

He had never seen garments like hers worn under a shift. He fingered a string of white that held a triangular scrap of fabric in place over her breasts.

Why would a woman want to bind her breasts like this? Surely it canna' be comfortable.

He picked up his knife to slice through the thin fabric between her breasts, but something stopped him.

No, he would not remove this bizarre garment.

His fingers gently outlined the circle of one breast beneath the cloth. As the temperature in the hut jumped several degrees, sweat beaded across his forward and trickled down his temple.

Desire slammed through him, and he clenched his fist as he forced his gaze away from her breasts. His eyes traveled down the flat of her abdomen toward a slight swell where creamy white skin disappeared beneath another triangle of shiny fabric.

A low moan escaped unbidden from his lips as shadows of the dark curls hidden there taunted him and begged for release from their confinement.

Again, he held back his blade.

There would be time later. There must be time later.

All along he had planned to force her to marry him, but now that they were married, he wanted her to come willingly to him.

He must first break the fever and his own perspiration would not help her. Her skin remained hot and dry to his touch. He poured more water across the hot rocks to fill the chamber with fresh steam. Cupping water in his hands, he began to rub her arms, first the left, then the right. His touch was light, meant to wet her skin, not invigorate it.

He felt the weak, but steady pulsation in her neck and trickled water from his hand across her collarbone and the shallow space between her breasts.

"Muirnin," *sweetheart*, a name he had never called another woman, "Ye must fight the fever. Come back from the gates. Come back to me."

He drizzled water from her ankles to her thighs, daring not to touch her legs for fear the heat within him might explode and consume her with a fire much hotter than the flames a few feet from him.

He wanted her fully conscious, fully aware and fully wanting him when they consummated their marriage.

Chapter 33

I fought demons, wild boars, and even wilder warriors in the blackness that engulfed me. A thin voice reached into the void soothing me, and pushing away the visions of animals and men pursuing me.

Grandmother Moira entered the dreams and called a little girl away from play. I stepped back and watched the scene as though it were a movie on a screen, yet I knew I was part of the story.

I was the little girl.

"I'm coming," I said.

I hated to leave my friend when Grandmother had summoned me for dinner. I straightened my doll's skirt and sat her in her miniature chair.

"Now, Bridget," I said, wagging my finger and speaking with all the solemnity a six-year-old can summon to instruct her doll. "I'll only be gone a few moments. Remember, mommies always come back."

I kissed a porcelain cheek, then tucked the doll back into her chair. Every day, several times a day, I told Bridget I would be back. That was my solemn promise. It was important to keep a promise.

And I always would. I wouldn't be the kind of mother who promised to come back and didn't. No matter what, I'd always come back. I would never leave my baby.

In the dream, I reached out to pick up the doll as the dream shattered into a million pieces and a new fragment of memory popped up. Still a child, I snuggled into my grandmother's lap for a bedtime story.

"The Princess," I requested.

My favorite story. I wished I was young once again and nestled in my grandmother's arms. Moira nodded and began with the words of a well-rehearsed story, stopping every few minutes for me to add a line from the tale I had heard a million times.

It was the story of a faraway place and a long-ago time when knights roamed the green hills and fought for fair ladies. My grandmother's descriptions were so vivid that even now I could close my eyes and see the great oak woods and hear the chattering squirrels and the friendly red fox.

I had always longed to go there to that magical place of peace and happiness where I might find my mother, the princess, sleeping on the heather with a knight sitting guard over her.

The place was Aasleigh, and I whispered the name.

A white light came into my dream world to direct me to another place. I felt urgency and knew that only when I reached my destination, could I rest.

I stepped away from the tableau of my grandmother and the child version of me, and began walking toward the light.

"Come back to me," a male voice beckoned from the shadows of the dream world.

It must be David.

He must be there with my grandmother. He was looking for me, worried because he didn't know where I had gone.

"I'll always come back," I tried to tell him. "You have my promise."

But the light pulled me toward it.

I felt such peace and calm. This had to be Aasleigh, the land of my childhood dreams.

He called me again.

But something was wrong. It wasn't David. Someone else summoned me. Someone whose spirit was stronger than mine tugging me away from the light, away from Aasleigh.

I struggled for a moment, then decided to let go. It wasn't my time yet. He needed me.

I turned away from the light and groped through the darkness for the way. Someone was there in the shadows with me.

A warrior.

Come to rescue the princess. He had made a promise.

I reached out to him and he scooped me up into his arms to carry me through the darkness. When I nestled against his chest, I felt safe and protected and loved.

The journey to consciousness came slowly and painfully.

I heard his voice, one minute in my dreams, the next awake, though not fully, but trapped somewhere in that nether world between dreams and consciousness.

At first, his words made no sense, then I realized he spoke Gaelic and my brain slowly began to translate his words.

"Muirnin, sweetheart, come back to me."

I opened my mouth to answer him, but no words came out. Only a moan as a white-hot wave of liquid pain poured over my left shoulder, down my back and arm.

I dared not move or breathe or even open my eyes.

He continued talking and I settled into his arms and listened. "Ye must fight the guardians of the gates. Fight the fever."

What is he talking about? What guardians? What fight?

My eyelids fluttered as I tried to open them, but I felt as though even that much effort might be too much for me. I didn't want to do anything that might bring a return of the pain in my shoulder.

I slipped back into the darkness for a few minutes. Or a day, I didn't know which. The next time I tried to awaken, I threw off the shadows of my dreams like a butterfly slowly emerging from its cocoon.

Cautiously, deliberately, I raised one lid and then the other.

Hell!

I've died and gone to hell, and Connor is here with me.

Hell was red and rock and hot. I knew that. The nuns had taught me well.

Connor's bare chest glistened with sweat and I dared not move my head enough to see if I was also naked.

But, my skin tingled from the steam settling on it. On all of it!

Naked, lying across his lap in hell!

The thought of being naked and confined to Connor's arms for an eternity of roasting shocked me enough to rouse me from any lassitude the heat had induced.

I mustered whatever strength I could and sat straight up, ignoring the piercing pain.

"What do you think you're doing?"

Connor startled. "What? I was reciting the chant."

"Chanting? Don't you think it's a little too late for that now?"

"No. But I guess you're right. I've received an answer from the goddess."

"You prayed to go to hell and here we are?"

"Nay, muirnin, I prayed ye would return to me."

"Then, what is this place? It sure is hot in here. And you're— where's your clothes?"

"I took them off."

He put his hands on my upper arms and gently tried to lay me back down, but I resisted.

"No, you don't. Just because you have your shirt off and we're in hell doesn't mean you can have your way with me."

"Muirnin—"

"Stop calling me that!"

"Caitrín—"

"And don't call me that either. My name is 'Kat.'"

"Kat"—my name came out sounding like "caught"—"this is not the Otherworld. Ye did not pass through the gates. Ye are alive."

"Alive and hurting." I slowly leaned back into his arms and let him cradle me. "What happened?"

"What do ye remember?" he asked, laying a hand on my right shoulder to gently knead my neck with his thumb.

"The warriors. A crowd. They cheered."

"Go on. What else do ye remember?"

"I hurt. My shoulder."

"Yes, it was an arrow. Ye were struck by an arrow."

"Does that mean Donal attacked?" Fear strangled my voice into a whisper.

"Aye, it was Donal."

"We survived? What about the others? Where's Niall? Lia?"

"I do not know. I brought ye to an island down river from the valley."

"This is an island? We're not in hell? Are you sure?"

"This is a hut built against two rocks. Ye had a fever and I hoped to break it."

"How long has it been since ..."

"Two days," he said.

I looked into his dark eyes, framed with a mix of relief and concern, and said, "We must go back to Croaghnac. Your place is with your people."

The stillness of the night, just before dawn painted the canvas of the sky with streaks of purple and orange was Niall's favorite time. He walked along the wall and paused to look at the valley below from a vantage point where a warrior with bow and arrow could defend the fort during battle.

Campfires dotted the darkness like sparkling stars on a midnight sky. Three days of fierce fighting had ended Donal's attempt to take the valley.

On this fourth day, the last of the enemy in the valley had been found and killed, and now, Niall could send warriors down the river to search for Connor.

The chieftain was safe. Niall knew in his heart that every day without Connor's return meant that Caitrín still lived.

All of their lives depended on Connor's ability to keep her alive.

And so much the better if she came back pregnant.

Niall chuckled to himself at the fury Donal would feel then. His grandson a Malley! Perhaps Connor had been right to pursue that crazy plan of his.

But, it all hinged on bringing Caitrín back alive. The fianna had held off Donal's warriors, but most of his force, including Basta, had retreated.

Connor needed to mount an attack and the sooner, the better. The warriors were ready, all they needed was their chieftain to lead them. Niall must find him as soon as possible.

Chapter 34

Connor inhabited my dreams and my wakefulness. Always there, quick with a sip of water or a word of encouragement. No one had ever cared for me like this. I luxuriated in the feel of his arms around me, and the reassurance of his constant presence.

I slept most of the time, waking occasionally, and each time remaining conscious a little longer. Connor timed his trips away from our campsite so that he was with me every time I awoke to coax me to try a little more food or water.

Once the fever broke and the red streaks extending down my arm faded, my wound began to heal. He continued to dress it daily with fresh river weed bound with strips of fabric. He had fashioned a sling for my arm when I was ready to begin using it.

On the morning of the fourth day, as he tended my wound, he asked, "Do ye recall being wounded?"

I shook my head. "No, the last thing I remember is walking down the slope to the field."

"What do ye remember about that?"

"You were with me." My voice trailed off as I searched for the images in my memory.

"Aye. Where were we going?"

"To the games. No, to a feast? I don't know. The warriors were cheering. But I don't remember more than bits and pieces after that. Shouts. People running. Niall was there. I remember hearing him tell you to take a boat."

"That was after ye were wounded."

My shoulder throbbed suddenly and I rubbed my upper arm.

"Yes, my shoulder ... the pain, blood. I saw blood on my dress."

I looked at my shift. Connor had washed out most of the blood, but a small stain marked both sides of the tear. I suddenly realized I wasn't wearing my slip, with its precious cargo, and link to my past and passage into this time.

"My clothing. I was wearing an undergarment. Did you discard it?" I tried to control the panic in my voice so as not to arouse any suspicions.

"It is here," Connor said, handing me a wad of white nylon and lace, the pocket and ruby undiscovered. "I could not put it back on ye.

"That's all right. I'll replace it later." I hugged it close and felt the gemstone through the fabric.

He returned to our conversation. "Ye do not recall what was happening when the arrow hit ye?"

"No. I only remember the most awful pain I've ever had. Sharp, like I'd been stabbed. I fell, and I think you caught me. There was so much confusion. Noise. You took me into one of the tents."

So, she didn't remember their wedding, the ceremony, her vows. There were good reasons not to bring that memory to her mind. Not to let her know they were married.

If Donal finds us, he might spare her life if he believes we are not yet husband and wife. He'll kill me no matter what, but she might live if she is still a virgin and he can fulfill the bridal contract with Colum.

Connor's decision to forego consummating their marriage, however, was taking its toll on his resolve. A battle raged within him.

The strain of caring for her, of being so close to her for days and nights waged war with keeping her safe. He had seen and touched her, keeping in check his own needs and desires even now as she recovered her strength.

It would be so easy to take her as his wife.

And she wanted him, he could tell. Yet, he held back to protect her.

He avoided looking into her eyes for fear she would guess he was hiding something from her. Not just to keep the truth from her, but also to protect his own heart.

He had replaced her shift when he could no longer bear to see her partially clad breasts. But, clothed, she was nearly as desirable as naked. Now, he simply imagined what he knew lay beneath the soft nap of the shift.

He clenched his fists, and said, "Rest now. We can talk more later."

She nodded and was asleep before Connor's internal battle resolved itself.

I must not tell her. She canna' know we are married, and whatever happens, I must not make her my wife.

A quick swim in the cold waters of the river gave him the opportunity to both check for any warriors, and quench the desire that was quickly driving him to forget who she was.

Try as I might, I could not recall the details. I sorted through pieces of memory. There was chaos, shouting and footsteps, great confusion. I remembered panic, not being able to get my breath. Falling, then Connor lifting me in his arms. Niall floated in and out of the memory fragments.

"Take her to the islands."

A boat. Feeling cold. Very cold.

Then, blackness so deep the stars could not break through. I had been on a journey.

I did not know where, but I remembered a voice calling me. Wherever I had been, Connor was there. Through it all, he loomed like a guardian angel watching over me. I sensed his presence.

He pulled at my consciousness like a stubborn dog fighting for a bone. He wouldn't let me go.

At night, he held me protectively, his breath warm and moist on my neck. When I awoke in pain, he massaged my shoulder until the spasms disappeared. In the daylight hours, he fed me, tended my wound, helped me stand. He spoke soothing words, some sort of prayers I sometimes struggled to translate.

Finally, I was awake and more aware. The shoulder no longer ached constantly. And I was restless to get on with life.

Where I would go, I didn't know. And didn't much care so long as Connor and I were together. I marveled at how quickly I had come to love him.

We had not talked much, after I awoke. At first, it took too much energy, then I simply didn't know what to say. But as my strength returned, I wondered what we could discuss.

Seen any good movies lately?

What'cha reading?

Didn't you just hate the ending of that show?

So, think the Browns will make the Super Bowl? This year? This century?

Yet, for all we lacked in common, the bond between us grew stronger by the day. I looked for him as the first rays of the morning sun sifted through the thatched roof of our shelter.

I could no longer imagine a time when he wasn't part of my life, and I did not think about returning to my former life at all. I'd been given a second chance at life, with Connor.

Certainly, it was different than my life in Cleveland. There was no comparison. But that difference made the colors here seem a little more vivid, the sunlight brighter, my feelings stronger.

And love—I was still amazed that I had found love—more precious. Connor filled my every waking hour. When he wasn't with me, I thought of him and longed for his presence, the feel of his fingers kneading my muscles, the back of his hand against my cheek, his arms cradling me as I walked.

I wanted to touch him as well. To trace the muscles of his arms, to massage the bronzed skin of his broad back, to kiss the thick mustache that curled down from the sides of his mouth, to explore the body that lay against mine every night.

But, in spite of our proximity, there was always a space between us. As my strength returned, I began to ask myself why he had not made love to me. He planned to marry me. He had made that plain from the moment he had kidnapped me.

Yet, in spite of our proximity and isolation, he hadn't made a move.

Something unspoken, invisible, yet maddeningly persistent came between us.

Recovering quickly from my injuries, I felt a restlessness growing within me. As I thought more and more about it, I realized that I wanted him with an intensity I'd never felt before.

We were a man and a woman, marooned on an island. And this wasn't "Gilligan's Island."

I searched his eyes for a glimmer of desire. It was there all right, bold and brash, yet he tried to hide it by looking away quickly.

So, why does he hold back? If he wants me as much as I want him, why not?

Perhaps he believes we should be married first.

Although I was unfamiliar with the mores of his times and people, that didn't seem like the right answer. Certainly Basta had had no difficulty coming on to me.

No, something else holds Connor back. I see lust in his eyes, and there's been more than ample opportunity ... what is it?

Frustration grew when he didn't pick up my subtle signals at all. But I also didn't want to be blatant and ask, "Would you like to make love?"

This had never been a serious problem before. If I had been at home in Cleveland, I'd have invited Connor for dinner. And left the rest unspoken, yet mutually understood.

I had not been shy about sex with David either. We'd dated for several months and then, slept together. No long discussion, no flowery sentiments or pledges of commitment. When the relationship deepened, we began to have sex. We'd been committed to each other for years before deciding we might as well get married.

When had David told me he loved me?

I couldn't even remember. I tried to imagine the words coming from his mouth, but all I could hear was Connor's deep voice and Gaelic lilt.

What are the rules of the game in this place and time? What do women of Connor's clan do when they want a man? Do we have to be married first?

Surely Connor wasn't a virgin. But I knew he hadn't been married before.

Perhaps I should broach the subject of his previous experiences. But talking about sex also didn't strike me as the proper thing to do.

His language might be very different from mine, and the correct words weren't on the vocabulary list my grandmother had taught me. What if I ended up asking him for something entirely different from what I wanted?

As I felt stronger, I realized I was becoming almost short-tempered every time he approached. One evening, I thanked him for all he had been doing that day to keep me comfortable. I took his hand and brought it to my lips and kissed it.

Then, he smoothed the hair from my brow and kissed my cheek, before rolling over and going to sleep. I stared into the darkness for hours before pounding the bedding in frustration.

What if I take off my clothing? What would he do? Would he get the message?

Flashing him the next time he came into the hut didn't really appeal. I needed some pretext for disrobing so that if he rejected my advances, I wouldn't feel completely foolish.

Asking him to check my shoulder wound wouldn't work. He'd been tending it for days and seeing nothing but that little bit of skin.

Bathing would work. I've got to persuade him to take me to the river for a bath.

"How far is the river?" I asked.

"Ye are not strong enough to walk there yet."

"Then, carry me," I said, words sparkling with a challenge.

"And what is it ye wish to do at the river? Ye are not ready to travel the white waters."

"Bathe," I answered, running my fingers through my hair, and groaning when I snagged a tangle.

"Bathe?"

"Yes, it seems like ages since I felt clean. It would do me good, trust me."

"The river is not the best place for that. The water is cold and the current is swift. Ye do not have the strength yet to fight it," he said.

"The air is warm now and the sun bright. You could go in with me. Not to bathe, of course, but to be sure I am not swept away."

"If ye got your shift wet, ye might get a chill."

"I would take off my clothing. I plan to bathe, not catch pneumonia."

Chapter 35

His brows came together as he considered what she had said.

Naked. She would bathe naked? Why?

There was determination in her voice that told him he had better offer some alternative before she tottered off to find the river on her own. Perhaps the place he had found on the other side of the island. A small tributary broke from the river and wandered through the island until it ended in a deep, rock-lined pool of still water. She could safely bathe there.

He sucked in a deep breath.

Seeing her naked would give him more than mere will power could handle. Perhaps he might concentrate on the icy temperature of the water to cool his ardor. Perhaps he could take her to the pool, and persuade her not to take off her clothing. Perhaps he could avert his eyes, and stay away from the pool himself.

Perhaps the sun would not shine and darkness would cover the face of the earth.

"I will take ye to water, another day," he said.

"Why not today? I feel strong enough, and the air is warm. It is the perfect day."

Not perfect for anything except love-making. No, it must be a cloudy day, a rainy day. A day when the gods withhold their promise of spring.

Sleet!

That would make a perfect day. Sleet that stings the skin and chills the flames. Sleet that turns to ice and encases the body.

She rose and said, "I'm ready now."

"Now?" He swallowed hard against a lump that had jumped into his throat.

A lamb going to slaughter would be happier.

He carried her in the hopes that he would exhaust his energies on physical labor before they reached the pool. However, she weighed even less than the day he kidnapped her and the journey was far from strenuous.

The afternoon sun warmed the rocks lining the edge of the pool, but did little to increase the water's temperature. He set her on a sunny ledge along the bank. She dipped her feet in and squealed, but, undeterred by the icy water, she began to remove her shift.

Time to go.

He suddenly felt uncomfortable and started to move away, but she said, "You may need to help me. I can't raise my arm enough to take this off."

Connor nearly said a word only meant for the company of his fianna.

Did she not know what she was asking of me?

He had removed her shift and undergarment in the dimness of the shelter and then replaced it later after the fever had broken. But now, when sunlight danced across her red-gold curls, when her eyes matched the blue of the water, when her lips were full and inviting.

Now, when one touch, one brush across her bare skin, even accidental would erase all of his resolve.

Now when one look at her pale, soft, perfect breasts would … He closed his eyes, set his jaw, and pulled her shift over her head. Roughly and with no apologies.

This is no way to protect her.

He looked up at the sky for something to distract him. Not a cloud, not even so much as a wisp of white. Where was that rain, that sleet he had requested from the goddess?

He glanced back at her as she began to remove the strange undergarment securing her breasts. Feeling the heat rise in his belly, he quickly averted his gaze, and stared at the frigid water of the pool, wishing it would send its chill through his veins.

His hands itched to touch the fascinating cloth. To see how she had undone it. Her movement broke his concentration again as she slid out of the shiny white garment she wore to protect her womanhood.

Sweat beaded on his forehead, and he felt as awkward as a young boy who had not yet taken a blade to shave his cheeks. He could not look away, no matter how hard he tried. The image of her bare buttocks burned through his brain.

"Perhaps I should check to be certain no one has found this island," he said, his voice sounding hollow to his own ears.

"Do you hear that?"

"What?" He gripped the handle of the sword strapped to his waist. "Ye heard someone?"

"No, silly, birds. I hear birds singing. If there were someone nearby, the birds would be calling alarms, not singing, wouldn't they? I think we're perfectly safe here," she said as she slid into the crystalline waters.

His heart pounded in his head, drowning out the calls of those birds. Her lovely body disappeared beneath the water, and he tried to convince himself she was safe now.

He could observe her and still maintain his resolve. The water would cover her from his gaze. But he had already seen enough that the sight of her gliding through the water froze him where he stood.

He could neither avert his eyes, nor stop the liquid fire in his gut. And he had to command his breathing to slow.

"You were going to check something?" she said.

Had he imagined her voice seemed more sultry? Beckoning?

"What? No, ye are right, all is peaceful."

His belt felt too tight and heavy, constricting his breathing and movement. He undid it and laid his sword on a rock near the pool's edge where it would be within quick reach.

"Then, why don't you join me?"

Water droplets sparkled in her curls like a handful of jewels sprinkled across her head.

"Ye want me to get into the water?"

No, he could not. He had to remain at the edge of the pool. But it would not hurt to dip his feet into the water and that might cool the blaze that surged through him.

He untied his boots, pulled them off and dropped them next to his belt. Sitting on the ledge where she had removed her clothing, he contemplated taking off his own. It would be cooler and give him something to do other than stare at the curve of her neck where it met the water and the vague shape of her breasts beneath the surface.

"Sure?" She playfully flicked a splash toward him.

Her smile begged, no, dared him to plunge into the pool.

If he entered the water, all would be lost. He knew it, and yet felt powerless to stop what he, and the gods had set in motion.

"I would get wet," he said.

He unwrapped his belt and tossed it aside. The sun's warmth, welcome in the coolness of the water, felt oppressively hot on his sweaty skin. His clothing prickled his neck and perspiration trickled down his back.

"You might. Do you think you'll melt?" She faced him and swam toward him, the water lapping across the slope of her breasts. Breasts completely free of that protective garment. Breasts that begged for his touch more than his gaze.

Melt? No, but steam might rise from the pool.

He pulled off his tunic, acutely aware of the effect she had on his body. An effect that even the coldest of water would not diminish. An effect she would soon discover.

For days he had watched over her, prayed for her life, tended to her every physical need. At night, he had listened to her breathing, held her in his arms and fought the urge to possess her body until he could have her heart as well.

I've taken the warrior's vow to protect ye, with my own life, if need be. But I want ye so much!

Looking at her, he remembered another vow that he had promised as her husband.

Husband!

The word felt as foreign as a sip of milk to an adult. He rolled it around his brain again.

She is my wife.

But I cannot make love to her. I cannot enjoy that which she offers me now. I saved her life once. The only way to protect her is to ...

He searched her eyes and saw her desire nearly as obvious as his own. And he knew he was sunk surer than if he had tied boulders to his ankles.

If he got into that pool, she would be his wife in more than his mind alone.

He slid full body into the water.

"Come to me," he said to her.

She shook her head, spraying drops of water from her curls like a dog after a romp in the river.

"You come to me," she said, her voice softly challenging him as she floated two arms-lengths away near the center of the pool.

How dare she tease?

Did she not understand the fire within his gut, the desire that tore at his soul? He would lay down his very life for her, yet he could not do the one thing that would save her life. He could not turn away from her at that moment. He had to have her.

"Do not—" he started to say, as she suddenly disappeared beneath the water.

Where had she gone?

His heart began to pound as he scanned the surface for some sign of her.

Damn her! I didn't save her from an arrow to lose her to the spirits of the depths.

Just as he was preparing to dive in search for her, she touched his foot and her hands followed his legs upward. He reached down and grabbed her arms as she slid up the full length of his body, warm and solid against him. Her breasts brushed his chest and one of her legs wrapped around his thigh.

Suddenly, she was no longer a desperately wounded woman barely clinging to life, nor a fairy sent to steal his soul, but a full-bodied, nearly perfect woman molding herself against him.

And, she was his wife, pledged to him by the gods, and the words from her own mouth.

Blood rushed from his head and his mind could no longer focus on the dangers of what he was about to do. There was no choice left. No turning back now.

She rested her hand against his upper arm and the muscles tightened at her touch. With a wet fingertip, she traced a thick vein up to his shoulder.

"Don't ever—" he started to say.

She placed both hands on his shoulders and pushed down in the water until his mouth met hers and she clamped her lips over his, swallowing the admonition he was about to deliver.

A tidal flood of unfamiliar emotions crashed over him.

No other woman had ever been so bold with him. No other woman had invited and taken in the same moment. She wrapped her arms around his neck and coaxed him into deeper water.

"Come float with me," she said.

Floating was the last thing on his mind.

She was his. His wife. His lover. She was woman, not fairy.

Woman, indeed. The mother of his children, of his clan. He possessed her body and soul.

And she owned his heart.

His hand brushed up her neck to capture a lock of her hair and twine a wet curl around his fingers. Damp, dark red, like the sunset on a summer's eve. He carried her to the deepest part of the pool, encircling her with his arms until he felt her relax and float gently within his embrace.

She brushed against him and slipped away again, teasing, enticing him as his desire mounted.

Touch. Retreat. Touch. Until he thought he might go mad with desire.

Then, he held his arms open and let her return on her own terms and, even when she swam into the circle of his arms, he did not close it on her.

She came to him. Of her own accord. She clung to him. Weightless in his arms while his mouth began a search.

His tongue traced her collarbone to the sensitive juncture of the hollow of her neck. He licked a droplet of water from her skin and continued up her neck until he reached an earlobe.

Flicking his tongue, nibbling with his teeth, desire crashed across him like a rogue wave, sweeping him under a sea of urgency. Never before had he wanted a woman as much as he wanted her.

"Please," she whispered in a voice husky with desire.

Connor did not need any more encouragement. He swept her to the edge of the pool and lifted her from the water. Laying her on his clothing, he covered her body with his own.

Wet flesh against wet flesh, yet he did not feel the chill of the air.

She opened her mouth to his tongue, and he traced the soft fullness of her lips. Still he took his time, touching her, exploring her body, all of her, open to him to his mouth and his hands.

He kissed each of her fingertips, stroking and licking before moving to her palms, then up to the pulsating point of her wrists. He nibbled her arms, gently, carefully so as not to cause her pain from her shoulder.

He brought his lips to her breasts, fondling her nipples until they peaked, and she groaned with pleasure. She excited him beyond the point where his brain could even fashion the word, "No."

Then, when he could hold back no longer, he parted her legs and slide inside, wordlessly begging her to forgive him.

Chapter 36

Hours later, in the darkness and silence of the night, I curled against Connor. I should have been asleep long before. Exhaustion soaked me as thoroughly as the icy water of the pond had, but at the same time, I tingled with contentment and happiness.

I stared into the darkness as if it held, like some crazy eight ball, the answers to my questions.

"Do I love Connor?" I would ask. The answer would float up to be displayed.

"Does he love me?"

Questions I wanted to ask, but answers I wasn't sure I wanted to know.

Couldn't it be enough to simply lie with him, to awaken next to him in the morning, to hold him and love him and never ask any questions? Wasn't that part of my dream? Why did questions have to interrupt?

But, this was no dream.

I had traveled two thousand years to find the one man, the man of my dreams, the man I wanted to spend an eternity with.

What our future might hold, I didn't want to know. For now, the present was more than enough.

My skin still tingled from the wet tickle of Connor's mustache as he explored my body with his mouth. My heart raced at the thought of his hands on my breasts and his hard thighs pressed against mine.

The intensity of my own desire had surprised me. The fierceness of our passion overwhelmed me.

The fire, the rawness, the force of my explosion carried beyond time and place. I had never experienced such a feeling of surrender, and at the same time, conquest.

We made love on the bank of the pool and again, when we returned to our shelter.

Yet, with each new touch, each kiss, each shiver of ecstasy, I felt as if I had never known such intense fulfillment before.

I reached out to touch him.

"Ye want more?" he murmured sleepily.

"No, just wanted to be sure you are still here."

"Forever, muirnin."

I wanted so much to believe in forever.

I wanted to tell him I loved him, but I held back. My feelings were new and tender and not quite ready for the light of day. I knew what forever felt like. I had been there.

"Forever" wasn't part of our vocabulary yet.

I snuggled against him, bare breasts against his back, invitation enough for him to reach behind and stroke my hip.

"So ye do want more," he murmured as he turned over.

Yes, I did want him again, and again.

Forever.

Chapter 37

Near the end of the fighting in the valley, four men of Donal's fianna became separated from their comrades.

"Ferghus, what is that I see?" one of them asked his companion.

"It looks to be a boat. Let's be off in it then. Anything is better than facing a Malley sword."

Four warriors crammed into one small boat nearly sank it, and certainly did not make for an easy voyage down an already treacherous and unfamiliar river. Nightfall rapidly approached and they knew they could not reach the sea before dark. They paddled furiously past the first two islands, then decided to land on the third one as the sun slipped behind the mountains.

"Still Connor's land," the self-appointed leader of the group said. "No fire tonight."

"No food either," Ferghus grumbled.

"Nay, but at least ye got out with the meat still on your bones."

"Aye, I'll live to fight another day. That is, if we make it safely to the sea and survive it."

The warriors spent a cold, damp night huddled on the beach, sleeping in shifts, but with hands on their swords, one blink from consciousness. As the sky began to lighten from deep purple to ever-changing shades of blue streaked with rose, they rose and prepared to push their curragh back into the inky waters.

At first morning light, Connor had a fire to rebuild. He had been so distracted the night before, he had not smoored the fire. He brushed aside the ashes to uncover still-warm embers, but not finding any, he piled fresh kindling and pulled his flint stone from his pouch tucked beneath his shirt.

Wrapped in my brat against the early morning chill, I came out of our shelter to watch what he was doing.

"I've always wondered about that. Starting a fire with rocks and twigs. Would you show me how?"

He refused, saying, "Fire was given to man by the gods."

"Then, why do the women of your clan tend it, use it and clean up the hearth?" I asked, rubbing my hands up his back to generate some heat of my own.

He did not have an answer to that, and the massage distracted him from any clever reasoning. So, he held out his flint stone and allowed me to try scraping.

Pursing my lips, I focused so much energy on the stones it was a wonder the wood didn't spontaneously combust.

Connor kissed behind my ear and along my neck, kindling a different kind of fire. "Perhaps ye are better at building a blaze in a man," he said, encircling my waist with his hands.

"And what might I strike my flint against?" I asked as I surrendered the stone to Connor.

He grinned and knelt to light the pile of twigs. "It is not knowing how to strike so much as it is generating the right friction. For that ye need no practice."

"Oh, yeah!" I pushed him over and fell atop him, tickling him in the recently discovered sensitive spot along the side of his waist.

He stopped me by imprisoning both arms with his and capturing my mouth with a long, breath-stealing kiss. "Perhaps ye should come back to the bed with me," he said.

"And if I did, what would you do to a prisoner such as me?"

He wasted no time telling me what he preferred to show me.

On the beach, the warriors prepared to leave the island, when the leader lifted his head slightly and sniffed.

"Wait!" he said, laying his hand on another's forearm. "Smoke!"

"There is someone on this island?" Ferghus asked.

"Friend or foe?"

"Does it matter?"

"Only if he has a sword aimed at ye. But there are four of us. If he's building a fire, he must have food."

They agreed to spread out and follow the scent until they found the fire and the person who started it.

In the lean-to, Connor clamped a hand across my mouth, and I tickled his palm with my tongue until I noticed the sudden flash of warning in his eyes.

"What?" I started to say, but he tightened his hand over my mouth while his eyes told me to be silent. Then, I heard something, too. Outside our shelter. Rustling in the bushes. No animal would come that close to our campfire.

Connor grabbed his sword, and handed a small dagger to me. He touched my leg in a gesture I understood meant I should hide the knife in my boot as I had seen him do.

Then, following his hand directions, I moved to the far wall of the shelter and pressed against the stone. He stole to the draped door and waited.

The warriors, drawn by the smoke of the small fire encircled the small campsite. They approached warily, certain from the cessation of sound in the shelter that their presence had been detected. Standing to one side of the doorway, one of the men shoved the tip of his sword through the branches of the wall and another man did the same, in another place.

I bit my lip as the sword plunged through the wall and narrowly missed Connor. He backed from the doorway until he stood in front of me, protecting me with his body. The attackers pulled down the make-shift wall, and we came face to face with four sword tips all aimed at Connor's chest.

I gasped.

In an instant, I knew he would die before surrendering to them and I couldn't bear the thought of watching them run him through.

I started to step from behind him and my movement startled one of the warriors who lunged at Connor. He raised his sword and brought it down flat-bladed against the warrior's shoulder. The man thudded to the ground and the others launched a simultaneous attack.

Connor advanced toward them, sword swiftly parrying their thrusts. While two of the men engaged him, the third took advantage of the confusion to grab me.

I screamed and struggled, but I was not yet strong enough to fight the man whose arm clamped around my waist as he dragged me from the shelter.

By the time he reached the boat, his two companions, out-of-breath and bloodied joined him. They shoved me roughly into the curragh and pushed away from shore quickly.

"Connor!" I cried, hoping he was still alive to hear me.

I knew they would not tell me the truth about Connor's fate so I didn't bother to ask.

I wrapped both arms around myself and held tightly until the motion of the boat became so violent I had to cling to the sides. As soon as they pushed away from the shore, the river's current picked us up like dandelion down on the wind and swept us down the river.

The men, experienced warriors, not sailors, fought the rushing waters, barely keeping the boat upright and away from the boulders that threatened to break apart the small vessel. We bounced from one eddy to another, one wet-slicked rock to the next past several more small islands before the river straightened out.

From narrow and tortuous to wide and swift wasn't much improvement. Looming cliffs replaced the sandy shores along the river as it once again narrowed to a barely passable width about the same size and character, I thought, as a roller coaster at Cedar Point, an amusement park near Cleveland.

I tightened my grip on the sides of the boat as it plunged through the mouth of the river, and dropped onto a huge wave that picked it up like a bottle thrown into the ocean.

We were fortunate that the waves quickly swept us away from the coastline instead of dashing the curragh against the rocks along the face of the cliff. Looking back over my shoulder, I understood why someone might have difficulty finding the opening to the river fjord. There were dozens of false crevices.

The sea seemed a good bit rougher than the day I had told Connor there was no way I'd climb down a cliff and get into a small boat. The dark gray, boiling waters of the river were nothing compared with the stiff white peaks and the steep, rolling slate blue waves of the great northern sea.

The tiny boat climbed to the top of a wave, crested and slid down the back into a valley of water as the next wave towered over them, threatening to engulf them before another stomach-churning ride up. Faces blanched with fear, the warriors dropped their paddles and seized the sides of the boat.

Overhead, sea gulls swooped down as if to warn them not to proceed. But it was too late.

Icy sea spray soaked through my clothing and sent violent shivers through me. Just as I began to wonder whether I would be able to continue clinging to the boat with numbed hands, a rogue wave crested over the top of the boat and ripped me from my seat.

I gulped a breath of air as I plunged beneath the water. Uncertain which way was up, I kicked furiously and within a few seconds, bobbed back to the surface, coughing and gasping for air.

I floated and looked around for the boat. Nothing but gray-blue. I could see neither land nor sky. The horizon disappeared blending with the sea into solid color with only an occasional gull to distinguish between the two.

I kicked to stay afloat while the water soaked my clothing and began to drag me under. I couldn't determine which direction to swim, but that didn't matter, for, within minutes my legs felt like heavy, wooden blocks. I looked around frantically for the boat, for the shore, for help.

"Connor!" I screamed, my voice lost in the raging sea and wind.

The cold sapped my meager strength quickly. When my legs and arms no longer responded to commands from my brain, I closed my eyes and sank into the frigid water.

"Connor!" was the last word I said, and the last thought in my mind before the sea swallowed me.

Chapter 38

Connor blinked away the darkness and nausea that accompanied any movement. With one hand he felt his scalp for a wound and finding nothing but a lump, decided he could safely move.

Safely, but not without agony. Every motion sent stabs of pain throbbing through his head. He could not wait for the agony to moderate to a dull roar.

He had to find Caitrín. He pulled himself upright and staggered past the bloodied body of one of the warriors unfortunate enough to get within reach of his sword.

At the river, he found the tracks of the others and of the curragh they used to escape. Scooping cold water with both hands, he splashed his face and commanded his head to stop hurting.

He considered the possibilities. Donal could have sent his warriors to find his daughter.

Had he defeated Niall and the Malley warriors? Or were Donal's warriors fleeing the valley and stopped on the island by chance?

"I would have taken on all of them!" he shouted at the river. Without a curragh, he could not follow them to the sea and he felt certain they had not returned to the valley. They weren't sailors and would not know how to handle the rapids on an return trip. No, they'd head for Donal's land whether Donal was there or sitting in the fortress of Croaghnac.

Connor had to go after them, but he certainly couldn't do it without a boat. Returning to Croaghnac would allow him to get a curragh, but he had no idea whose warriors he might encounter when he reached the valley.

Nor could he wait for a boat. He'd have to swim. Swim in icy waters.

He believed he could make it to the closest island, rest and warm up there, then move on again. There might also be rocks large enough to offer momentary respite.

If the gods were with him, he'd reach the valley by nightfall.

He removed his sword, boots and tunic and plunged into the river, trying to stay near the edges of the water and out of the channel where the water ran swiftest. Within minutes, his feet numbed and his arms burned with the effort of pulling himself through the current.

He climbed onto a rock where the sun slowly warmed him, then resumed swimming until numbness forced him out again.

As he approached the first island, Connor heard her call his name as clearly as if she stood on the shoreline summoning him. He scanned the beach, the rocks, the trees beyond and saw no one, yet he knew he had heard her.

"Connor!"

He heard her call his name again with panic in her voice. He wanted to race toward her, but he froze. She was not there.

There was no way she could be on this island. His mind must be playing horrible tricks on him.

His head ached and the frigid water consumed every bit of his energy. Swimming required utmost concentration. If he stopped to think of Caitrín, he'd be swept downstream into the rapids. He pushed her voice away and told himself she was safe.

She had to be.

The warriors would not dare touch Donal's daughter. She didn't remember her wedding and, if she didn't tell her father about being with him on the island, she might remain unharmed.

A sense of doom settled on Connor stronger than the weight of icy water tugging on his legs. Alone with nothing but the currents, the demons of the depths, and his own exhaustion to fight, Connor imagined every scenario he could think of.

Donal's warriors had her, but they had no intention of returning her to her father.

Basta had captured her, and was making love to her at that very moment.

She had managed to get back to Donal, and he learned she wasn't still a virgin.

She was a fairy after all and had returned to the fairy world.

Each thought became more ridiculous than the last. Drawing himself up onto the shore of the last island, he collapsed, too weary to even rub warmth back into his arms and legs.

Thoughts he'd tried to suppress returned quickly.

Caitrín, when he lifted her from the pool and made love to her the first time. Closing his eyes, he imagined she knelt over him, warming him with her hands. He captured her firm buttocks and rolled her over into place beneath him, then marveled at how she fit him as if she were made just for him.

His heart ached as much as his head. *Where was she?*

Connor made it to the valley in complete darkness, only aware of where he was because of the light of campfires dotted across a black horizon.

Were they friend or foe huddled around the fires?

He barely had the strength to pull himself from the water, let alone defend himself against Donal's warriors. Every muscle quivering with fatigue, he collapsed on the bank of the river and prayed he had not alerted any sentries to his presence.

His hopes were dashed by the sound of footsteps running toward him. A pair of hands grabbed him roughly and dragged him to his feet while a second warrior held a sword to his neck.

"What name do ye give?"

Connor thought he recognized the voice of the man with the sword.

"If I answered 'Niall, son of Alred' what response would ye offer?"

"I'd offer a feast of thanksgiving to the goddess," boomed a voice from beyond the two guards. A voice Connor knew well.

Niall brushed past the warriors and clasped Connor's forearm in greeting. "Help him," Niall instructed the guards.

"Are ye wounded?"

"Nay, just exhausted, wet and cold."

They took him to the nearest fire and Niall sent for dry clothing and food. As soon as they were alone, Niall asked Connor, "Where is the woman? Did she not survive?"

"Warriors took her. They came by boat. Donal's men, I think."

Chapter 39

The first thought I processed: *I'm alive.*

I could not kick my legs, nor close my fingers into a fist. My hands and feet were no longer part of my body. Only my mind seemed to still be working, and it plodded from one thought to the next in slow motion.

I'm alive. Cold and wet.

Followed by the awareness of solid ground beneath me.

I lay on sand. Not a smooth beach, but one strewn with rocks, some smooth like the pebble pressing my right flank. I managed to reach down and could not push it away. Rolling onto my back, I looked up at a dark azure sky shaded with the stroke of a purple brush and studded with a scattering of small white lights.

Questions about the sun's whereabouts and why I was so cold hit at the same time.

But several seconds passed before I could frame answers that sunset was not long from now, and I was thoroughly soaked. What to do about either one took even longer.

I began to move slowly, flexing my fingers, and wiggling my toes. Many more minutes passed before I could raise my head, and push to sit upright. I found myself alone on a rocky beach, waves lapping a few yards from my feet.

I had complete recall of how I came to be there, of every second of the terror before I gave in to the ocean and whatever gods or spirits Connor attributed to the sea.

As I sank, strong arms grabbed my waist and pulled me upright. Somehow, one of the warriors had managed to grab me. But before he could do more than that a wave tore me from his hands again.

Was he still alive? Were any of them?

I saw no one on the beach, and no sign of the small boat. I studied the waves. Hard to believe this was the same ferocious ocean that had swallowed the curragh and its warriors, and had nearly drowned me. It was perfectly peaceful now.

At the edge of the narrow strip of sand, a cliff rose from the beach. That was a challenge that would have to wait until morning. The sun had dipped beneath the watery horizon without so much as a sizzle and the chill of the evening seeped into my clothing as fast as the frigid water had.

I needed shelter and I needed it fast.

"C'mon," I said to myself, with a voice hoarse from coughing and shivering.

I stumbled toward the cliff seeking a cave or crevice or any opening in the wall large enough to sit and be surrounded on three sides by rock. Rock that had been warmed all day by a spring sun might radiate heat and keep me warm during the chilly night.

I took off a sodden brat and draped it over one boulder to speed its drying before sitting with my back against a smooth boulder and knees drawn up to my chest. Pulling off my boots, I laid the small dagger within reach. Out of the wind and safe, I dozed until morning.

Something woke me before the first light.

I dreamed that Connor was there, his arms around me, his lips brushing across mine. I opened one eye and thought the dream world was better than reality and I should stay there a little longer.

But lapping of waves against the rocks intruded on my slow awakening, and I remembered where I was.

I checked my arms and legs. A few bruises, but otherwise okay. My clothing had dried. I quickly felt for the secret pocket. The lump reassured me the ruby was still with me. I looked around me at the expanse of beach.

The beach. Gone.

The waves..

Oh, my God, the tide is coming in!

Chapter 40

As exhausted as he was, sleep did not come easily to Connor. He dreamed of Caitrín, her pale skin against his own bronzed arms, her hair a handful of crimson flowers in his fist. His lips tasted her sweetness as she opened like a rose to his touch.

He awoke with a start and the feeling that she had been there next to him in his sleeping furs.

Morning dawned gray and chilly, matching Connor's mood. Caitrín's abduction gnawed at his gut, along with the premonition that she was in danger clung to him like a mountain fog.

He rose early to begin considering his options. He could take a few warriors and go by boat to Donal's land. But he expected enemy warriors would be waiting for him, and without his entire fianna, he could be easily defeated.

He could lead the entire fianna across land. But, even on horseback, that would take longer than he wanted. However, he'd be in a much better position for the siege that would certainly follow.

How long could Donal hold out in his tower?

Connor had no idea, but assumed it might be a long time.

However, this was spring. Planting season. Donal's food supplies would likely be low. He wouldn't have reserves.

The other consideration was Caitrín.

She was the great unknown. His bride, although she didn't remember their wedding ceremony.

His lover, but he hoped she would not confess as much to her father. Her safety, and possibly her life, depended on her silence.

Whose side would she choose?

What of her feelings for him?

She had not told him she loved him, and he had not confessed that he loved her. Indeed, the words had barely registered in his own heart.

Did she love him? Would she tell her father?

While Connor hoped she did not, at the same time, he wanted her to shout her love for him from the top of Donal's tower.

Even though Caitrín spoke to him of forever, he couldn't be certain about her feelings for him, especially if she were now back in her father's tower.

Blood might still be stronger than the fragile bonds of a marriage she didn't know had occurred.

By the gods, what am I thinking? Could she possibly love me?

Do I love her? What do I feel for her?

He wanted her. He feared for her safety. He was crazy with fear for her. But he also knew he could not afford the luxury of these feelings now.

Caring was dangerous, it made a warrior vulnerable.

Love had never been a part of his plan. He had not wanted to love the daughter of his enemy, and now it greatly surprised him that he did.

Love. He bristled at the thought of it.

Love could only bring disaster. My own parents proved that. Love killed them both.

He wandered into the empty dining hall. Memories of Caitrín lingered in this room like the puff of smoke after extinguishing a fire. In his memory, he saw the furniture strewn about by the fight when the women of the clan armed themselves with cooking pots. The room still echoed with the song Caitrín led. He smiled, then frowned as the image of her made him desire her all the more.

The scruffy dog, who had been befriended by Caitrín, trotted from the shadows of the room, whining as though he'd lost his only friend.

"Ye miss her as well," Connor said to the mutt. He held out a hand to the dog, only to be rewarded with a growl.

Connor needed to find Niall, and short of bellowing his name, the chieftain took the stone stairs two at a time to Niall's chamber on the second floor.

When he reached the room where he expected to find the counselor, he neglected the courtesy of announcing his entrance before barging through the drape that covered the entrance. The room was empty, the sleeping furs stacked neatly as if they had not been touched for some time.

Connor abruptly left and went in search of his friend and advisor. He found Niall near the gate, surveying the warriors' preparations to leave.

"I must go after her," Connor said.

Niall nodded. "Let's talk over a meal. Ye should eat before ye leave."

They returned to the hall, sent a servant to fetch meat, bread and a skin of mead while they retired to Connor's chamber. Niall quickly filled in the details the chieftain wanted to hear, how many warriors had been lost, how many injured, and how much food they had.

"I am anxious to resolve this," Connor said.

The sooner this is done, the sooner I can resume life with my wife.

Connor glanced at Niall and caught him studying his expression. He knew the old man suspected something had happened on the island, but Connor was not ready to tell him he'd taken Caitrín as his wife, nor to admit his feelings for her.

Their marriage was supposed to be all about expedience, not caring, not risk. And certainly, not love.

Rising from his seat, the chieftain walked to the window to look out.

"Something troubles ye?" Niall asked.

Without turning, the chieftain replied, "Aye. While I swam, I heard her call my name as clearly as if she had been next to me. Ever since that, I have had a feeling something is wrong. Caitrín is in great danger, even though she is likely with her father by now."

Niall walked up behind him, and laid a hand on Connor's arm. "Ye have feelings for her?"

"She is my wife!" Connor turned abruptly.

"Aye, that she is," Niall said, lowering his voice, "in more than name only?"

Connor felt torn between his duty to clan and his feelings for Caitrín. He loved her, yes.

However, the urgency of defeating his foes to rescue her might push him toward rash decisions Unlike his father, he would not allow his feelings for her to determine his fate. He must set aside all feelings and focus on a strategic plan.

"Your father faced a similar dilemma, ye ken. When your mother carried ye, and Donal attacked the fortress. The siege lasted much longer than anyone expected and the food supplies dwindled until we were forced to take some action. Her travail began as Malley led the warriors against their enemy," Niall said.

Connor knew how the story ended.

The story was the tale of his childhood. His heart had been engraved with the part about Malley leaving the battle, being wounded on the way back to the fortress.

The warriors brought their dying chieftain to the cave where the baby was about to be born, how his father's last breath came just as Connor drew his first breath. He grew up with the burden of being responsible for their deaths, as well as for restoring the clan's honor and avenging his father's death.

He did not need to be reminded of his duty.

Niall irritated him for comparing the two situations, for implying that Connor would allow feelings for a woman, especially the daughter of his enemy, to impair his judgment.

The situation was different now.

His wife was not expecting their child. She didn't even know they were married.

Should he fail, she could remain with her father and still be married to the highest bidder.

Should he succeed ... he could not foresee the direction that path might take.

What troubled him most was the feeling that even though he had done what he could to protect her, it had not been enough.

She was gone. Slipped through his grasp like the icy waters of the river. Was she in danger now? Was she back in her father's tower, completely unreachable to him? Her father would never make the mistake of allowing her out unguarded again.

For the first time in Connor's life, he resented the course he had taken. He had spent too many years seeking revenge on his enemy. Suddenly, he wanted something different.

"We must end this war," Connor said quietly.

Niall agreed. "So, what plan do ye have?"

A late, sleepy sun spread golden-rosy fingers across the mountains grabbing a hold to pull itself over the horizon as the two huddled together intent on coming up with a strategy that would defeat Basta, rescue Caitrín and end the war with Donal.

A mountain zephyr, completely without logical direction, whipped across their path first one way, then the completely opposite. Connor could not have anticipated the weather on the other side of the cleft would be drastically different than that in the valley. Long sheets of rain as gray as a winter day and nearly as cold pelted them as soon as they emerged from the mountain passageway.

Although the trek down the mountain was not easy, it was rarely this treacherous. The fianna struggled against rain and wind made the horses nervous forcing the warriors to strain to control them on the slippery path. Connor moved among his men, encouraging and instructing them.

"We have only a short distance before we reach the slopes and can ride. Hold onto the horses."

They all knew the dangers. One misplaced foot, one slip of a man above and the whole group could go down with him. Connor rallied them as they fell in line behind him, following him out of respect as well as kinship. They'd been with him through much worse.

They needn't have worried about being detected by any of Basta's warriors who might be lurking in the area. Even though the weather made the whole mission more miserable, Connor silently thanked the gods for providing cover for his warriors.

He pulled his sodden brat around himself against the chill of the rain and wind. No need to pull out his sword yet, they had not seen any signs of others.

Connor's fianna moved slowly and silently through the downpour until the steep, rocky path began to level out across gently rolling, grass-covered hills. This path, though easier, still held danger for the horses whose feet could slide on the wet grasses, or be trapped in unseen mud holes.

Fortunately, the rain that greeted Connor's fianna that morning ceased by the time they reached the flatlands. They mounted their horses without a word of command and began to cross the plains.

The chieftain didn't need the sun to guide their direction nor estimate their time. He had made the journey so many times that he knew the landmarks. By the time he signaled the men to slow, their horses were lathered. They stopped well short of the druid's forest where Connor and Caitrín had spent their first night together. From here, the journey would be on foot.

Only that strip of trees and a wide meadow lay between them and the enemy and Connor wanted to take advantage of one last opportunity to plan their approach.

Chapter 41

I stared at the white foam inching up the beach toward my feet.

The tide!

"If you don't want to get wet again, you'd better move," I told myself as I scrambled into my boots, and grabbed my brat, quickly wrapping it around my shoulders.

Less than a foot of beach remained above the water line with angry-looking waves rolling in quickly. I looked up at the cliff to find what looked like hand and toe holds. Certainly, the only avenue of escape.

I can't believe I'm doing this. I can't even sit in the top row of bleachers at the football stadium. Please don't make me climb a rock wall. With no security harness. And no cute muscle-bound trainer ready to catch me.

A brisk breeze arrived with the dawn and whipped my hair across my eyes as I began to feel my way from notch to notch along the face of the cliff.

Don't look down. Whatever you do, don't look down!

I stared straight ahead or a few inches up, but never down. Not even at my own feet. Hand over hand, barely able to use my left arm, I inched my fingers and toes into narrow crevices and pulled myself up.

In spite of the chill in the air, sweat trickled down my temples. My arms ached, and, if it weren't for the soft leather of my tunic, my knees would have been scraped raw by the time I reached the top and climbed over the edge.

Only then did I allow myself to look down. I gasped when I saw how far I had scaled. Easily as far as the cliff Connor had wanted me to climb down in my wedding gown.

Turning away from the dizzying view, I studied the path before me, a slope strewn with boulders, worn smooth from wind and rain. Yellow and white lichen, and tiny pink flowers poked from fissures and cracks between the rocks. Had a master gardener planned this garden it could not be more incredible.

"I guess the only way to go is that way." I wished I had a little dog to accompany me. Even Connor's straggly mutt would have been a good companion. And he certainly would warn me of warriors and wild boars.

I thought ahead to where I must go.

The meadow with its fairy gate ... could I find the portal?

I touched the pocket where my gemstone lay hidden, and felt reassured by its presence. I might still be able to go home. The morning sun pointed my way south.

All I had to do was follow the line of cliffs to the tower, then, in its shadow, look for a meadow of flowers. The portal was there amidst the blossoms. Somewhere.

Find the portal, and I could return to my own time.

This was my big chance.

But what about Connor? Had he survived? Was he now looking for me?

I studied the path along the cliffs, then turned to face the sun, still dripping with dawn's orange hue. Connor's valley lay somewhere in that direction. Could I walk for several days, find the cleft in the rock and Connor's valley? Should I?

Niall's words, "The day will come when ye must make a choice," echoed in my mind.

Is this that day?

Memories of my time with Connor on the island flooded through me, causing my breath to catch in my throat and tears to well in my eyes.

Well, if this is the day of decision, I choose Connor.

I had to know.

Was it real? Our love? My love? Does he love me also?

I tuned east.

I started walking toward the horizon, calculating it would be more than a day's travel on foot. The slope eventually began to level out and moss and lichen gave way to grass and heather. By mid-morning, I came to a meadow that reminded me of the one we had crossed shortly after my kidnapping.

I felt certain it wasn't the same one, but there was a forest at the far side.

As much as I didn't want to go through woods full of wild boars and strange warriors again, there didn't appear to be much choice. If I wanted to continue on a southeasterly course, I had to go through that forest.

I clenched my fists, determined that nothing, not wild animals, nor enemy warriors would stop me from getting back to Connor. I plowed across the meadow into the cool, shaded wood.

Did this glen belong to the demented druid? Recalling the wild boar attack, I considered pulling the dagger out of my boot and keeping it ready. But I knew I could never throw it with as sure an aim as Connor had. I'd be better off running, screaming, climbing a tree, or throwing a stick.

"Lions, tigers, and bears, oh, my," I said, trying to summon Dorothy's courage.

In the forest, I picked my way slowly and quietly as if I were entering the back of a courtroom while the trial was in progress. Beasts, strangers, and a drunken druid didn't need to know I was in their woods.

I found a few nuts that had survived winter's foraging animals. But I didn't know what type of nuts they were and whether I could safely eat them. They served only to remind me I hadn't eaten for a day.

Breaking every rule in the Girl Scout camping book., I was traipsing through a forest with no food or water.

I had not gone far when the sound of laughter startled me.

I quickly bent down to slide the knife from my boot, and cautiously pushed aside the foliage to see a man and woman sitting on a fallen log.

Their light-hearted conversation floated like musical notes across the small clearing. They sat on a log in front of a small fire over which a small animal was roasting on a spit.

It smelled stomach-growling delicious. Any resolve to back away quietly and leave the pair to whatever they were doing instantly evaporated at the thought of food.

I studied them more closely while trying to plot how to steal their breakfast.

Rusty red curls cascaded and bounced across the woman's shoulders, as she threw her head back in merriment at something the man had said. They didn't seem to be the least bit afraid of ferocious boars and evil men or a druid with Alzheimer's?

The young man leaned toward the woman and held her chin as he kissed her. She wrapped her arms around his neck and pulled him closer.

Holy cow! They were going to make out while I was squatting here dying of hunger.

Someone had to break the ice. I rose and lost my balance, and fell through the bush into the clearing.

"O, hello!" I said, followed by, "Sorry to interrupt," as I scrambled to my feet.

The man suddenly jumped to his feet, drew his sword and turned to face me.

"There's no need for that. I'm sorry to have intruded on your privacy, but I've been shipwrecked and, now I'm slightly lost and need help. Could you share your breakfast with me?"

The woman stood and turned toward me.

And, I gasped as I came face to face with my twin.

The two of us moved closer until we stood less than an arm's length apart. The man looked from her to me.

Were it not for my shorter hair, he might not have distinguished between us.

"Do ye have the same father and mother?" the man asked.

I shook my head, unable to find a voice to speak.

No wonder Connor was confused.

I could see minor differences between us, but the casual observer would not be able to tell us apart.

Caitrín didn't have the tiny scars from pierced ears that I had let grow closed years ago when I developed an allergy to the nickel in most earrings. Donal's daughter was less than an inch taller than me and I sensed she might be a few years younger, probably in her late twenties.

If I were being honest, especially with myself, I'd have admitted to having a few more wrinkles at the corners of my eyes, but in the absence of a mirror, I wasn't going to make that claim.

"You must be Caitrín," I finally said.

The young woman nodded. Eyes wide with shock and unable to answer, she opened her mouth, but no sound came out.

"I'm not a fairy."

I had a feeling she might be thinking that. Realizing I could almost read her thoughts was too eerie in itself. I didn't want to ask why we, born thousands of years apart, looked as similar as twins.

Finally, Caitrín stammered, "Who are ye then?"

I had no idea how to explain who I was and why I was here.

"Let's just say, I'm a friend. We'll talk, but alone."

I turned to the man and asked him to leave for a few moments so we could speak privately.

As he left the clearing, I asked, "Do you mind sharing some food with me? I haven't eaten since yesterday morning and I'm starving. Who's the guy, by the way?"

Caitrín motioned for me to join her sitting on the log, and took out a small dagger to cut away a piece of meat. She handle the knife to me, and answered, "My husband. Well, we're not exactly married. But he is the one I want to marry and we have pledged ourselves. Just not before the clan."

"And you've run away together," I finished the explanation as I took a bite of the meat even though it was still very hot.

The woman nodded as color rose in her cheeks.

I was quick to reassure her. "It's okay with me. The problem is, it's not all right with your father. You were supposed to marry someone else, weren't you?"

Caitrín nodded. "How did ye know?"

"Talk of the town," I answered, then noticed the look of confusion on the young woman's face. "Never mind. This meat is so good. Want a bite?"

I handed the dagger back to her and she broke off a piece for herself while I continued our conversation.

"Let's talk about your father, for a moment. What are we going to do about him? He's not too happy with you. And he thinks that Connor—you know Connor, chieftain of the Malley clan?—has kidnapped you. There's a war going on right now over this."

"There's been bad blood between them since before I was born. But why would my father think I am with Connor? I left a message."

"I don't think he got it. So, what do you think about going back and telling your father?"

The woman backed away from me. "I don't think it would be a good idea."

"Well, he's liable to find you anyway. Soon as he defeats Connor, and realizes you're not with him, he'll start looking for you. It's only a matter of time. I could go with you and try to mediate. Perhaps he'll accept the news better than you think. You might even say I was sent here to stop this feud. That's why we look so much alike."

I smiled at the clever explanation I had offered. Made no real sense but in a world where fairies and druids could make magic or mischief, it sounded like a winner to me.

Maybe Donal would buy it also as some sort of celestial occurrence. The gods had sent someone who looked like his daughter to end this clan feud.

Remembering my failed fairy test, I liked this new explanation a lot better. The gods sent me. Which one probably didn't matter. Anyone with any superstitions could easily see the resemblance between Caitrín and me and jump to some wild conclusion. Might work.

Caitrín studied my face. She held her hand up, palm toward me and I did the same. Palms together, Caitrín gasped. I did, too. We really were twins, even though that was physically impossible.

"I know. Like seeing yourself in a mirror, but the glass isn't there," I said. Then I thought about my words and shrugged. "But it's not mirror image either. Oh, well, we've got work to do."

Her eyes told me she didn't know what a mirror was. *Must not have been invented yet.*

"Tell me about your father."

"He's in his tower."

"He has returned already?"

That could only mean one thing. Connor must be dead. Donal had already defeated the clan of Malley.

A shiver swept across me at the thought that the war was over and Connor had lost.

Caitrín nodded. "He waits. Connor will attack, and my father prefers to fight on his own land. The gods of the mountains do not favor him."

"Then, Connor is not dead? How do you know all of this?"

"Aidan goes into the camp at night. That was how we learned my father blamed Connor for my disappearance, and sent warriors to Croaghnac."

"So, now Donal is back, and without the daughter he sought. And Connor, if he is still alive, will bring his warriors here for another round of fighting. We must stop this war."

I paused to see if I had Caitrín's support.

"Don't you see? If it continues, many innocent people will die. Maybe not just this generation, but the next. This feud has already gone too long. The future of your clan is at stake. Both sides have done bad things. But you and I have a chance now to stop it now. Will you help me?"

"Ye are talking to the wrong person," Caitrín said gently, laying a hand on my shoulder. "Save it for my father and Connor."

"Do you think either of them will listen?" I asked.

Caitrín shrugged her shoulders. "Probably not, but what other choice do we have?"

Chapter 42

Donal slammed down an emptied goblet of mead. "By the gods, I have never seen double before, and I've scarcely had three cups of mead. I know I am not drunk!"

He bellowed for a servant to refill his cup, then pointed a finger at me and asked, "Who are ye?"

I shifted slightly and did not answer immediately. Donal walked across the chamber to face Caitrín and me. He was a huge man, both tall and rotund, with little other than his red hair to enforce the claim of his paternity of Caitrín.

He stopped in front of his daughter, and started to raise his hand as if to slap her, but I said sharply, "Don't touch her!"

I knew I couldn't pull off a "because I said so" response should he challenge my command. This man obviously did not respect my judicial authority, and was far more likely to put me to the ultimate fairy test.

But I held my ground on the basis of the "gods sent me" explanation, which I had yet to offer. Fortunately, my stern tone worked sufficiently.

Donal turned, stared at me with a look that might have cowered one of his servants, but not me. Then, he backed off.

Caitrín finally found her voice, saying calmly, "Father, I have returned to tell ye I have married Aidan, and we seek your blessing on our union and the child we will have."

"Child?" His face grew redder, and his fists tightened into white-knuckled balls.

Taken off-guard by her abrupt confession, I gasped.

My, she knew how to add the drama.

Pregnant? Already? Why didn't she tell me this before?

Donal paled, and sat heavily on his chair. A servant rushed in to fill the goblet again. He stared at his daughter, then at me before upending and draining the cup.

"Does this man come to speak on your behalf?"

"No, father. I speak for both of us. And I remind ye that I have loved him for a long time. That I begged ye to consider him long before ye sold me into marriage with a foul, old man. I ran away because I knew I would have to dishonor that contract. I thought that I might save your reputation. I know now that I was wrong and beg your forgiveness."

I hoped the girl's soft-spoken plea for mercy would work. As I watched, Donal's face softened slightly.

The expression in his eyes, however, did not match his words when he said, "I must think on what ye have said. Go to your chamber and take your servant with ye."

Servant? Well, okay, I could deal with that. At least Caitrín distracted him enough he didn't pursue my identity and I hadn't had to use my crazy theory.

And he might have sent us to the dungeon, if they had one.

After they left, Donal dismissed his servants and paced in his chamber. Two women. Close enough in appearance to be twins.

Some strange twist of fate or magic?

It mattered not which.

The stranger could be a fairy for all he cared. He wasn't even angry with his daughter for betraying his plan to marry her to Colum. The warrior was old. He'd be dead soon enough, and then she could marry the man of her heart, if she chose.

By some stroke of luck, Donal now had two daughters.

He felt pleased with himself, although he'd not even had a hand in this. New opportunities presented. He had promised his daughter to two men, and now he had two women to fulfill both bridal contracts.

How could he have been so blessed by the gods!

The women were right—it was time to end the war. And now he had the means to do that. Basta would kill Connor to have Caitrín and, none-the-wiser, he'd get the short-haired look-alike.

Coulm would have his daughter, as was the original plan. As long as neither man found out about the deception, it would work.

But, Donal had to act fast, before his daughter's pregnancy was obvious. Marry them both quickly. The twin stranger first to Basta and then, his daughter to Colum. He summoned the leader of his fianna to send messages to both warriors.

Caitrín's room was near the top of the tower, up a narrow, circular stone staircase that gave me goose bumps as we climbed it in semi-darkness. Exactly the dungeon I had expected, but high in the tower, instead of down below ground. A stark room, dirty, and drafty, with thick walls and narrow, open windows.

Like Croaghnac, the interior did not deliver on a promise of grandeur and beauty fit for a clan king. And Donal himself did not resemble a warrior-chieftain, at least not in the same way Connor did.

Donal reminded me of a weasely con artist who appeared one too many times in my courtroom.

"Just give me one more chance ... I've seen the light. I'll do good this time."

Nope, I didn't trust Donal, the drunk, any more than Sam, the con man.

I walked across the room, looking closely at the furniture, a wooden platform piled with sleeping furs, and a plain wooden box, something like a trunk.

"So, now what?" I asked Caitrín.

Caitrín plopped down on the furs and said, "We managed to get past the warriors in the camp to get here. Father knows I can do the same again any time. He'll post guards this time. So now, we wait. Until he is in a better mood. I've seen this before. He needs time to think, to scheme, to figure out how he can keep the bridal fees and yet, save face with Colum. That's why I told him I was pregnant. That was his out."

"So, you're really not?"

"I don't know."

"Oh, my! At least he can't get a test from the local drugstore."

To the younger woman's puzzled look, I said, "Never mind."

A servant brought in a tray with bread, cheese and a slab of meat that didn't look too appetizing. The cheese had green mold covering one corner. I asked the man if I might borrow his knife to trim the mold away.

He handed me a small dagger and I began to slice the bread, remove the mold and cut the meat. I worked as slowly as possible, pausing to eat a piece of bread, tasting the cheese, offering food to Caitrín.

When my back was turned to the servant, I whispered to Caitrín, "Get rid of him."

Caitrín nodded slightly and said loudly, "Ye may go now, but when ye return, bring us something to drink."

The man left, but I noticed that he lingered outside the door as if he were guarding, or spying on us.

"What are ye doing?" Caitrín asked.

I put a finger to my mouth, signaling Caitrín not to speak, then looked around the room until I found a place to conceal the dagger.

The younger woman understood and moved so that she could block the servant's view should he glance into the room while I hid the knife between a wooden chest and the wall.

"My father did this on purpose, ye know," Caitrín said.

I gave her a puzzled look and Caitrín continued, "Sent us moldy cheese and rancid meat. He just wants to remind me who's in charge."

I picked up the meat and walked to an opening in the wall that served as a window and tossed it out.

"I like ye," Caitrín said, eating a piece of bread while I checked the view from the window.

The window faced the cliff where Aasleigh would someday be. Campfires dotted the landscape where the whitewashed, thatched roofed buildings that would someday cling to the crest.

Someday, there'd be a pub with a crooked sign there, and a bridal shop with a ruby waiting for me, and the spire of the church on that rise, and beyond that a meadow of wildflowers with a portal to the past.

How far away that time and place seemed now.

I laid my hand on the stone ledge at the base of the window and thought of all I had left behind. David was no more than a quarter mile, and two thousand years away.

But I also realized that I no longer missed him or wanted to return to him. A solitary tear slid down my cheek as a lump formed in my throat.

It wasn't David or homesickness that left a gnawing emptiness in my heart. It was Connor.

Where was he? Was he all right? Would I ever see him again?

There could not be two more different men than Connor and David. I supposed I loved them both, but in different ways. Now, it was Connor I wanted. I craved his presence, his touch, his embrace. I wanted a future with him.

David, I simply missed. Separated from Connor, I felt as if some part of myself had been amputated. Something vital was missing, but I wasn't sure what.

I only knew that my heart ached as if it held something new and precious, and fragile. Something that only Connor—both the guardian and the cause of my affection—could cherish and protect.

I loved him.

In that moment, staring at dancing fires on the cliff, I realized how much I loved Connor.

A different love, yes.

I could barely fashion the words to describe it, but I felt it. Deep within, like the tumblers of a lock all clicking together, like the pieces of a puzzle sliding together effortlessly, like a hand fitting into a glove and knowing it was meant to be there.

I whispered his name for the sea breeze to carry across field and forest and mountain range to his ear.

"Connor. I love you."

Brushing away the tear about to slide down my cheek, I scanned the horizon again. The portal between the worlds was out there just beyond the camp in a meadow of wild flowers.

Now I had no desire to search for it. The ruby knew, and was silent in its hidden pocket.

"Why are there such bright fires in the camp?" I asked Caitrín, who had come to the window.

Caitrín yawned, turned away and looked longingly at the sleeping furs. "Those are beacon fires. The warriors will soon be here." She walked toward the bed.

"Warriors other than Donal's and Basta's?"

The girl nodded. "Father has sent for them. For Colum as well. The fires are likely for him. He'll come by boat."

"Okay, so what's Donal up to? Do you suppose he plans to marry you to Colum even though you told him you're carrying Aidan's child?"

Caitrín climbed under the furs and pulled them up to her chin. "I don't know. He must have something planned."

How much do you want to bet it isn't a good something either?

I didn't say so out loud because, even though Caitrín admitted her father's faults, he was still, after all, her father. The mid-day sun wasn't going to chase away the sense of foreboding that clung like a shadow. I retrieved the small knife from its hiding place and sat on the edge of the bed.

Donal was up to something, and it sure didn't feel right. I figured he might ignore Caitrín's claim to be already married and with child, and still marry her to Colum, but why?

Could Donal be hoping to lure Connor from Croaghnac? Would he use me as a hostage?

Darn, why didn't I think of that?

That was a possibility I should have considered before I suggested to Caitrín that we return to the tower. Running one finger tentatively along the blade of the dagger, I watched with fascination as a thin red line turned dark with a single tiny drop of blood.

Connor would walk into the very trap he had planned to lay for Donal. I've got to get out of here and warn him.

I smeared the drop of blood across the blade and handed it to Caitrín. "I have my own dagger," I said, pointing to my boot where a knife was still tucked. "No security scanners in this tower."

Caitrín gave me a puzzled look, and I gestured with my hand for her to ignore my words.

"Caitrín," I said, "is there a way out of here without being detected? Can we get past the guards?"

"Yes," she said. "Why do ye ask? What are ye planning?"

"I'm not sure yet, but I don't like waiting around here for whatever your father has in mind for us. Something's going on outside. I think we need to get out of this tower and investigate."

I didn't know why I felt such urgency. Where we'd go, I also didn't know, but perhaps we could return to the forest where we had left Aidan.

"We need to get away from here as soon as possible."

"Where should we go?"

"You tell me. First, we have to get out of the tower without being seen or stopped. Can you do that? Then, cross the cliffs. Do you think we could make it back to the forest? We did it once, can we do it again?"

Caitrín shrugged and threw her brat across her shoulder.

"Sure. But before we leave ..."

She took out the knife I had given her and sliced off a handful of her own curls.

I gasped. "What are you doing?"

"Let's make it more difficult for my father," Caitrín grinned. "Help me. If ye do not help me, I'll surely make a mess of it. Here," she handed me the knife, "cut it like yours."

"Well, okay, but this is liable to cause you more trouble."

Caitrín laughed. "At least we'll be in it together. I always wanted a sister, and it looks as if the gods have granted that request in a most unusual way."

I picked up a lock of dark red curls hanging down Caitrín's back and cut it to collar-length. Within a few minutes, a pile of hair covered the floor at Caitrín's feet. She ran her fingers through her cropped curls and shook her head.

"It is so much lighter. Why did I never do this before? I love it! Do I look like ye now?"

I stepped back. "Very close. I think someone would have to see us together and know us well to tell the difference."

Caitrín scooped up the pile of her hair and crossed the room to the window where she tossed her curls out and watched them flutter to the rocks below. With a smile of satisfaction she turned back to face me.

"Take off your brat and trade it with me."

I didn't object. I unwound the garment, and handed it and the brooch to Caitrín who did likewise with her own.

"Now, let my father try to marry off one of us. He'll have to determine which one," Caitrín said.

"Let's just hope we can get away before he has the chance to make that choice," I said, returning the small dagger to her. "Ready to try?"

Caitrín nodded. "Come then, let's be off. I know a way. Even better, we'll take a guard with us. Then, I know no one will stop us."

"How are you going to pull this off? A guard? One of your father's warriors? He won't rat on us?"

"By that I take it ye mean tell my father where we are. No, he is completely loyal to me. He loves me."

"I see, I think. But, you sure have a lot of people in love with you." I wasn't jealous, just worried about the wisdom of putting our escape plan in the hands of some teenaged warrior with a crush.

We hurried down the stairs, Caitrín leading the way to a large central room where half a dozen men seemed to be engaged in discussions involving much shouting and gesturing. She motioned for me to wait while she approached one of the warriors and spoke to him. Within seconds, we had our escort who looked and acted very official as he accompanied us through the tower.

Ominous, heavy gray clouds had rolled in from the sea by the time we emerged from the tower. Crossing the cliffs seemed to be the most dangerous part of our journey. We would be easily visible from the tower.

Our path took us directly through the warriors' camps past the beacon fires. Then, there was a broad meadow before we reached the relative safety of the forest. The darkening sky looked as if clouds could open with a deluge at any moment.

I moved alongside Caitrín to speak to her in a low voice that the warrior could not hear. "Do you suppose Aidan will still be where we left him?" I asked.

"I hope so," Caitrín said.

I noticed a worried look in her eyes. "Something's wrong. What?"

Caitrín nodded toward the warriors' camps. "There's more of them than we saw from the tower."

I inhaled sharply. "Not just more, but, wait, there's Basta!"

Both of us stopped suddenly and our guard continued without us. "Down!" I hissed to Caitrín. We both ducked down next to a campfire as if we were checking the food cooking over it, or warming ourselves, both of which anyone examining more closely could tell was not plausible.

"What's he doing here?" I whispered, keeping my head down.

I tugged my brat over my head like some sort of scarf and Caitrín did likewise. But, we would definitely attract attention if we continued to squat next to a fire with cloaks pulled over our heads.

There was nothing, not a tree, or horse, or wagon or tent.

Nothing to conceal us. No way to get past Basta other than to walk past him.

"We've got to get away from here without being seen by Basta," I said.

Chapter 43

Connor glanced toward the sky. Rain.

Both a blessing and a curse. A thick curtain of rain would muffle the sound of their approach, giving them the element of surprise. But it would also increase the chances for disaster.

The gods rarely favored a battle fought in bad weather.

He and Niall huddled with several of the warriors. They planned to divide, Niall taking one group to the south along the cliffs while Connor led his group from the east.

There would be no place for Basta and Donal to go but into the tower or the sea.

Niall and Connor separated from the group for a few private words. "Something has changed," the counselor said.

"Aye," Connor said. "I cannot tell ye what it is."

"Ye didn't mean to love her."

Connor nodded. "I didn't mean to love her, but I do."

Niall laid his hand on Connor's shoulder. "Then, ye must do this. Ye must bring her back. It would only be proper for her to bear Malley sons at Croaghnac."

Niall grinned as he clasped Connor's forearm in farewell. Then, he departed with his company of men, as the sky melted into a constant drizzle that turned the landscape slippery and colorless.

Connor's fianna secured their horses to trees at the edge of the forest, as his men silently slipped into the woods where the canopy of leaves would give them some protection from the storm. They'd wait until they thought Niall was in place, then advance through the woods.

The chieftain sent two warriors ahead to scout the area, and told the others to keep alert. He pulled his sword from its sheath, and strapped a small round shield to his left arm.

Like the others, he had removed his tunic and brat and painted himself for war. Blue streaks that resembled lightning bolts zig-zagged across the broad muscles of his chest and shoulders. He declined face paint. He wanted to be certain Basta and Donal recognized him.

They listened to the sounds of the forest, animals burrowing in until the storm passed, the storm ruffling the tree branches to let occasional rain drops find their hiding places, until the scouts returned and confirmed what Connor suspected.

Basta camped along the rim. Donal had retreated to his tower. And, one of the scouts overheard warriors speak of a celebration.

A wedding feast to be held that night.

Connor knew immediately it would be the wedding of Caitrín and Basta. There was just one small problem ... she was already married to him. And he intended to be her only husband.

Bile rose in his throat. He had given his brother one too many chances.

"A feast will give us the perfect opportunity to surprise them. Spread the warriors out through the forest to wait, but do not relax your guard," Connor told his men.

He selected two runners and sent them south with the news to Niall.

Connor was actually pleased to have the cover of rain even if it did make them more miserable. The storm would also restrict the movements of their enemies. And discourage the wedding celebration which might have to be moved indoors to the tower.

Confine them all to a small space where they cannot escape our swords. That thought pleased Connor.

Connor's closest advisors gathered in a small clearing and Connor joined them, sitting on a fallen log. Someone else had been here, and recently. A small fire pit, although cold, had not been out for long. Connor gestured and three of his men slipped among the trees to find other clues to the presence of the campers.

Within a few moments, one of his warriors returned with a young man who introduced himself as Aidan, son of Hurta, one of Donal's counselors. Connor's eyes narrowed as he considered Aidan's claim to be Caitrín's lover. He had not been one of the warriors who took her from the island, yet somehow, he had been with her earlier that day.

"She wanted to stop the war, and she planned to tell her father we are married," the young warrior said.

Connor heard only two words, "war" and "married."

What?

Caitrín thought she could stop her father by confessing she had married this warrior?

228

How could that be? Had she been married before I stole her? Why had she not told me?

He did not want to hear any more. He did not want to know how Caitrín met with her lover before returning to her father.

Connor did not want to think about Caitrín making a fool of him by acting as a wife. If Donal had used her to set a trap for him, the chieftain of the clan Malley would be certain Donal met his blade.

Basta, too.

Then, Connor would deal with Caitrín. Her betrayal would not go unpunished!

Chapter 44

Caitrín and I squatted to eavesdrop on the warriors' gossip about the celebration.

"We've got to get out of here. Could we be servants sent to gather flowers?" I whispered to her.

She shrugged slightly. "Let's head for the meadow as if we are on a mission and cannot be bothered to stop and explain it to anyone. Just keep your head down and hair covered."

Before we could move toward the meadow, a warrior spied us and approached.

"Who do ye servants think ye are?" he demanded. "The cooking tent is over there." He pointed and grabbed my arm, shoving me in the direction of a group of servants I had not noticed before.

Caitrín hurried after me and together, we disappeared into the cooking tent.

"Okay, we've got a little breathing space now," I said quietly, as I pulled the brat down from my head. "If we can hide in here until the storm starts, perhaps we can escape then."

Caitrín looked around for some task that would look as though we were busy enough not to be disturbed by warriors or the other slaves.

"Here," she said, "Let's work the dough."

We squatted in front of a slab of wood placed on the ground and began kneading two lumps of what had once been white dough before being pummeled by dirty hands and pressed into a dirty block on the ground.

"Remind me not to eat the bread," I whispered as we pushed against the mound and discovered it wasn't easy squatting and working dough near our feet.

We worked as slowly as we could, heads tucked down, stealing occasional glances at the people coming and going past the open entrance to the tent.

"This poor bread will be as rubbery as an old tire before I'm done with it," I whispered to Caitrín.

One of the servants brought us cups of broth and vegetables. Caitrín knew her from the tower, and spoke to her.

"Aye, I recognized ye," the old woman said. "But I knew here must be a reason Donal's daughter is hiding in the warriors' camp. I would not betray ye."

"And we greatly appreciate that, as well as the broth," Caitrín said. "What is going on in the camp?

"We're preparing for a feast, a wedding, tonight. Ye are being married to Basta."

Shock registered on Caitrín's face, but I suspected Donal would not give his daughter to Basta.

No, I'm the one he'll try to push off on Basta.

As soon as the servant left the tent, I shared my fears with Caitrín. "It doesn't make sense for your father to give you to Basta. First of all, he'd get no bride price. And, if what I've heard is true, Colum has already paid for you. No, your father means to marry you off twice. That is, he'll use me to impersonate you in the ceremony with Basta."

"It's meant to be a punishment, I am sure. You to Basta and me to Colum, no matter what I have told him of my love for Aidan."

"Well, in either case, no marriage is going to happen. First, he'll have to find us," I said.

"Not hard to do. We haven't even managed to get beyond view from the tower. There's a camp full of warriors between us with only whatever safety the forest can offer. And, it's beginning to rain."

"I know, but we can do this. Neither one of us is getting married tonight," I said, with what I hoped was enough confidence to convince both of us.

The tent shuddered, the edges of the fabric walls fluttering with the change in the wind. A distant rumble, growing louder by the moment, signaled the approach of the storm. Large drops, a few at first, then more and more as if the rains tested the camp and found it hospitable before moving in for a deluge, splattered on the ground outside the tent.

"Good," said Caitrín, "Rain will help us get past the guards when the time comes."

She pulled aside the tent flap to peer into downpour. "The men have disappeared into tents for shelter from the storm. I think we can slip out and make our way toward the meadow without being seen. We'll get wet, but this may be our only chance."

I agreed and we quickly pulled our brats over our heads, and left the tent, sloshing through the downpour to the perimeter of the camp without encountering any warriors. My heart pounded in my ears, nearly as loud as the rain. I scarcely noticed the cold shower soak through my clothing until my teeth began to chatter.

Could there be a more miserable afternoon? Even Cleveland's lousiest weather didn't seem to be as bad as this.

At the far edge of the meadow, a flicker of movement caught my attention as I peered through the curtain of rain. For a split second, I remembered the wild boar.

As I studied the figure emerging from the forest, I realized it was a man, not animal. I grabbed Caitrín's arm and pulled her down in the knee-high, wet grass. Pointing toward the silhouetted figure creeping through the stormy dimness, I said, "We've got company."

Friend or foe?

We couldn't wait and find out.

Caitrín gestured to our right, and we began inching in that direction, at an angle to both the camp and the advancing warriors. Keeping low, we moved through the grass as the unknown warriors began to creep toward the camp.

At the mid-point in the meadow, Connor's men stood, swords drawn and shields strapped to their left arms. Shouting battle cries, they ran forward, surrounding us while we huddled, as yet unnoticed in the grasses.

The warriors appeared far fiercer than I could ever have imagined. The blue and black designs they had painted on their naked bodies streaked in the downpour. Rain pinged on their metal shields, and their feet thudded as they ran across the sodden field.

I buried my head against my arm as the warriors reached the camp, and began slashing indiscriminately.

A flashback of confusion and pain swept over me. My shoulder ached to remind me of the arrows and screams of another attack. Biting my lip to stop me from crying out for Connor, I froze.

Caitrín grabbed my hand bringing me back to the present.

"We've got to get out of here," she screamed above the din.

Metal clanged against metal, shouts, moans, and grunts filling the air. Two warriors engaged in a sword fight forced us apart as we dodged out of their way.

I slipped on the wet grass, and fell hard trying to avoid landing on my injured shoulder. Above me, two warriors exchanged blows with their swords. I tried to roll away, just as one of them, blood spurting from an abdominal stab wound, thudded to the ground next to me. I stifled a scream and scrambled back to my feet.

Panicked, I looked for Caitrín. A warrior had seized her arm. I lunged for the man, and caught him around the knees, knocking him to the ground. Caitrín squirmed free, picked up the dagger I had dropped, and thrust it into the warrior's chest.

She pulled me up and we prepared to flee. Our actions, however, caught the attention of several other warriors who quickly made their way to us, and captured us. The two men, holding as human shields, faced each other.

Chapter 45

In the camp, the sounds of battle began to diminish. Warriors fought against each other, each side claiming small victories, as the wounded fell to the ground, and the uninjured claimed an enemy's sword.

Then, a drama being played out at the edge of the meadow attracted the attention of both sides.

Two warriors, each painted with different colors of war paint, faced each other. Between them, they held Caitrín and me.

Two identical women, different only in the colors of our clothing. One of us wore the brat of a chieftain's wife. The other, a chieftain's daughter.

The men backed away from each other until they were several arms' lengths apart, but still holding each of us around the waist. Their comrades gathered in a semi-circle behind them.

A lightning bolt split the sky with simultaneous thunder declaring the anger of the gods.

Connor!

I caught a glimpse of him in the flash. My heart jumped into my throat, thankfully blocking a call to him.

"What have we here?" Basta asked, getting a look at the struggling woman pinned in the arms of one of his warriors. "My brother's bride."

"I think not," I answered, thankful that the roar of the storm disguised my voice so that he might not realize he held the one who barely spoke his language.

Basta looked at me, then peered across the space at the woman now being held by Connor. He took a step toward his brother and stared hard, peering through a curtain of rain, then turned back to face me.

Gripping my hair and tilting my face toward his, he demanded, "Who does my brother have?"

When I did not answer, he slapped me across the face. I gasped and said, "Donal will not be happy with someone who harms his daughter."

"Donal's daughter!" Basta snorted. "But which one of ye is Donal's daughter?"

I remained silent, as tears, mingling with raindrops across the stinging imprint of his hand on my cheek. His warrior held me with both arms pinned at my waist, keeping me from wiping my tears or soothing my bruised cheek.

"And which of ye is an imposter about to die?" he asked, holding his sword to my neck.

The rain let up slightly, as a moisture-laden cloud dropped down onto the meadow. Thick mist replaced the downpour, and pea-soup fog crept like a cat rubbing our ankles.

Basta kicked up fluffy, white puffs as he began to pace back and forth, brandishing his sword in my direction each time he turned.

I glanced once in the direction of Connor and Caitrín. He, too, was questioning his captive, but had not struck her.

"How did ye get here?" Connor spoke into Caitrín's ear. He turned her around and leaned toward her face waiting for her reply. One close look at her revealed the answer to him. "Ye are not Caitrín."

"Oh, but I *am* Caitrín!" the startled woman said. "She is not!"

'She is not.'

Connor looked in my direction. *Had she not told him that many times? Not Caitrín, not Donal's daughter.*

But then, who was she?

Connor stared across the gap where fog sidled in and out. The import of his dilemma began to sink in.

He had Caitrín, the woman he had planned to abduct, while his brother had captured the woman Connor had stolen and had married.

When Caitrín shook her arm, he realized he was bruising her without meaning to. He let go of her.

Gesturing toward Basta, he asked the woman, "She did not go with him willingly?"

"Nay," Caitrín answered, her tone implying she was about to add, "fool" to her reply. "We were trying to flee my father before he married one of us to Basta and the other to Colum."

Connor swore softly under his breath. He glanced toward Basta again as he and the other woman completely disappeared in the fog. Both groups of warriors froze where they were. To move about in the poor visibility would be foolhardy since they were close enough to each other that they could not easily discern friend from foe, and near enough to the cliffs that a misstep could be disastrous.

Fog did strange things to sound as well as sight.

The neighing of Niall's horses as he and his fianna arrived bounced across the meadow as if they were a force of hundreds. The moans of injured and dying men added to the confusion.

He thought he heard her voice, calling to him, just as he had heard her when he was on the river.

"Do not move," Connor instructed his men. "And keep alert," he added.

He pulled Caitrín close, not to restrain her, but to offer her protection if needed. He wanted to call out to the woman Basta held, but to do so might endanger her. Basta might not know which woman he had captured. He couldn't risk revealing any information to his half-brother.

Chapter 46

"Send me to my father," I said to Basta. "I will plead your case."

I hoped he wouldn't ask what case because my offer made no sense whatsoever.

He did not reply immediately. I studied his face for any glimmer of similarities to Connor. If I knew more about this man, I might be able to manipulate him into releasing me. They had the same midnight black eyes, but even the harshest of Connor's glares could not match his brother's.

Evil saturated Basta, and oozed from his pores. Even looking at him sent a shiver down my back.

I did, however, have one hope. I could see that my words confused Basta. He wasn't the brightest light bulb in the package. That, I could exploit.

"I must think on this and, in any event, we cannot move until the fog clears," Basta said, signaling to my captor to release me.

I promptly sat down right where I had been standing. Let him try to move an uncooperative woman.

If I had to spend the night there, I didn't mind. I didn't want to move from the spot from which I had last seen Connor. He was out there in the fog. So close I might be able to hear him breathe, and he hear me whisper his name.

I peered into the thick gray curtain willing it to lift for just one glimpse.

Basta, however, wasn't about to spend any time sitting on the ground next to me. He spotted a tent, partially standing, like a ghostly sentinel, and he motioned for two warriors to move me to the tent until he decided what to do next.

What he and his warriors did not realize, was that the back of the tent had been torn open. The men shoved me inside and took their places at the entrance.

I wasted no time sneaking out. The fog was so heavy that I could not see the warriors or even Basta himself who could not have been more than two feet from me when he faded from view.

I huddled low to the ground, hidden in the thickest gray swirls while I crept in what I hoped was the direction that would take me from the camp and the cliffs. I did not know who belonged to Basta, to Donal or to Connor so I tried to avoid all of the warriors.

In this crazy weather, they might slash first and ask questions later.

Barely able see my own feet as the fog blanketed the grasses of the meadow, I slowed. Several times I paused when I heard voices. Most were muffled, but occasionally words came through as clearly as if the person speaking was standing next to me.

Caitrín's voice came first.

"Basta's warriors are sounding an alarm. That must mean they've lost her. She's managed to escape."

I froze and looked around to see if I could find her or Connor. Scenes shifted with the fog. I could see the tower one minute, then a few tents, and for a split second, the forest. But each view dissolved quickly in the ever-moving cloud.

Connor said, "In this fog? I hope she has sense enough to stay in one place."

I did not.

I could not. There was no way to tell friend from foe, safety from peril.

I kept moving, creeping in what I hope was the direction of the forest.

Within moments, the steady thud of a drum bounced through the fog. When I felt the low pulsating rumble of the bodrhan, I remembered the fairy music and drumbeat that had brought me to this place.

Connor. He must know I have escaped Basta, and ordered the bodrhan to help me find my way to him.

I turned my head in the direction of the sound, and began inching toward it. But the fog played games with hearing as well as vision.

First, I heard the drum to my right, then to my left. At a distance, then close. I dared not call out to Connor. I was hopelessly lost in the thick cloud of swirling mists when, a ram's horn pierced the night, as if it blew within arm's length from me.

Who? Which warriors sounded the horn?

The ruby in my slip pocket suddenly came alive, warm and vibrating. I clutched it through the fabric, and begged it to help me find Connor.

Then, without warning, the cloud of fog lifted for a split second, and I saw Connor and Caitrín not more than twenty yards away.

"Connor!" I called and waved my arm.

Connor looked directly at me, and held out his hand. I took a step toward him when blinding pain stabbed through my head like lightning, and the ground opened beneath my feet, sucking me into a vortex of nothingness.

I fell to my knees, squeezed my eyes shut and covered my ears with my hands.

"Connor!" My cry caught in my throat as I was swept into chaos.

Chapter 47

How long I had been unconscious, I didn't know, but when I blinked the head-splitting pain away, and opened my eyes, I saw a soft blue, unblemished sky above me. A thick, green hedge shaded my face from bright sunlight. I rolled to my side and sat up. The ruby, still clutched in my hand no longer felt warm, nor pulsated.

My clothing was still wet, and my boots mud-covered, but the fog had lifted. I reached out one hand toward Connor, and looked in the direction where he had been standing. A tree grew where I thought Connor should have been.

I glanced over my shoulder in the opposite direction. Behind the hedge, stone monuments leaned against one another in a crowded, little cemetery overshadowed by a stone church that looked vaguely familiar.

I must be mistaken.

I shook my head, squeezed my eyes shut and opened them again.

Connor?

The warriors, Basta, Caitrín, had all disappeared with the fading drumbeat.

The church, the graveyard.

No!

I looked again for Connor, and whispered his name, spoke his name aloud, shouted his name as the realization that I had once again traveled through the portal began to sink in.

I'm back in Aasleigh!

But when? Is David here?

Feeling no lingering ill effects from the pain that had stabbed through my head only seconds before, I stood and walked slowly through the graveyard toward the church.

The doors were locked, the priest and David apparently not there. Stumbling down the stone steps, I hurried up the cobblestone road to Norah Kelly's shop.

I pounded on the shop door frantically.

"Mrs. Kelly!" I turned the knob, but the door was locked. The curtains were drawn over the windows so that I couldn't see inside.

Please, Norah, be here.

"Coming ..." I heard her faint call.

She opened the door and gasped, "Oh, child, where have you been?"

She ushered me into her shop. Walking past the mirror where I had, not long before modeled a wedding dress, I caught sight of my reflection.

I barely recognized myself. My hair, normally cropped short, looked ragged and unkempt. I tucked a wild strand behind my ear. The haunted look in my eyes wouldn't be so easily tamed.

"Connor," I whispered his name.

His image appeared in the mirror and I reached up to touch the glass as if I could stretch across time to him. I could still feel his presence, as though he might come through the door after me at any moment. I imagined his embrace. His fingers entwined in my curls, tugging gently as he pulled me into his arms.

I must go back. I'm really not supposed to be here.

I looked at the door, and wondered if I should or even could return to the portal and cross back to Connor's time.

Then I heard the Norah clinking in the kitchen and vaguely recalled hearing her say something about putting on the tea kettle.

It sunk in then.

The portal had closed. I knew it. I felt it in my gut. Suddenly, I was just as trapped in this time as I thought I had been in Connor's.

I began to shiver, whether from shock or having been soaked in the other time.

Norah led me to the kitchen, and wrapped a blanket around my shoulders, sitting me on a wooden chair at her kitchen table. I welcomed her gentle silence as she rattled about the room, pulling tea cups and saucers from a shelf, shaking tea leaves into small round balls, pouring hot water into the teapot.

She seemed so calm, and reassuring, making me feel as if I had just dropped by to chat.

How could I tell her I had left in the middle of a clan war and travelled across centuries? How could I tell her I had fallen in love with a man who lived centuries ago? How could I explain what had happened over the past ...?

Breaking my silence, I asked, "What is the date?"

"June 21," she said. "You've been gone for seven weeks." Her words sounded so matter-of-fact that I winced slightly.

Seven weeks that felt like a lifetime.

Norah set a cup of tea before me. I hadn't realized how much I missed hot tea. And china cups. And the friendly warmth of a cottage kitchen.

"You know where I've been?"

I retrieved the now cold and quiet ruby from my pocket and placed it on the table next to my cup.

She nodded and sipped her tea, before saying, "Your grandmother went through the fairy gate. No one believed her stories. After many months, she returned. She couldn't stay here. That was when she went away from Aasleigh for good."

"She left the ruby here?"

"She was afraid of it. She thought it was a touchstone, she said, a guide through the portal. And, she didn't want to ever wander through the portal again. I always wanted to go, out of curiosity, I suppose, but the stone never spoke to me."

"David? Is he still here?" I couldn't wrap my brain around the loss of seven weeks of my life.

"Nay, he stayed for days, a couple weeks, looking for you."

She stood and rummaged through a pile of papers on the far edge of the table. "Here," she said, handing me a piece of paper. "He made these flyers. Everyone in the village searched for you. I knew what had happened. I knew where you'd gone, but the others, even the villagers, wouldn't believe me. They hadn't believed Moira either. So I kept it to myself."

"Did you know I would return?"

She shook her head.

Did she know I didn't want to come back?

"I don't know what to do now," I said. I looked at my soaked and filthy brat, the once beautiful shift, the leather boots strapped around my calves.

"I'll find you something to wear that won't shock the others."

She led me to a closet and pulled out a blouse and skirt that were slightly too large but doable for the time being. I'd lost weight. I could tell without a scale.

"A hot bath will help, as well," she said. "There's no rush notifying the authorities. Let's get you cleaned up first, then we'll go find Father

Flaherty. He'll know what to do next."

Norah was right.

Tears mingled with bath water as I scrubbed away layers of accumulated dirt. Even though the water was warm and rose-scented, I remembered the pool on the island, and swimming with Connor. I didn't want to dwell on the love-making that followed. Those memories were too tender and precious.

I'll never ... Connor is gone. Gone forever. Forever.

We promised each other forever. What happened?

I folded the shift and brat, not certain what to do with them. Norah suggested I leave them with her.

"To guard your secret," she added.

I had to wear the boots—she had no shoes my size for replacements. But the boots actually went well with the borrowed skirt, and only close examination would reveal they were hand-tooled, and not of this century. I slid the ruby into the skirt pocket. Unlike my grandmother, I wasn't afraid of the stone, and didn't want to be separated from it.

It was my only link to Connor.

Running my fingers through wet, tangled curls, I surveyed the reflection of my borrowed outfit, and continued to feel disoriented. Norah laid a sweater over my shoulders.

"Ready to go?" she asked gently.

"Ready," I answered, trying to puff up some courage.

At the rectory, a round, apple-cheeked woman greeted us. "Ye'd be seeking Father Flaherty, would ye? Come in, I'll fetch him."

Norah left me there. "You'll be fine, now, dearie. Just give yourself some time to adjust. Come see me before you leave, if you want."

I hugged her before stepping into the rectory. A door in the back of the house closed and I heard voices. Whispering. I'd hear a lot more hushed words in the future, I felt certain.

Over tea and biscuits, I tried to answer Father Flagerty's questions, but every explanation sounded foreign to my ears. I wasn't even sure I could trust my own command of English and frequently reverted to Gaelic.

Slowly, the story came out, in bits and pieces, often contradicting itself as I spoke. But I could not tell him the truth. I could not explain Connor and Basta and Caitrín.

I said I had been kidnapped, and had somehow escaped my captors. I didn't know who they were, where I had been held, or why they had taken me. I did describe the wild boar attack, a cave, an island in the middle of a river with enough detail to give credence to the story. I didn't know how far my abductors had gone, nor even what direction they had taken. I couldn't tell how I had managed to escape and get back to Aasleigh.

Fortunately, Father Flaherty didn't press me for too many details, especially when my voice cracked and my body shuddered as if I might break into a thousand pieces.

When he left the room to speak with his housekeeper about finding a place for me to stay, I decided I'd better come up with a simple set of details and stick to one explanation.

My mind felt clearer now. I no longer felt as if I should run back to the meadow to seek the portal.

This would be the first of many times I'd have to tell the same story. Memory loss from trauma sounded like the best bet, at the moment. The fewer details, the less I'd have to remember every time I repeated the story.

Norah was right—no one would believe me if I told the truth.

As soon as I was alone in a rented room over the village pub, I rehearsed a story a few times. I stuck to it no matter what questions the authorities asked.

"A big man, brown hair, dark eyes, straggly mustache. I don't know how many companions he had. Nor where he took me. I don't know if I could identify him. I spent some time in a cave, and some time in some sort of building. No, I can't lead you there. I don't know where it was."

I was equally vague about my escape. I could not explain my sudden reappearance in Aasleigh. I simply shrugged and smiled weakly, adding, "Perhaps I was drugged some of the time."

Any prolonged interviews brought tears and near hysteria that anyone who knew me would recognize as faked. There being no clinic or hospital in the district, no one gave me a physical examination nor discovered the barely-healed arrow wound on my shoulder.

After three days of questioning and getting nowhere, the authorities agreed to allow me to leave Ireland. Father Flaherty had contacted David who sent my passport and arranged my transportation to Dublin and back home.

From the moment I stumbled into the rectory until I left Ireland for good, I was never left alone for more than a few minutes. Even in a rented room, the pub owner's wife kept an eye on me. I could not have gone to search for the portal or the druid's forest or Croaghnac.

I stared at the ruins of Donal's tower, the only link to Connor, other than the ruby in my pocket, but I knew no one would permit me to wander among the stones and rubble that had once been Donal's home.

Everyone thought my mental status was precarious. The truth was, my emotional state was in worse shape. I could think clearly and rationally, but I grieved. Yet no one else, save Norah Kelly, recognized that I had lost something irreplaceable.

My heart ached as old feelings of abandonment crept from the well-guarded corners returning me to the child whose parents had died suddenly.

Every morning, I searched the horizon for a glimpse of Connor sweeping in on horseback to take me away. As the sun set behind the tower at night, I thought I could see Donal standing at a window in his tower.

I wondered what had become of his red-haired daughter, my twin. And Aidan her husband. I constantly thought of Lia and my promise to be her friend.

My only solace was the gemstone, which remained strangely quiet. I could no longer peer into its depths. It was a cold rock in my hand. I finally buried it in the bottom of a borrowed suitcase with a nightgown Norah had sent over for me.

I inquired about seeing her before I left, but was told she had gone away for a few days. Apparently, without a word of explanation or farewell, and no one knew where she'd gone.

I didn't blame her. I must have aroused memories of my grandmother that Norah never wanted to relive. Even though she was very young, she remembered much about Norah.

Sadness lingered in my heart, but mostly, I wondered about the world I had abruptly left.

How did the war end?

Did Connor survive?

Did he marry Caitrín as he planned? Did she bear him sons?

I spread my hands across my own flat abdomen. *Was there a chance ... could I be pregnant?*

Such thoughts set off a whole new round of questions, and of heartache. I moved through the mechanics of life, answering endless queries, eating, sleeping, longing to be somewhere else, sometime else with someone else.

Why can't I be glad I'm back in my own time? Why can't I let go of Connor?

I ached to return to the churchyard, and to look for the portal. I even contemplated riding a horse across the countryside to search for Croaghnac. But the authorities wouldn't permit anything like that. They were anxious to get me out of Aasleigh, and Ireland.

In my heart, I knew any search would be useless.

The portal had closed, and Connor was gone forever. It was time to shut the door on him, and what our life together might have been. I squeezed shut my eyes and buried my face in my hands as the car drove me away from Aasleigh.

Reporters met me at the airport, but I refused any interviews and dodged the photographers. Jostling through the noisy crowd to board my flight distracted me from having to say, "Good-bye" to Connor for the last time.

But as the plane flew over Ireland, I stared at the green squares of land beneath the wings.

He was there. Two thousand years ago.

In my heart and mind, he was still very much alive. I heard his voice say, "Yours shall be the name I call in the night and your face the one I look for in the morn."

And I whispered in response, "I shall serve ye and the honeycomb shall taste sweeter because it comes from my hands."

Where did these strange words come from?

I could not piece together where I had heard them or why I had answered with an equally strange vow.

"Good-bye, Connor," I finally whispered as the rocky shore of Ireland disappeared behind a cloud. A solitary tear rolled down my cheek. I touched the plane's window as if I could reach out and place my palm against his.

Then, I forced myself to let go of him.

Chapter 47

David met me at the Cleveland airport to drive me home.

"So, you were kidnapped. I knew it. How did you get away? Did they hurt you? I mean, in any way?"

I knew what he implied. "Had I been raped?"

"No, I wasn't hurt. At least, not by the kidnappers. I ...um... there was nothing like that."

I rubbed my shoulder, but didn't tell him about the arrow wound. Not yet, at least. I wasn't ready to talk about everything.

"I'd like to know why no one has been caught. Couldn't you show the authorities where you were held? We scoured the area and found nothing. I felt terrible about having to leave before you were found, but they assured me after such a long time with no clues at all that the chances were you were dead."

"It's okay. I understand." I shrugged. "There were several different places. But, I don't think the kidnappers will be found. They're long gone by now."

"You don't sound sad about that." David looked as if he expected a denouncement of my abductors.

I sighed. "I'm just tired. It was a long trip. There's a lot I have to tell you. Later. Thank you for sending the airplane ticket. I wasn't thinking very straight when I got back to Aasleigh and to tell the truth, I wasn't sure what to do to get ... home."

For some reason, I had thought David would still be in Aasleigh waiting. It hadn't occurred to me that weeks had passed, and that David had left. And had taken my passport, clothing and ticket with him.

"You can tell me everything about your adventure. I have all evening. I'm just disappointed the law didn't catch up with those criminals. If I could have gotten my hands on them, there would have been a speedy trial and the maximum punishment."

David was unchanged. As self-possessed and controlling as usual.

"Yeah."

I could not imagine David taking on Connor. I had no doubt who'd win that contest. We rode the rest of the way to my house in silence. David unlocked the door and I walked in feeling as though I had never been there before.

I looked around my home. Everything had changed and yet, nothing had changed. Each piece of familiar furniture looked foreign. But, it was the same place I had left two months earlier. I had disconnected and wasn't sure how to plug back into my own time and place.

David made a pot of coffee, without asking if I wanted some and sat down at the kitchen table as if he were prepared to camp there until I talked.

What could I say?

What could I safely tell him without revealing that I had fallen in love with my captor?

That even now I longed to be with him, to marry him and give him children? That I might even be pregnant with his son, heir of the chieftain of clan Malley?

There was no way to explain Connor, or Donal, or the clan war, and certainly not the time portal. And Caitrín. I wanted more than anything to keep her to myself, as if she were part of me. My secret twin.

Yet, I had to tell David everything.

One person had to know what I had experienced. I had to be able to trust him if we were going to try to rebuild our relationship. Otherwise all that had happened would only have been a dream, a nightmare.

In the telling, it became real again. My words came out in a jumble along with tears, as if the dam I had so carefully constructed to contain a flood of emotions burst.

But I didn't share about the ruby. Only Norah and Linda knew about it.

As I spoke, images of Connor kept me from seeing David's look of disbelief turn to horror. When I finally finished talking and looked at him, I realized he didn't understand. He didn't believe me.

He never would.

Jealousy tarnished every word he heard. And rightly so, I supposed. Connor, even though he had been dead for several thousand years, was a very real threat to David.

David had closed his mind to my story.

"Tell the truth," he begged, "Premarital jitters, one last fling before settling down, even being kidnapped would be better than this nonsense about a fairy gate, first century warriors and some sort of war. None of that makes any sense."

Nothing ye say makes sense.

I could hear Connor's rough-edged voice telling me the same thing.

My heart ached with loss, with memories. The loss of all of my dreams, of my past, my present, and my future. I had only uncertainty left.

Both men were correct.

Nothing in my whole life made any sense.

"And what am I supposed to do with this Connor, this man who kidnapped you? You sound as if you liked him. There's a name for that, you know." David's face reddened with anger.

"Stockholm Syndrome," I said wearily.

Chapter 48

"It's eighty-six degrees already this morning on the northcoast. Gonna' be a hot one in ole' Browns-town today." The radio dee-jay's banter annoyed me.

I didn't need to be reminded this would be another oppressively hot and humid day. What was with this Indian summer? Didn't the weather know fall had started?

"What am I doing here?" I asked myself aloud as I pulled into my parking space at the courthouse.

I trudged into my office, conscious of the stares from courthouse employees, lawyers and even total strangers. Everyone had heard about the time-traveling judge with PTSD.

I no longer had to turn down talk-show invitations, and only rarely caught a tabloid reporter at my front door. But the wild tale of my abduction by a two-thousand-year-old warrior remained fresh in everyone's mind.

Why had I ever told David, I asked myself over and over?

Because my period had been late.

I had thought, I had even hoped.

But, it was simply a few days late, and by that time, I had confessed the entire story to David. If I had been pregnant, I desperately thought that I needed one person, just one person to be sympathetic and comforting.

Unfortunately, it wasn't David.

He had not believed my story. He had not accepted a word of it. And worst of all, he didn't keep anything to himself.

Even Linda distanced herself when I tried to explain everything to her. She was already convinced I'd had a combination of nervous breakdown-alien-abduction-pre-wedding fling, with some sort of PTSD now. I suspected Bill just didn't want her around me in case my mental illness was contagious.

I'd been back in Cleveland for weeks now, but I couldn't hear any cases until I completed a psychiatric evaluation and was cleared by a panel of fellow judges.

No one wanted to take a chance some defendant would demand a retrial on the basis of the judge's psychological problems. Never mind that I personally knew a judge who was as psycho as any of his defendants, and several lawyers who would be perfectly comfortable in a locked ward of the state hospital for the criminally insane.

I went to my office to work on old files while I waited for what I liked to call my "sanity" hearing scheduled in early October. Two psychologists had seen me for several visits. All that remained was the judges' review, but vacations took precedence in August. After Labor Day, I hoped to be back to the bench by the end of September, but that looked less and less likely as dates kept shifting.

I glanced at the calendar on my desk. David hadn't called for a week. At first, he had been solicitous and sympathetic, at least in public.

When we were alone, he was suspicious, jealous and angry. Everyone wanted to blame some psychological disorder. He wanted to kill someone. Anyone would do. Especially if he was a kidnapping shepherd.

All I knew was that when I spoke about Connor, my voice softened and tears flooded my eyes again. I had to be very careful what I said, and how I said it.

Why couldn't they understand I had loved this man who saved my life more than once? And I secretly continued to love him ... in my dreams. And memories. And thoughts.

"Well, I can't compete with a criminal whether he is alive and well today or died several thousand years ago. Get some help," David said as he left the last time I saw him.

I couldn't focus on my work, had anyone even allowed me to return to it. At first, I wondered about being pregnant and imagined having Connor's baby and raising him on my own.

Now, my mind, my thoughts, my heart simply lingered in Ireland. The grief that flooded over me did not abate with time. My body had returned, but I left too much of myself behind.

I didn't know what else to do so I went to the office every day.

Go through the motions. Make them think you're okay.

That was better than hiding at home all the time. I plopped down my briefcase on the desk and walked over to the window. Putting my palms on the sill, I looked out the dirty glass at the city.

But, I saw the valley beneath Croaghnac, the meadow burgeoning with spring colors, the slate-colored strip of river cutting across it. Beltane tents with fluttering banners. A huge horse with a warrior astride galloping at breakneck speed across the land.

A small wicker boat and an island where I watched him sitting at the edge of an icy pool. He held a hand out to me, summoning me to swim with him.

I shook my head, and the images dissolved, leaving only the taste of love souring in my mouth.

Something had to change. I couldn't go on like this thinking of him, dreaming about him, seeing him, wanting him.

I could resign from the bench. Move to another city and practice law.

But, my name and face had been splashed across supermarket tabloids across the country. Interviewers called less often now, but I still had offers for my story. Book deals, movie options, Dr. Phil, a reality television series.

How long would it be before everyone forgot how I'd disappeared for seven weeks and come back with stories of life in the first century?

My credibility, my career, my plans for the future disappeared the moment I landed in Cleveland.

And to think how I desperately wanted to find the portal and return to this life.

Why did I ever want to come back here?

A rogue cloud whisked across the sun momentarily damping the glare of bright sunlight on the concrete beneath my office.

Rain today?

I thought of the storm that separated me from Caitrín and Connor the day I returned. Every time I tried to put Connor out of my mind, something triggered a memory.

A love song on the radio, a purple velvet sunset, a quick rain shower. A glimpse of the ruby nestled in my jewelry box.

Anything. Everything.

I found myself thinking in Gaelic and having to translate into English. I dreamed every night of riding bareback, cradled in Connor's arms across the heather-covered hills. I felt his arms around me, his breath on my neck, his kisses on my lips.

I heard his voice. "I give ye that which is mine to give and freely share all with ye. Yours shall be the name I call in the night and your face the one I look for in the morn. As long as I live and breathe I shall honor ye and keep ye in my heart."

When had he said those words to me?

I couldn't recall, but his voice echoed through my memory. I knew he had to have said that. I couldn't have dreamed it. But, when, and what did the words mean?

Had he loved me? He'd never said as much.

I'd seen love in his eyes.

I'd heard it in his voice when he called me from the dead. I'd felt it in his touch.

He loved me.

He must have loved me. I stroked my shoulder absent-mindedly, feeling the scar, the reminder of my journey.

Turning away from the window, eyes brimming with unshed tears, I surveyed my office, once a busy, happy place, a symbol of my accomplishments. Now it seemed empty and foreign. Like my home, nothing felt right.

I didn't belong here anymore. And, nothing I could do would ever make things right again.

No amount of counseling. No self-talk to put it all behind me and move on. I was frozen in time, wallowing in doubt, confusion, grief and fear.

Yes, that's it, fear.

I couldn't let go of Connor because I loved him, and I feared I'd never know a love like that again. I felt his presence and heard him call my name. Even greater, however was my fear that he had not loved me.

Me, not Caitrín.

Another voice intruded on my memories.

There will come a time when ye must make a decision.

Suddenly, I knew, with all the clarity of the Irish sunrise, what I had to do. For the first time in weeks, I felt a wave of energy surge through me. I flipped open my phone book and ran a finger down the page until I came to the first of three numbers I needed to call.

"I'm going out of town," I said calmly.

"Ireland?" My attorney asked with caution in his voice that sounded as if he wanted to reach through the phone lines and to stop me from making a terrible mistake.

"I think Paris might be better." I kept my tone light and normal-sounding. "I just need to get away for a few weeks, and sort out my priorities. Some place where I can be anonymous. You understand," I said. "I'll send you a letter with some matters I need for you to handle while I'm gone."

Next, I called a real estate agent, and put my house on the market. The agent, a friend from high school years asked the same thing, "Going back to Ireland?"

I started to evade the question again when my friend said, "If I were you, I would."

"Why?" I asked her.

"It's so romantic!"

I laughed. Nothing about life in the first century seemed romantic.

Nothing, but the chieftain who had waited for me among the wildflowers, who had saved me from a wild boar, who had made love to me next to an icy pool, who had showed me how to light a fire.

I made arrangements to get a key to her and sign whatever paperwork she needed.

The image of Connor holding out his hand to me would not leave me. He never said he loved me, and I had not asked.

One minute I was certain he did not, the next minute, I knew he did.

The possibility that I had turned my back on the love of my life gnawed on my heart.

I had to know.

If I tried to start a new life here, if I ever found another man to love me, I'd be haunted the rest of my life by Connor, and not knowing whether he had loved me. I had so many questions that I needed to answer.

What happened to him?

And Caitrín?

Did they manage to escape Basta and Donal?

Did Connor marry Caitrín after all? Or did she run off with Aidan?

There were no birth and death certificates I could check. No graves, no mention in some history book. These were ordinary people who had lived and died thousands of years before.

They left behind their names only, Malley became MacMalley and Donal gave his descendants the name O'Donnell. I had inherited both MacMalley and O'Donnell blood from my grandparents.

The war between the clans must have ended at some point. I smiled at the thought of Connor and Donal making some sort of truce. Probably at the birth of Connor's first son from Caitrín.

Yes, that must be what happened.

Unless Basta carried on the family name.

My last telephone call booked a flight to Paris, leaving that night. I didn't dare fly directly to Dublin for fear the press would find out, and some well-meaning person block my plans.

I quickly jotted instructions to my lawyer and asked my secretary to mail the letter for me. The temperature had climbed to eighty-eight with no hint of a lake breeze in the two hours since I had parked my car.

I climbed in, listened to the engine purr as if this would be one of the last times I heard it. Then, I drove to the bank, closed all my accounts, including my IRAs, ignoring the lecture I received from the back officer about the penalty for cashing in retirement accounts before the proper age. I had one credit card still open, with instructions to my lawyer to pay it off next month. The proceeds from the eventual sale of the house would go into a charitable trust.

My last stop before going home was a pharmacy where I bought antibiotic ointment, vitamins, toothpaste and travel-sized bottles of shampoo, and a few other necessities for a trip.

Packing was the easiest part of the day. I felt as though a huge burden had been lifted and my heart sang as I folded clothing into a suitcase. I placed the ruby in a box, and tucked it into my purse. Not willing to let it out of my reach since it might be the key to unlock my trip through the portal.

I should take Lia something.

I settled on hair ribbons and a hairbrush, which I tucked into my suitcase along with the purchases from the pharmacy.

I called a taxi. "Take me to the airport," I instructed the driver. "No, wait. There's some place else I'd like to go first."

I gave him the address of a house I hadn't visited in years.

When the taxi pulled up in front of the small red-brick home where I had grown up, I asked the driver to wait for a few minutes. I stepped out and stood on the sidewalk staring at the porch like I was ten years old again and about to dash up the three concrete steps to the narrow porch.

In my memory, I saw myself burst through the screen door and race through the hall to the kitchen where grandmother Moira would be starting dinner preparations.

I missed her so much.

"I've got something to tell you, Grandmother," I whispered.

I wanted to tell her about Connor, about the love I'd found in Ireland. Somehow, Moira would understand. Her blues eyes would sparkle, and I imagined what she'd say, "Follow your heart, darling."

Even if it means leaving everything behind?

Even if it means going back to Ireland to find the portal?

Strangely, I knew what Moira would answer to even these most impossible questions.

But, Grandmother, I'm frightened. That's a scary place to live. People die young of diseases we don't even have.

Women have no rights. There's a clan war. It could be centuries before the MacMalleys and O'Donnells learn to live together.

Moira, herself a MacMalley and her husband an O'Donnell, would wrap her arm around my shoulders, and say, "If you love him, you'll work everything out."

That's why you left me the ruby, isn't it?

Somehow you knew I would cross the portal. Did you ever wonder what your life would have been like if you had stayed? Did you find love there also?

My heart sang. For the first time in weeks, everything felt right, the tension that knotted my stomach into a lump drained away. I climbed back into the taxi without looking back at the house I would never see again.

"The airport," I said. "I'm ready now."

As I gazed out the cab window at the city, I felt a momentary pang of doubt.

What if I got to Aasleigh and couldn't find the portal? What if the portal didn't open again? What if I landed in the wrong time and couldn't find Connor?

What if I got there and discovered he had married the real Caitrín? What if he died in the battle with Donal?

No, I shook my head, Connor had survived.

I felt it as surely as if he stood before me, ready to scoop me into his arms. Only one question remained in my heart.

What if he doesn't really love me after all?

Chapter 49

By the time I arrived at the Cleveland airport, fear and doubt wre close to taking over, and I almost changed my mind about leaving.

But, as I waited in line at the ticket counter, I noticed a young girl who reminded me of Lia. The child clung to her mother's hand as her body language shouted, "Don't leave me!"

I knew then I had to go back. Even if Connor didn't want me, Lia deserved a chance at childhood, with a mother.

Me, not a maternal bone in my body, wanted to be a mother to Lia.

The flight landed in Paris early the next morning, and by then, I had a plan in place. I'd spend a few days in Paris, use my credit card to leave a paper trail, then disappear to London, then maybe Edinburgh.

Of course, officials could track me because I'd have to use my passport, but I didn't think David would bother to follow my circuitous route to Ireland. If he even came after me.

I took a taxi into the center of Paris, and found a small and expensive hotel on a side street near the Louvre. For the next three days, I'd be a tourist, visiting Notre Dame, the Eiffel Tower, museums. I collected a handful of postcards, bought a disposable camera and took pictures.

I worried constantly that someone—David—might try to stop me. As I walked, I glanced over my shoulder to see if anyone was following me.

Add paranoia to my list of psychological ailments.

I pretended to look at a miniature purple Eiffel Tower in a souvenir shop window while actually studying the reflections of passersby in the glass. Then I chided myself for watching one too many spy movies.

No one lingered behind me or stepped into a shop and out again. No one tracked my movements. I glanced at the date on a paper at a newsstand. One more day. Three days in Paris should have been enough that anyone looking for me would have figured out where I was and come after me.

I wandered into a bookstore near Notre Dame and, much to my delight, found a book about the ancient Celts. I perused it and decided to buy it, paying cash so that there would be no credit card record.

The next morning, I paid my bill, and told the hotel clerk I had decided to visit Switzerland and Austria while I was on holiday. He wished me well and called for a taxi for me.

At the airport, I used my credit card to buy a ticket to Zurich and then, at another counter, paid cash for a ticket to London. I left the first ticket, credit card and the postcards on a ledge in the restroom, hoping someone would steal them. Attempts to use my card all across Europe might distract anyone who tried to follow me.

So clever. I should have been in the CIA or a Bourne movie.

I never made it into London from Heathrow airport, but immediately boarded a flight for Edinburgh. A day later, I reached Dublin, arriving in the early afternoon.

There, I found a driver willing to take a wearying trip and, for a generous tip, forget he had ever driven someone to Aasleigh. I didn't know how long I might have to wait for the portal to open again, but I had enough money to stay for six months, and felt reasonably certain I wouldn't be there that long.

Aasleigh greeted me like a long-lost daughter. The village was just as I left it. Its three minutes of fame had faded, and it had gone back to sleep. I carried my bag to the priest's rectory and waited on the steps until I heard sounds inside.

Father Flaherty was surprised to see me, but I gave him a well-rehearsed explanation about needing to put the events of the past few months behind me, and this was the perfect, quiet place to hide from the press.

I planned to write my memoirs and wanted real inspiration from the place where so much had happened.

The story sounded real even to me.

Father Flaherty certainly couldn't object to that reasoning. But he did quip that if I were of a mind to time-travel again, I should not leave anyone waiting at the altar for me.

I smiled and promised I would not. With his assistance, I rented a cottage on the edge of town, tucked behind a thick hedge that offered all of the privacy I needed.

The townspeople kept their distance. While it was true I had brought them business and publicity, they considered me a foreigner and crazy.

Only Norah welcomed me with open arms.

"I had a feeling you'd be back," she said, handing me a satchel. Inside were my clothes, laundered and neatly folded. The brat still smelled of wool, but without the campfire, dirt and horse-sweat embedded in it. The shift was as soft and beautiful as the first time I wore it. She'd even managed to mend the tear in the left shoulder.

I thanked her. But I did not share with her my plans to try to return to Connor. I had a feeling she already knew the real reason I was here.

My cottage was a wonderful place of solitude and soul-healing. In the distance, the surf swished rhythmically against the cliffs and a seagull cried a welcome. Late-season blossoms filled the salt air with the sweetness.

I studied the book I had bought in Paris. The more I learned about the Celts, the more I understood some of what I had seen, and lived. My days became set. I rose with the dawn, made a pot of tea and read. Throughout the day, I wandered, explored, talked to the sheep in the fields, and the birds in the forest.

One day, as the morning sun painted the horizon with bands of purple, rose, pink and orange, I sucked in a deep breath. All of the stress of the past months, all the feelings of alienation, all the pain of abandonment melted.

I felt like I was home again.

I had purchased a journal in Paris, and decided to write the entire story of my journey through time. The ending, I hoped, would never be written if I was successful in my attempt to return to Connor.

I walked the hills, climbed the rocks of the ruins of the ancient tower. Standing on the very place where Donal must have watched his Beltane games and planned the wedding celebration for his daughter, I turned toward the cliffs and tried to imagine seeing a man carrying a woman in white.

Connor was there, I felt him.

Rather than dismiss those feelings as some sort of mental illness, I chose to indulge them. I talked to him as though he were standing next to me. I read passages of my journal to him.

"Do you love me, Connor? Did you go on without me? Or did Basta and Donal defeat you?"

I couldn't imagine that for a moment. Connor somehow must have won. He had lived a good life with Caitrín and their children.

But that solution didn't feel right either. I needed to know if Connor continued to feel the same emptiness and purposelessness as I.

I couldn't move on in my life until I knew if he had moved on in his.

That was my "out." I tried to convince myself that even if he didn't love me, I still had to know what had happened to him.

Croaghnac.

I might find some answers in the ruins of Croaghnac.

If Aasleigh wasn't on the map, there was no way Croaghnac would be, but I decided to hunt for the oldest map I could find. A neighboring village might have a library or bookstore where I could find an old map. I visited Father Flaherty to ask about arranging for a ride and he remembered a map he had in one of his books.

"Dates from the nineteenth century, I believe," he said, rummaging through books on a solidly packed shelf in his compact church office. "Ah, here it is."

He pulled an aged tome from the shelf and opened it on a table near a window. "Let's see what we can find here."

"I'm looking for a valley between the mountains east of the village. A river runs through the valley. There are several small islands." I stopped, and didn't explain why I thought we might find those geographical features.

He traced the map with his finger and said, "Not enough detail in this map, but wait, let's check another one." He turned the page and found almost what I hoped for.

A narrow ribbon of river bisecting a high mountain meadow before tumbling down to the sea. But this river never broadened enough to support tiny islands. Still, rivers do change over the centuries. Floods and droughts could have altered its course and even eliminated the islands.

I touched the page, and my memory supplied the valley with its brightly colored tents and pennants flapping in the wind. I saw Croaghnac, proud, ancient, the home of warriors and kings and slave girls.

"Ye were there Connor, I know it," I whispered.

Father Flaherty's map book had the page I sought, but not the answers I needed. Did Connor really exist? Or was the whole thing some sort of crazy dream? Could I be insane, as many still thought?

The next afternoon, I hired a horse and rode toward the mountains to the east of Aasleigh. With the memory of the map, I could find a way into the valley. At the edge of the foothills, I climbed as high as I could toward the gray-faced cliff where once there had been a cleft passageway into the valley.

A rock slide, a shift of the mountain, time or the magic of the aés sídhe had closed it. I touched the solid rock wall, and shouted Connor's name.

"Where are you? This is Malley land," I cried, my hands pressed hard against the stone as if my will could split the stone so that I could pass through. "Connor, I belong to myself and I give you that which is mine to give as a free person."

I didn't know where those words came from, they just popped into my head as I said them to the wind.

More answers were not found in the highlands, but in a dusty, cluttered, dimly lit shop. I had heard about the place from Norah.

"Books in Gaelic, with the charms of the olden days," she had whispered, as if saying it aloud would beckon the fairies. "Just what ye need."

I thanked her and immediately walked to a neighboring street. A tiny building opened into a narrow alleyway, easily overlooked if one didn't know it was there. A door chime rang loudly and slightly off-key as I entered, and, like Norah, the owner called a greeting from somewhere in the dim recesses of the store.

I paused at the doorway, watching dust motes slide down a beam of sunlight. They could have been fairies frolicking on the ray. This place had that sort of air about it. I sensed I'd find the right book here, and I did.

I purchased three books, one of them written in the ancient language on delicate, musty-smelling, yellowed parchment pages. Enchantments, folk lore and fairy tales, the shop owner had said.

Somewhere, in one of these books, would be my ticket to Croaghnac. I'd find something about the portal, the way back to Connor. Perhaps a magic spell, perhaps an explanation. Perhaps the diary of someone who had crossed from one time to another and come back again.

I opened all three books on the small table in my cottage and leaned over them, searching, translating, and making notes on a writing pad. I found an occasional mention of gemstones and their magical powers, but nothing specific to the ruby, even though I already knew its power. As the days stretched into weeks, I studied the books to try to pinpoint when the door might open again.

A subtle shift in the weather did not go unnoticed. Winter, with its fierce winds and temperatures hovering below freezing would soon take over the coastline. I counted my cash, and calculated how much longer I could wait.

I still had the ruby, and its sale in Dublin would bring a small fortune, but I could no more sell it than bargain away my future. I believed it was the key to unlock the portal, should I ever chance upon it again.

All of my efforts now had to be focused on finding the portal. Nearly cross-eyed with fatigue, I worked late into the evenings.

When I wasn't studying the books, I wrote in my journal unfolding the story of Connor and his clan.

Nights brought little rest. Every time I closed my eyes, Connor was there, tugging on my heart, giving me more of his story, our story, as yet unfinished.

"Muirnín," I heard him say softly.

Sweetheart. Why had he called me that?

Yours is the face I seek in the morning.

Over and over I heard the same words, phrases that sounded like some sort of ceremony, but I still didn't know where they came from.

My readings led me to the conclusion that the most likely time for the portal to open might be the end of October. Halloween, Samhain to the Celts. The night when the spirits of the dead roamed freely and mischief reigned over the land.

The clans would hold feasts to appease the spirits and to mark the beginning of the long, dark season. If there were any night that the portal would be wide open, it would be that night.

The gate had opened on two other dates celebrated by the Celts, May 1 and June 21.

I circled October 31 on a calendar.

Chapter 50

Then, I fastened my thoughts on Connor. There must be some way to draw him to the portal to meet me.

That is, if Basta and Donal had not killed him.

I visited the cemetery daily, pulling weeds, brushing dirt off the stones, listening for the music. Weeks came and went, and a new chill grabbed hold of the October breezes, puffing the thatching of cottage roofs. The wind sang to me as it brushed weeds against the cemetery gate.

Sometimes, a flute played eerie notes that floated on the breeze, but no drum throbbed. The portal was silent, the fairies sleeping yet. The ruby, in my pocket, remained quiet as well.

"There'll be ice on the morn," the pub owner warned me as I passed him on the street. I nodded and tucked my chin into the scarf around my neck.

What would freeze that night? The surf? The streets? Or my feet?

I learned the next day when I rose to find a thin layer of ice on the water in a pitcher in the kitchen. My cottage didn't have central heat, and I had forgotten to add extra coal to the fire. I thought of Connor's fire-building lesson, and tears filled my eyes.

"I'll do better tonight, my love." I wrapped my brat around my shoulders and started breakfast.

I could see him standing by the camp fire, hand resting on his sword as his brother Basta swept in on horseback. So much had happened in my "other life," as I had begun to think of my time with Connor.

I felt more connected to it than to the life I had left behind in Cleveland. I doubled my efforts to finish the journal.

"It won't be long now."

The calendar reminded me. October thirtieth. One more day.

I slipped the doeskin boots over my feet. "I'm coming, Connor, and you'd better be there to meet me!" I said aloud, hoping some fairy would take the words to him.

Like a ghost peering over my shoulder, the feeling of his nearness clung to me all day. As I went about routine chores, I'd glance up quickly expecting to see him in the shadows of the corners of the room.

"Soon, muirnin."

Darkness came early in this northern clime drawing closer to winter solstice. By the time I finished dinner and cleaned the dishes, the night wind whistled through the rushes of the roof.

"I've got to clean up a little, then I'll join ye," I said aloud to Connor.

A knock on the door of the cottage startled me, and I rose to answer it, half-expecting to find Connor standing on the other side.

Instead, David greeted me. "I've come to take you home."

Home? This is my home.

I stared at him, my mouth open but soundless.

Why did he have to show up now and spoil everything?

David pushed past me and dropped his bag in the center of the small room. "Not the idyllic honeymoon cottage I planned for you," he said, wrinkling his nose. "Don't know what attracted me to it in the first place. Just trying to give you the wedding of your dreams. Hhhumpf, things have changed, haven't they?"

He turned and looked at me. "You look like a native. Enough of this nonsense. Pack your things. We leave in the morning."

Standing next to the table, where my journal lay open, I quickly flipped it shut before he could glance at my writing.

"Why? What are you doing here?" My voice sounded strange to my ears as my breath caught in my throat.

"The board cleared you. Fortunately, they didn't know you were in Ireland, dressing like a shepherd girl. And I certainly won't tell them. If we get out of here quickly and get you back to Cleveland without some sort of further nervous breakdown, I'm sure this minor transgression will soon be forgotten, and you can get on with your life."

"But why did you come to tell me this?"

"When the board cleared you, you got your job back. I decided to forgive you. We can still be married. But not here. We'll find a JP back in Cleveland."

The room began to spin, and I grabbed the table to steady myself.

"Forgive me? For what? Do you think I had any choice in the abduction? It wasn't my fault. I tried as hard as I could to get back to Aasleigh. I--"

"I know, I know," he interrupted me. "No need to rehash old news. But to come back here? What were you thinking? God, this place is cold. It's only the end of October. I'd hate to be here in the winter."

End of October to you, but beginning of my life.

I took a deep breath, and walked over to the stove. The handful of coals I threw onto the red glow radiated heat only a few feet into the room. The wind had picked up outside and even with the foot-thick walls of the cottage, I could hear its mournful wail, and feel its power. We were in for a blow that night.

While David pulled a chair near the stove to sit where he might feel its meager heat, I moved away from him to close the interior shutters over the windows.

"I can't imagine anyone choosing to live here," he said. "It's so ... primitive."

I secretly smiled thinking how much he'd hate Croaghnac. Especially the dining hall.

"This is really the first bad weather they've had," I said, controlling my voice so that he would not detect any emotion.

"You sound like a native." He threw that at me as if it were an accusation.

"Listen, David, I'm really surprised you came to bring me news of the hearing. But, I'm not ready to go back, and I'm not sure I want to return to the bench at all."

He ignored my words, and rubbed his hands to warm them. "They blamed all your strange behavior on that new thing, Post-Traumatic Stress Disorder. That's what cleared you with the panel. Couple more sessions with a shrink, and they'll welcome you back with open arms."

"And if I don't want that?"

"How could you not want that? You can't stay here forever, you know. Sooner or later the money will run out. I'm just being practical."

Bile rose in my throat, and I struggled to keep him from noticing I was anything but calm about his presence. "I appreciate your concern. I'm ... I'm just not ready to go back yet."

I began to panic.

I was so close to Connor. So close. The portal would open soon, possible this very night, and I had to be there, and ready.

I didn't want David to interfere or distract me.

I had to concentrate on Connor, to draw him to the portal. All day I had felt his presence and talked to him. Where was he now?

"How long will it take you to get it together? A day? Two? I can wait that long."

David was talking again, and I feared I'd missed something he had said.

Drawing in a quick breath, I said. "I don't know. I was working on a journal. A memoir, I guess you'd call it."

He continued, "Well, it's all settled. A day. Two at the most and I'm taking you home. Your house sold, by the way, but your lawyer is holding the money for you. You can stay at mine until we're married."

Married?

A chill swept up my back. *Why does he want to marry me now? After everything that happened?*

The room began to close in on me. I backed a step away and felt the edge of the table behind me.

"I can't think about this right now. Give me a little time to let it all sink in."

Wasn't it obvious to him that I no longer wanted to marry him? That I loved another man? Didn't David understand that I had come here to be closer to Connor?

Connor!

I wanted to scream his name. I stared at the door of the cottage willing it to burst open, for Connor to storm in and spirit me from the room.

David cleared his throat, and I looked at him, catching a glimpse of a leer in his eyes that reminded me of Basta.

I shuddered. Alone in a cottage with a man I had almost married, I suddenly realized I didn't know him at all.

I wasn't safe. I could no longer trust him. I had to get away. But how could I?

How could I pick up the satchel of toiletries and leave the cottage to go to the cemetery?

How would I find the time portal and the path to Connor?

What if David followed me?

If this time were like the previous times, I'd hear the ram's horn and the drumbeat. But adding to my worries was the storm brewing outside.

Would the music come? Would it be loud enough? Would I be able to find the right place?

I had planned to go to the cemetery at midnight and spend every minute of October thirty-first near the portal waiting for it to open. I couldn't explain why I thought this would work.

No, it sounded like the scheme of a crazy person, not one who had just been cleared on a Post-Traumatic Stress Disorder defense.

First, I've got to get rid of David.

I glanced at my watch. Precious little time before midnight.

"Where's my manners? You've been traveling for what, twenty-four hours or more? You must be exhausted, probably want to get some sleep. Why don't you take the bed?" I suggested. "I don't mind sleeping out here."

"Why would we not sleep together?"

He looked at me with distrust more than curiosity.

I shrugged my shoulders, trying to act as calm as possible, and said, "It's been a long time and I'm not ready. Besides, the bed's narrow."

"You liked that once. Don't worry about not being ready. It'll all come back to you. Like riding a bike." He chuckled.

"No, David," I said a little more sternly.

I didn't want to provoke him, but I was firm in my resolve that I would not sleep with him, nor go back to Cleveland with him, nor marry him. "You sleep in the bedroom and I'll stay here. Just let me get a few things, and my nightgown and you can have the room. You must be tired after the long trip."

I grabbed the satchel, and my linen shift and laid them on the table, hoping he wouldn't notice my strange choice of "nightgown." Then I sat at the table watching the clock while David remained near the stove. Neither of us spoke until David finally broke the silence.

"You're right, it's getting late, and I am tired from traveling. You're sure you don't want to join me? I'm too dead to do anything more than sleep tonight." His tone was as close to conciliatory as he could be.

"No, you go ahead. In fact, what about a spot of Irish whiskey to help you sleep?"

I remembered seeing the bottle in one of the cupboards and wondering why the cottage's owner had left it there.

"Good idea." He nodded, and watched as I poured a glass of dark brown liquid into a porcelain tea cup.

"There you go," I said, handing it to him. "Drink up and you'll sleep like a baby."

He finished the drink and headed for the bedroom. I waved over my shoulder as I rinsed the cup, and replaced it on the shelf over the wash basin. Within minutes, his snores resonated from the room. I tip-toed to the bedroom door, and pulled it closed as quietly as possible.

Eleven-forty-five.

Hurriedly donning my shift, I wrapped the brat around myself. Slinging the satchel across one shoulder, I slipped silently from the cottage.

The wind pushed me up the path as if I needed help to get to the cemetery quickly.

Such a fierce night!

I understood how the legend of the banshee originated as the wind shrieked through the headstones with a noise like an old woman calling out the names of the dead.

The weather had turned so nasty that I need not fear that anyone would find me. Not even evil spirits or fairies would be out in such a storm.

With fingers numbing from the chill, I opened and re-latched the iron gate at the cemetery, and hurried passed the graves of my ancestors. The overgrown flower bed had withered and the brown ghosts of the weeds crackled in the wind.

But, I still recognized the place where I had heard the music and fallen to the ground in May.

I huddled against the ground, the wind flapping my brat like the sides of a poorly staked tent. Stinging nettles of icy rain began to pelt me. I held the ruby tightly in one hand, begging it to respond, to help me find the portal.

Pulling the edge of the brat up over my head, I whispered a quick prayer that I would not die of exposure before the portal opened.

Suddenly, I realized I had left on my watch. I had not removed it at the cottage, fearing David would find it and know I had left him again, this time voluntarily. I quickly stripped it off my arm, and stood to throw it toward the cemetery.

At that very moment, the sound of the ram's horn reverberated through me and the drumbeat pounded more within me than in the air.

The wind snatched the edge of my brat and tore it from my head. Rain, laced with sleet slammed into me, immediately soaking through the thin fabric of the shift. I stumbled forward, dropping my watch and nearly losing the ruby as the force of wind, rain caught me.

"Kat!"

The muffled call, nearly lost in the storm, startled me. Looking back across the cemetery, I saw a dark figure trying to open the gate.

David!

Chapter 51

Icy rain and wind conspired against David's efforts to unlatch the gate, buying me a few precious sections. He tucked his head down and rattled the gate to try to force it open.

I heard the music, much as I felt the drum, but I did not know whether to move toward it. I'd gone through the portal from this spot among the wild flowers and brambles. I couldn't risk missing the doorway, yet I also couldn't allow David to catch me and try to stop me.

"Connor!" I screamed into the storm as I flung myself away from the cemetery.

Tears and rain blinded me, and pain tore through my head. I squeezed shut my eyes, and buckled to the ground, praying I would die right there if the portal did not open.

Strong arms scooped me up. I could not open my eyes, I was so fearful I would see David carrying me away from the meadow and cemetery. I was afraid he had reached me before the portal opened, and now he was taking me away from there.

Away from the man I loved and wanted. Tears mingled with the rain pouring down my cheeks.

Was Connor destined to remain the man of my dreams only?

Would we never be able to reach across the centuries? Would I never know if he loved me? And would I never stop loving him?

The wind quieted, and the rain stopped. I assumed that David had brought me into the shelter of the church. I slowly opened my eyes, but the room was so dark I could not see him.

He set me on my feet, and I began to shake from the cold as well as my raging emotions.

"David ... I ... " my teeth chattered, interrupting the words.

He stripped the wet brat from my shoulders, and began to rub my arms vigorously. I shrank as his touch sent an involuntary shudder through me. I wasn't ready for intimacy with David, yet he was pulling me into his embrace. I planted both palms against his chest and pushed, but I was no match for him as he wrapped his arms around my shoulders, engulfing me in his warmth.

Something was wrong.

I wasn't sure immediately what it was.

Smell?

I didn't sense anything other than the sodden fabric of his clothing. I touched the fabric beneath my hands, rough woven, not David's overcoat, not his sweater, not anything I knew him to wear.

Then, I reached up and ran tentative fingers down his smooth cheek to the corner of his mouth and found his mustache.

Not David!

But, was it Connor?

Did I dare say his name?

I didn't have a chance to say anything before his lips fastened over my mouth. He took away both my words and my breath.

Some small part of me tried to resist the stranger's kiss, but the heat of his body pressed against me sent new shivers, this time of delight, through me.

His kiss sent my heart into the thundering beat of Basta's wild ponies, and my body into a frenzy of desire that had been restrained too long. I matched his intensity with my own, our bodies coming together until we were molded as one.

His lips parted and I opened to his tongue, letting him explore, ignite, caress, invite. Every fiber of my being sought, and found at the same time, sweet release.

The bonds of time fell away.

All that existed for us was that moment of suspended time between two worlds. His hands could be no quieter than his mouth as he stroked my back and neck, twining his fingers through my hair as if trying to capture every curl. Slowly, he lowered me to the sodden brat, crumpled on the floor.

But, I would no more be still lying beneath his body than I had been standing. I rolled against him until he turned and I was atop. Then, my hands slid the full length of his body until I found what I wanted.

With one fluid motion, I grasped the handle of his dagger and pulled it from his boot sheath. Pressing the blade against his neck, I said one word.

"Connor?"

He knocked the blade aside, sending it skittering into the darkness. "If ye can kiss a man like that, then ask who he is, ye are not the woman I came for."

"Ye came for me? How did ye know I would be here?"

"I did not know. But, I heard ye calling my name."

"When? When did ye hear me?"

"Ever since ye left. In the darkness of the night, on the wings of an eagle as it soared across the sky, on the whisper of the breeze at the dawn. Ye called me many times. And I tried to answer. I tried to find ye. I waited here, in the shadow of Donal's tower. And ye have finally come back to me. What is it ye want, woman?"

"Then, I *am* here," I said, satisfaction and wonder mingled in my voice.

Connor stood, and helped me to my feet. He took my hand, leading me from the hut into the muted gray world of a full moon so bright I thought I saw the man-in-the-moon wink at me.

"Now, do ye know where ye are? And with whom?" he asked.

I looked at him for a full minute. "I do."

A gentle breeze swirled across my still-damp tunic, bringing a new round of shivers.

How? Why? What?

So many questions flashed through my mind, but I felt no urgency in seeking the answers. I merely wanted to savor Connor's arms around me.

"Look to your left," he directed. "Do ye see the fires at the base of the tower? There is peace between the clans."

"The battle? How did it end?"

"Donal was furious with Basta for allowing ye to escape. Basta stabbed Donal, and Donal's fianna killed him before he could flee. The war ended that night."

"And Caitrín? Did she marry?" I held my breath, praying he wouldn't confess that he'd married her.

"Yes."

He paused. I turned to face him. I had to see his eyes when he told me he loved her and had married her.

"What?" he asked. "Not to me. No. She married Aidan, the man she loved."

I threw my arms around his neck. "What about Colum?"

Connor threw his head back and laughed, the sound I remembered and loved.

"Colum never wanted to marry her to begin with. He prefers his freedom."

"And you, do you prefer yours?" I touched his cheeks with my fingertips and looked deep into his eyes. The answer was there, in the depths of his soul.

But I wanted to hear him say the words. "Why did you wait for me?"

"Do ye hear the surf at the base of the cliffs? Which is louder? The waves or the beating of my heart? Do ye see the face of a man who could not let go of a dream?"

He answered my question as if he were discussing the riddle of the universe.

"But there was no hope for my return."

"Oh, but ye are wrong. It was not hope that brought me here, and instructed me to build a hut. I knew ye would return as certainly as I know the sun now slumbers, but will arise again when the moon surrenders the sky to it. I knew ye would return to me because the cords of my heart wrapped around ye so tightly ye could not escape. I knew ye could never forget me."

I half-pushed, half-slapped his shoulder and caught him off-guard. He fell backward with a thump, landing on his seat.

"You are the most arrogant man I have ever met! Arrogant! Conceited! Difficult!"

"I am Connor, son of Malley!" he interrupted.

"This is where I came in and where I am leaving!" I said.

"I forbid it!" he shouted.

"Ye what?"

The sight of a warrior, a clan leader sprawled on the ground commanding me brought a fit of laughter.

"I forbid ye to leave me. I should have done that long ago," his voice softened and dropped in volume and anger. He jumped to his feet, but stayed an arm's length from me. "If I could have stopped ye from leaving before, I would not have spent so many nights here waiting for ye."

"No one forced you."

"No, I waited here for only one reason. Because my world was empty after ye left. I told myself that if ye did not come back, I would take the fairy's path myself and go to ye."

"You would leave your clan?"

"I would leave life itself. I am Connor, son of Malley, but without

276

the woman I love, I am nothing."

I could never be quite sure I fully understood his words, especially now when every word I had longed to hear matched what I thought he said.

"Niall told me the words to say to make it right for ye," Connor continued. "He told me to tell ye I love ye and want ye to be my wife. That is not what I would say."

"Say, then, what is in your heart."

He reached out, took my hands in his, and said, "Yours is the name I call in the night and your face the one I look for in the morn. As long as I live and breathe, I shall honor ye and keep ye in my heart. I shall honor ye above all others until the day I die. I love ye, Kat-leen."

"You said my name."

"Aye. There is no mistake whom I love."

Memories of the first time he spoke those words flooded over me. I knew what to say.

"There is no mistake. I love you, Connor, chieftain of clan Malley. My life and death are equally in your care, and I shall honor you above all others until the day I die."

ABOUT THE AUTHOR

By background, I am a nurse, writer and photographer, living on the east coast of Florida. My husband, the man of my dreams, and I have six children, and fourteen grandchildren.

After I finished this book, Kat wouldn't let me go on. She continued to tell her story in an upcoming book, which, as yet, has no title. You can find an excerpt of the first chapter on the next page of this book. This next book should be available in the fall of 2015.

You can find my other books at www.amazon.com and at my website, www.celticloombooks.com.

Other Books by Joyce Good Henderson
To Rule the Wind
I Speak for Éire
Victoria's Promise
Woven on Fate's Loom

Who Am I that I Should Go?
From Book to Business: Starting a Successful Writing Business
Before You Call Mom
So You Have to Do a Science Fair Project
Strategies for Winning Science Fair Projects

Excerpt from the sequel to Wedding of My Dreams ...

I quickly discovered that I actually love this place, even in winter, when the dark days are worse than Cuyahoga County in February. The chill in the air, the pristine snow on the ground, and very brief glimpses of sunshine wrap me in the magic of this time and place. And in Connor's love. His unbelievable love. Unlike anything I have ever known. Time stands still when we are together. I think less and less about what I left behind.

Then some random thought will cross my mind and I'll experience a sudden pang for some of the trivial parts of life. No watches, no clocks, no calendars here. I sometimes miss time. Or rather, the consciousness of it. I used to be so aware of time. Clocks in every room. I never wore a watch without a second hand. I've even been known to time lawyers' addresses to the jury.

"Move it along," was my favorite admonition. Like I had someplace better to be.

Connor has acquiesced to all of my foreign ideas and requests, like washing our hands before we eat, and using a scrap of cloth to capture coughs and sneezes. But when I explained that I want to keep track of the days, he couldn't understand why. Nevertheless, he brought me a smooth pole, about two-inches in diameter. I carve a notch for each day and tie a strip of leather after a month has passed.

Since I arrived just after midnight on November first, tracking the days and weeks has been easy so far. Now, if I can just remember the names of the months. I would write them down. If I had paper.

There are two very practical reasons for me to keep a record of time. I traveled here the first time on May 1, Beltane, and returned to my own time on June 21, the summer solstice. I hoped that the fairy portal might open again on October 31, Samhain. I came back to Aasleigh, the time-lost village on the northwestern Irish coast to wait for the portal to open. While I waited, I studied all that I thought I might need to survive in a more primitive time. I visited the meadow where I had first fallen through time every day, waiting for the fairy music prelude to the opening of the time portal. I brought with me the ruby I had carried both times before. Whether the blood-red gem has anything to do with time travel, I haven't any idea, but it seemed like a good idea to recreate the identical conditions.

October 31, Halloween, Samhain to the Celts, the gate between centuries opened again, and I came back to find myself in Connor's arms.

I had learned that the Celts believed the portals between the natural world and the fairy realm opened several times a year. I'd already crossed on three of them and I didn't know when the next might occur. I wanted to identify any other possible dates, and stay as far as possible away from the meadow where the unseen gate could swoop me away to some other time.

Guarding myself from an inadvertent slip through a time portal was one reason for my improvised calendar, but the most important goal for keeping track of time lay in my greatest fear:

I could get pregnant.

www.ingramcontent.com/pod-product-compliance
Lightning Source LLC
Chambersburg PA
CBHW070316260626
47160CB00003B/857